Everybody Lies

A Novel By Melanie A. Smith

Wicked Dreams Publishing

Table of Contents

Prologue — Frankie

Dolly sits on the floor next to Pandy. They drink tea while I wait for Momma and Jack. Jack is Momma's new friend. Momma says he is a nice man, but I don't like him. He smells like cigarettes. And he brings me peppermint candies. I hate peppermint candies. Momma says it's because he likes me. But I know she's lying.

"Francesca, dinner is ready, come to the table, *now*," Momma calls from the kitchen.

I watch Momma and Jack carry plates to the table, so I get up. I wait for Jack to go back in the kitchen, then I sit down in my chair. The plastic is squishy and sticky under my bottom.

Momma and Jack bring the rest of the food and it's finally time to eat. Tea parties always make me hungry. Momma gives me a big spoon of the beef and noodles. *Stro-guh-noff.* I say it slowly and quietly to myself. Jack gives me a funny look. He's always giving me funny looks that Momma doesn't notice. Just like the kids at school.

"How was school today?" Momma asks me.

"My teacher says I'm the best reader she's ever seen in first grade," I answer proudly, happy that she finally asked. "She gave me a book called *Little Women*."

Momma looks like she doesn't believe me. "I think you probably misunderstood her. That book is far too advanced for you. You're only six."

I frown, unhappy that she thinks I'm not a good enough reader for *Little Women*. "But I've already read some of it, and I like it," I protest.

"Don't lie," Jack snaps at me. He's been mean before, but I don't like being called a liar, and I can't stop myself from saying something back this time.

"I'm *not* lying," I insist. I jump down from the chair to get the book from my backpack, so I can prove it.

"Francesca Marie, I did not give you permission to leave the table," Momma yells. I stop, knowing I'll be in big trouble if I don't.

"But Momma, I can show you —"

"I said, *sit down*," she insists. "I'm going to have a talk with your teacher tomorrow about age-appropriate books. You'll bring it to me after dinner. I won't have you reading it anymore."

1

"Oh please, Sam, she's *not* reading that book. She's obviously lying," Jack says again.

"I'm not a liar, you're a liar." The words come out of my mouth before I can stop them.

Momma's eyes go wide. Jack's face turns red, but she puts her hand up and I know she wants to talk instead.

"You apologize right now, young lady. You know better than to speak to an adult that way." Momma's voice is too quiet.

I know that quiet. But I'm still mad because I'm not lying. And I know Jack lied to her. And even though she told me never to use my gift to hurt people, I don't care right now.

"But he lied to you last week when you asked why he was gone so long. He wasn't taking out the garbage. *He* is the liar," I scream back.

Jack isn't red anymore. Now he's white. And that makes me happy because I know that means he's scared. Momma is quiet now. Jack looks at her.

"She's just a kid. She doesn't know what she's talking about." *Lie.* "You gonna let her talk to me like that?" Jack's voice sounds scared too. Because I told on him.

"Francesca, go to your room, please," Momma says softly but firmly.

I swallow hard and nod. I'm quiet as a mouse as I unstick myself from the chair and stand up.

"She doesn't know what she's talking about," Jack says again. *Lie.*

I back slowly into the living room.

"I *was* takin' out the garbage, just like you told me to. I just got sidetracked talkin' to Jimmy." *Lies.*

The little voice inside me always knows. Now that they can't see me anymore, I turn around and run to my bedroom. I close myself in my room and hide in my closet, hoping Momma isn't mad at me.

I listen to their muffled voices. They get louder. They yell for a long time. Then the front door slams and the pictures on the wall shake.

Finally, Momma comes. The closet door slides open and she sits on the floor next to me. She looks really mad.

"I'm sorry, Momma," I whisper. "I didn't mean to, it just came out."

"I know, and I'm glad you told me," she says, sounding very tired. "But you have to keep it to yourself. The things you know can cause trouble."

I don't understand. "You really didn't want to know that Jack lied to you?"

"That's not the point. If people know what you can do, you won't be safe anymore," she says.

"Why not?" I ask.

My mother brushes a long strand of my dark hair behind my ear. "Because they'll think you're a freak, Francesca," she says impatiently. "And we don't need that kind of attention. Besides, most people really don't want to know the truth anyway."

"But I always want to know the truth. How do you know what you should and shouldn't do if you don't know the truth?"

"You can never know the whole truth, Francesca. People lie on purpose, but they also lie by accident. And people lie to themselves. There is no such thing as just the truth," she explains. "I think you're old enough now to learn the only real truth. That everybody lies."

Chapter 1 — Frankie

The room is dimly lit. I stand against the wall, my feet shoulder-width apart, both hands on the gun that hangs loosely in front of me. My eyes scan the other side of the room through my lightly tinted glasses, watching the shadowy figures come and go. Waiting.

Finally, I catch sight of my target. I exhale as I confidently lift the weapon, aim, and fire. And I nail the motherfucker right between the eyes.

The lights snap back to full brightness abruptly. I holster my gun and pull my ear protection off.

"Dammit, Frankie, you're supposed to get him in the chest," Mac grumbles, coming out from behind the safety glass.

I shoot him a grin. "That's hardly a challenge," I scoff.

Mac scratches at his flaming red beard and scowls at me. "Don't be thick," he chides. "You're not a goddamn sniper — you're supposed to be learning defensive shooting. If this was in your little club it wouldn't be so easy. It'd be dark, loud, an' a whole hell of a lot harder to hit your target. Aim for the torso. Harder to miss and shoot some drunk fecker instead."

I can tell he's really annoyed, because his Irish brogue is thicker than usual. And I can't argue that he has a point. "Fine, fine," I reply. "Reset?"

We've been at it nearly two hours, but I can't help enjoying something I'm so damn good at.

Mac shakes his head. "Another day. I'm starved," he insists, rubbing his round belly.

"I guess I could eat," I allow. With a sigh I remove my safety glasses and pull out my hair band, letting my bright pink waves cascade back over my shoulders. I work my fingers through the roots at the back of my head, rubbing the tension from the spot as we pack it out of the range.

"Tacos?" Mac asks, climbing into his junky old pickup truck that's probably as old as he is. And that's saying something. You'd think for being such a successful guy he'd have a nicer set of wheels. But it's part of his charm, I suppose.

"You know me, I'll never say no to tacos," I agree as the old engine rumbles to life. "So who is the meeting with this afternoon?"

Mac stares straight ahead, navigating traffic on the backstreets. "New money. He wants in on the casino buyout."

4

"Ah. So you're not looking for my skills in wooing moneybags out of his cash. You want me to tell you if he's dirty."

Mac is one of the few people who knows about my ability. And only because I know he can keep his mouth shut.

"Got it in one," Mac agrees with a smirk. "You still sure you don't want in on the deal?"

I laugh. Mac is a persistent old bastard.

"I've got my hands full at Baltia, but thanks," I reply drily. I'm not sure why he even asked. He knows I live and breathe that club these days.

"Awww, come on, for old time's sake?" he presses.

I can't decide if he's teasing or not. "All my cash is tied up right now," I insist. "And that'd be one hell of a favor for old time's sake. Even for the return."

Mac mentored me toward my goal of owning a nightclub. Having more than thirty years' experience in almost every type of adult entertainment business that exists, from casinos to bars and nightclubs to strip clubs, he took me on as his assistant and trained me. A little too well, perhaps. I got out from under his wing as soon as I felt confident that I knew what I needed to in order to go for it. And while he taught me a lot, he expected more. I was his work horse for the better part of a decade. Not that I'm complaining, but I've already got enough on my plate.

"How is the club? You gonna be in the red at the end of year one?" he asks curiously.

I laugh. "Of course I am," I reply. "But I'll be making money hand over fist by the end of year two. Don't you worry."

"There you go getting cocky again," he warns with a shake of his head.

I press my lips together to suppress a smile. He's not wrong — I'm probably being overly confident. But then, I was a good student and I've done my homework. And the club is finally taking off, as per plan. The plan that's been ten years in the making. I think I've earned a little confidence.

* * *

The meeting is quick, and Mac's investor was clean. Just a young, enthusiastic tech millionaire looking to diversify. Don't get me wrong, he dropped plenty of lies in the meeting, just nothing unusual. The same bullshit everyone spouts.

I go home to shower, change, and eat before heading to the club. It's a Saturday night, always our biggest night of the week, so I opt for something "club dressy" but still comfortable enough. If I've learned anything these last eight months, it's that running a nightclub is practically a sport, but one you have to look good while doing.

I opt for black pants with enough cling to be sexy, but plenty of give in case I need to kick some ass. Metaphorical ass, of course. We have bouncers who handle the other stuff.

My shiny purple, halter-neck corset-top is also both alluring and still holds everything in properly without being sweltering. I roll my long, pink locks up into a simple twist and pin it in place. The halter and hair-up combo has the bonus of showing off the half-sleeve tattoos on both of my arms that connect over my upper-back. A pair of black, four-inch platform boots adds to the dangerously hot look but also puts me at an even six feet tall. Perfect for seeing eye-to-eye with most males who might think they can intimidate me.

And I'm not just talking about patrons. Being a female nightclub owner who looks considerably younger than my thirty-four years with tattoos, piercings, and crazy colored hair, well, just about everybody challenges me at one point or another. My employees. My suppliers. The deejays, band managers, agents, dancers, and other entertainers. Everybody. It's why my two biggest hobbies are boxing and shooting. You can't be too careful or too prepared, I say.

As soon as I'm inside, everything else falls away as it always does, and I've got my game face on. It's three hours until doors open at ten p.m., but most of the crew is already bustling around, getting everything ready for the night. Bartenders are checking stock, the cleaning team is working on the floors and bathrooms, and Ace, my stage manager, is talking to who I presume to be the band manager for tonight's act.

I watch everyone from next to the coat check for a minute, admiring the scene. This club was dying when I bought it, and I've worked my ass off to bring it back to life. It took forever to clean up all the old concert posters on the wall with fill-ins and a coat of lacquer, making it look less like a fading rock club and more like a purposely styled, modern tribute to the club's history. The old wood paneling was replaced with a sleek, gothic print wallpaper with dark, heavy curtains at the entrances to match. The old bar to the left of the entrance was completely ripped out, allowing us to fill the whole wall with a streamlined, steel designed bar-front onto which we could project any number of shapes, colors, and images throughout the night. The bar-height tables and chairs spanning the deck across the front of the club were all replaced with a similar design to the look of the bar itself.

But the sunken dance floor behind the seating area was simply refinished, its dark wood polished of scuffs, and it gleams with a new sheen. The stage at the back of the venue was also mostly just spruced up. I didn't want to kill what had made this club famous in the first place. The acts that have played here over the years are legendary. Every nick and dent on the stage are commemorations of their collective performances. Thankfully we've managed to keep the interest of some of the hottest bands around, blessedly smoothing the transition of ownership.

I spot my club manager, Nils, heading toward me from the hall on the other side of the bar that leads to the back offices. The tall, lanky Swede swaggers across the floor like he owns it. A former runway model, I think he just can't help it. But his good looks and charm are the shiny outside. Inside, he's a shrewd and precise club-managing machine. I wouldn't have survived this long without him.

"Mr. Larsson," I greet him in mock formality.

He does approving elevator eyes over me as he approaches. I return the favor. His fitted, designer black slacks and black button-front shirt are perfectly tailored. His shirt is unbuttoned just enough to show off his hairless, sculpted chest but doesn't give away *too* much. And his patterned dress shoes probably cost more than my entire outfit. He is, undoubtedly, ridiculously hot. Though far too much of a pretty boy to be my type. Which is yet another reason he was the best pick for the job.

"Ms. Greco," he retorts in a saucy tone, leaning in to kiss me on the cheek, and as usual I note that he smells better than most women I know. His shoulder-length blond hair tickles my collarbone as he pulls away.

I tip my head toward Ace, who is standing on stage with his hands in his pockets, looking at his shoes while the guy he's talking to gesticulates wildly. I can't tell from here if Ace is upset or not.

"What's going on there?" I ask curiously.

Nils gives the pair a glance and shakes his head. "That's Nick Pappas. He manages a bunch of acts we'll be hosting. I understand he used to do business with the previous owners as well. He's a real piece of work."

"Aren't they all?" I ask with a sigh. "Do I need to step in?"

Nils shrugs nonchalantly. "Couldn't hurt."

I give him a smirk, because his reserved, Swedish politeness always cracks me up. And I really know that's Nils-speak for, "Yes, please, go schmooze so I don't have to be the one to brown-nose this guy."

I check my makeup in the mirrored bar behind Nils's back and am pleased that I can see the smoky eye and bright red lip that are my go-to are still perfectly done. Heading down the stairs, I can feel Nils's eyes on my back. I assume he must have had it out with Mr. Pappas already, because he's clearly very interested in how I do with him.

Ace looks up as I approach, relief blossoming over his face. Since Mr. Pappas's back is to me, he doesn't notice as I hop the step up to the elevated platform. He is still gesturing wildly as he babbles.

"Gentlemen," I interrupt. "How are things going?"

Ace looks like he could kiss me, and I press my lips together, so I don't laugh. Mr. Pappas finally stops talking and spins around. Short and dark, his olive skin is greasy, and his suit is cheap.

"I think we have a misunderstanding about the —" Ace is cut off by Mr. Pappas whipping back around and glaring him into submission. But then, Ace is a go-with-the-flow guy, not really into confrontation. His grungy jeans, seventies band T-shirts, and hippie vibe certainly speak to that. He's great with the musicians. But stuck-up assholes like this guy don't really show him much respect, unfortunately.

"What junior over here isn't getting, is that I *specifically* requested separate restroom facilities for my guys. Now, you've done this before, and I don't understand what the goddamn problem is," Mr. Pappas spits. He looks me up and down. "Why don't you go get your boss? I'm sure he can straighten this out."

I take a subtle breath in through my nose and let all the things I can't say run through my head quickly before I respond. *He's about five minutes younger than you, asshole; no you didn't; and no, we haven't.* My next thought, however, I can say.

"You're looking at her," I respond with a sweet smile, extending my hand. "Francesca Greco."

Mr. Pappas's jaw drops momentarily as he stares hard at my chest, but he recovers quickly, roughly grabbing my hand. His shake is overly firm, and I suppress the urge to roll my eyes.

"Well, good," he grumbles. "Yeah. It's, uh, nice to meet you." He drops my hand and rolls his shoulders, eyes still fixated on my breasts. "So about the facilities."

My mouth twitches as I suppress an annoyed sneer. "I understand the previous owners may have been able to provide that; however, with bringing things up to code, unfortunately those restrooms are now shared between my employees and the performers, leaving the restrooms on the other side of the building dedicated to customers," I explain. "I apologize for the inconvenience, but I assure you my employees will not get in the way of your client's use of the facilities."

If I thought that was going to placate him, I was sorely mistaken. He turns as red as my lipstick, looking me in the eyes for the first time, and I know this is going to take every ounce of charm I possess.

"I was promised *dedicated facilities*," he all but yells in my face. *Lie.*

I fight the urge to roll my eyes at the inner voice. I didn't really need it to know he's full of shit.

"Do you remember who promised you that?" I ask, still sweet.

He blinks hard. "Well, no, but —"

"Okay, did you get it in writing then?" I press.

He scowls. "Well, no, but —"

"And you do understand that we're legally required to comply with health and safety codes that govern the purpose and use of facilities as allowed by our permitting and inspections," I continue.

"Well, yes, but —"

"And I know you wouldn't want us to risk getting shut down because we were caught violating those codes, since my club manager tells me you have other acts booked here in the future," I reply.

His shoulders slump, and if he had a tail, it would be between his legs. "Of course not," he grumbles.

"Good, then we're in agreement that your client will use the same facilities as per usual, and our employees will do their best to stay out of their way," I say with a smile. I lay a hand on his arm. "I appreciate it, Mr. Pappas. Not everyone understands the long list of rules we have to follow. You must be very good at what you do, knowing so much about clubs and all."

In my head it's said in a much more sarcastic tone. But out loud I manage to sound sincere, or a good impression of it anyway, and it has the desired effect. He perks up and puffs out his chest a little and Ace's eyes go wide with mirth.

"Yeah, I do," Mr. Pappas replies. "I'm glad I could help." His eyes drop back down south of my face, and I know he's calmed down and the storm has passed.

"Good," I reply brightly. "Well, it was a pleasure to meet you, Mr. Pappas. Please be sure to let me know if there's anything else I can do to help. But right now I should check in with my manager to make sure our VIP area is set up for the band."

"Uh, yeah, yeah, it was good meeting you too," Mr. Pappas replies, clearly a little confused as to what just happened. He looks between Ace and me for a few seconds before shaking his head and going backstage.

Ace bursts into giggles. "Thanks, boss," he says between snorts.

One of the roadies looks up from setting up the drum kit. "That guy's a dick," he says in a low voice. "I'm glad you didn't let him push you around."

I shrug. "I've seen worse," I assure him. I turn back to Ace. "And next time come get me or Nils sooner, okay? Between Nils's charm and these tits, we have all the weapons we need to distract asstwats like that."

The roadie snorts and Ace offers an apologetic smile. I shake my head and wander off to find Nils to talk promoters.

* * *

By midnight I can barely hear myself think. The band is in full swing and the whole club is packed wall to wall. It's actually my favorite part of the night. Being a human lie detector makes one-on-one conversations exhausting and irritating after a while. But being alone is a special kind of torture for me too. Being in a crowd, though, is strangely soothing. The energy, the excitement, the mass of bodies moving to the same beat, with the same purpose. It invigorates me. Always has. I let my hips sway as I lean against the railing, longing to lose myself in the crowd below me as they rage to the intensity of the music. Being boss has its downsides.

But it's been a good night overall so far for the club, so I really can't complain. Great take at the door and from ticket presales, and that's not even accounting for alcohol sales yet. Very few fake IDs, no fights, no drunk people passed out in corners. Well, maybe one or two. But Nils is pretty good at getting the bouncers on things like that before I even notice.

I'm perched in the corner of the VIP balcony, reveling in the atmosphere and scanning the crowd when I see Nils making his way past the velvet ropes and up the stairs. He's clearly headed for me. I give him a questioning look as he approaches.

When he gets to me he leans his mouth to my ear. "Johnny says there's a guy at the bar asking about you."

I look up into his ice blue eyes and raise an eyebrow as if to say, *So? A lot of guys ask about me.* There had been a few articles and news pieces when I bought the club and in the following months as we renovated. Great press, but they'd brought out some weirdos. Nils just shakes his head and motions for me to follow him. This one must be different.

At the bottom of the stairs, Nils pushes me toward the bar before returning to his rounds. Confused, I slip behind the bar and tap Johnny on the shoulder. He holds up a finger letting me know he's finishing the order he's working on.

I look down the length of the bar trying to spot whoever could be asking after me. In case it's someone I actually do know. But since the bar covers the whole wall of the club, it's hard to see everyone vying for a place at the counter, trying to get the attention of one of the four bartenders on duty. Not to mention it's dark, loud, and I'm starting to lose steam ahead of the second wind I usually get around this time.

Johnny finishes up and pulls me by the hand through the service door into the private storage area behind the bar we use for the security monitors. The doors are heavy enough to muffle the sound so we can hear each other. Johnny grabs a bottle of water and slumps into a high-backed chair at the bank of monitors on the far wall displaying feeds from the various security cameras around the club.

"Nils told you there's a guy looking for you?" he checks. He leans his broad shoulders into the soft backrest.

Johnny's short, dark hair is sweaty, his collared dark blue polo shirt also slightly damp. I resist the urge to chastise him for sweating all over the chair. We all sweat buckets every night. It comes with the territory. So instead, I nod and take the chair next to him.

His dark eyes flick up to the farthest monitor, showing the opposite end of the bar than we'd been on. He puts his finger under a large, hulking guy seated at a stool pulled into the corner. "That guy."

I squint at the image. He looks big. Dark hair. Dark shirt. Lots of tattoos. But his head is bowed, his face hidden from the camera.

"He asked for me? What did he say that made you have Nils come get me?"

Johnny is usually my first line of fending off the creepers, so I'm curious why he thinks this one is legit.

"He didn't ask for you. Mentioned you is more like it. But he called you Frankie, and he's been sitting there all night like he's waiting for something," Johnny replies, finishing his bottle of water. "I'm gonna hit the head before I go back out. Cover me and put eyes on him. Dave knows what's up, just let him know before you go over there." Johnny gets up and heads toward the door on the opposite wall leading to the staff restrooms that had been the subject of heated debate earlier this evening.

"I need exact words, Johnny," I call after him, staring at the screen and trying to discern more about the mystery man.

"He said, 'This is a cool club. It's Frankie Greco's place, right?' That's it." Johnny disappears to the bathrooms.

Now I understand why it raised a flag. There are precious few people who call me Frankie. Mac, my best friend Emma, and my family. That's it. Nobody at the club calls me Frankie. None of the news outlets had either, I'm sure of that. Not that it's a super uncommon nickname for Francesca. But it's just enough to be odd, without being threatening, exactly. Only one way to find out who this guy is and what he wants. With a shake of my head I get back up, throw an apron on, and tuck a few escaped pink strands back into place.

Heading back through the door, I poke Dave as I pass him to work the opposite end of the bar. He barely looks up, but I see him nod and send Jess back down toward Johnny's area to cover. I pass the fourth bartender, Peter, and he barely acknowledges my passing as he struggles to keep up with the throng.

I focus on paring down the line that's formed in Johnny's absence. After serving half a dozen drinks there's a small lull, so I lean against the back of the bar nonchalantly and grab a bottle of water. I scan the bar as if I'm just checking on everyone. The guy is so tucked into the corner, he's the last thing I see. But this time I'm only ten feet away from him, so I get a good look. Or I would have, had our gazes not locked as soon as mine settled on him. His eyes are dark and intense, and I get the sense he's been watching me the whole time.

Unexpectedly, my breath catches in my throat and it's like someone stuffed cotton in my ears. All the noise around me drops into the background. I struggle to breathe, telling myself it's an adrenaline response. He's not "mainstream" handsome, but he's attractive in a way that makes my insides tighten nonetheless. He has dark hair that is short on the sides, but long and wild on top. His jaw is a little too square and has a significant five-o-clock shadow, his nose is perfectly straight, but his full mouth is crooked under it. His thick eyebrows are set over his big, dark eyes in a way that makes him look like he's laughing. But the muscled and tattooed arms that extend out of his short-sleeved black T-shirt are no joke. And I wish I could say I'd seen him before, but there's not even a hint of recognition. Well, beyond my body recognizing that it would like to see more of that perfect physique hinted at under his tight-fitting shirt.

Before it can be classified as gawking, I stroll over to him, pretending to respond to his look as if he were asking for service. *Oh, I'd be glad to service him all right.* I can't help the thought, but I internally chastise myself for it anyway. I've never fucked a customer, and I don't plan to start with my dark, alluring, and potentially creepy stalker.

I lean in and use my carefully practiced bartender-in-a-loud-club voice. "Need anything?" I ask as casually as I can.

One of his eyebrows flicks up and he smirks, pointing at the empty beer bottle in his hand. The look is so ridiculously sexy that a flush creeps through me. I swallow hard and nod, taking the empty bottle from him. I reach behind me into the cooler and grab a new one, removing the cap as he watches before handing it to him.

He tosses a bill on the counter as he accepts the beer and takes a long pull. I pocket the cash and give him change. And before things pick up again, I decide to just go for it.

"I heard you're looking for Frankie Greco."

He sets his beer down and chuckles. "That's some grapevine you've got here."

His voice is deep and luscious and it sends shivers down my spine. God, why am I reacting to him this way? Down, girl. It's not like there aren't heaps of gorgeous men in here every night. Thankfully, I've had a lot of practice on my poker face, so I shrug in response, not wavering. He gives me an appraising look.

"You're her?" he asks skeptically, raising one of his thick brows.

I raise my eyebrow right back. "Maybe. You a friend of Mac's?"

He's the only one I can think of that might send this slab of a man into my club asking after Frankie Greco. But it's also bait.

"Yeah, Mac mentioned this was your place," he replies casually. *Lie.*

The familiar internal voice is like a punch in the gut, even though I was expecting it.

"Try again," I say tightly.

His eyes grow hard and he gives me a look somewhere between cautious and ravenous. But before he can respond I'm distracted by a wave of frat boys asking for shots. When I glance back at the corner, a lone twenty-dollar bill sits on the counter and the mystery man is gone.

Chapter 2 — Julian

Fuck. That round ass, come-fuck-me pink hair, and those gorgeous red lips that I can't stop thinking about having wrapped around my cock completely distracted me. And when those velvety blue eyes locked on me, I swear I almost came in my fucking pants. Control is practically my middle name, and I'm not some wet-behind-the-ears kid looking for a quick fuck in a dirty club bathroom. But fuck me if I couldn't breathe properly from that moment on.

Much less think and work the situation like I usually would. Because there was no guessing the most alluring woman I'd ever locked eyes on owned the fucking club. And it made me sloppy. I should've known not to show my hand. I'm normally much more subtle than that. I have to be. It's my job. She's just a job.

I'm totally fucked.

Chapter 3 — Frankie

When I finally climb out of bed early the next afternoon, something about the encounter with the mystery man has me riled up far more than it probably should. My whole body feels restless in a way that the physical exertion of the night should've quashed. Unfortunately, Mac is unreachable on Sundays, rising early to hoof it out of the area to places that are beyond isolated so he can fish in peace. Meaning I can't even check in with him until tomorrow on the off chance he actually does know who this guy is.

I wander around my tiny Santa Monica apartment totally on edge. I contemplate going for a run, but while I'm mentally worked up, I'm not really in the mood for physical exertion. Suddenly, I have the urge to do something drastic.

I grab my phone off the counter and place the call before I can overthink it.

"Hey darlin', what's the haps?" Emma greets me.

"Hey babes," I reply hurriedly. "Got time for a chat this afternoon?"

"A chat and ..." Emma trails off, knowing there's more.

"A dye?" I admit.

Emma laughs. "About time. You've been pink almost two months. What are we doing? Back to blue?"

"I was thinking my natural color," I respond.

"Wow, really? Do you even know what your natural color is anymore?" she jokes.

"Ha. Ha. Ha," I snip drily. "Can you take me to a four? That should be close enough."

"Sure can. Gimme an hour and be ready to pay me in pizza."

"Thanks, babes," I reply. "I wasn't kidding about the chat though."

"And I wasn't kidding about the pizza," Emma shoots back.

* * *

In Emma time an hour means two. So imagine my surprise when an hour and fifteen minutes later she appears.

"Whoa," I say, answering the door. "You're early."

Her hands are full of supplies, so she pushes me out of the way with a round hip. "Oh please, I'm not that bad," she gripes as she goes through the open bathroom door just off the living room and plops her stuff down.

I close the front door and head back to the living room to sink into my favorite squishy chair. "Yes, you are," I tease. "You were almost two hours late *to your own wedding*."

She emerges, hands on her hips, glaring at me. Her naturally pale-blond hair is pulled up in a tight bun and she is, as usual, wearing far too much makeup on top of an insanely gaudy pink, sequined romper. She's outrageous in every sense of the word, and it's one of my favorite things about her. We've been best friends since we were six and I love her to death.

"Doesn't count," she replies, folding her arms over her ample chest. "You can do whatever you want on your wedding day."

I raise my hands in defeat. "Peace," I say with a grin. "Now are we gonna do this or what?" I rise from the chair.

"Someone's in a hurry," she remarks. "What crawled up your butt today? Rough night at the club?"

I press my lips together. I may know when people are lying, but Emma Martin has the most finely honed intuition on the planet.

"I wouldn't say rough," I hedge. "It was a good night overall, actually."

She looks at me expectantly. "But?" She puts her hands back on her hips.

"Some guy came in asking for me," I respond, grabbing a dining room chair and hauling it into the bathroom.

She follows me in. "You're going to make me pull this out of you, aren't you?" she teases.

I sit in the chair with a sigh, knowing it'll trigger her to start on my hair. And I'm not disappointed as she starts brushing it out. "No," I finally reply. "I guess I just don't know what to make of it."

As she sections my hair and mixes the dye, I fill her in on everything surrounding the mystery man. She's started slathering my hair with the smelly cream by the time I'm done.

"So you're what, mad that the hottie got away?" she asks. "Or worried that he's a stalker ax murderer?"

I laugh. "Both, maybe?" I admit. "I don't know. Something about the whole thing really bothered me."

Emma's nostrils flare, a sure sign that she's trying not to laugh at me. "I bet."

"What's that mean?" I gripe.

She catches my eye in the mirror and grins. "It means you need to get laid, Frankie. How long has it been?"

I try to do the math in my head but can't even remember enough to recall specifically. At the very least the better part of a year. "A long time," I allow. "But that's not what this was."

"Mhm," she hums dismissively. "So what are you gonna do about it? Are we dyeing your hair so he doesn't recognize you while *you* turn stalker on *him*?"

"I don't think I could stalk him even if I wanted to. I don't even know the guy's name."

"Did he use a credit card?" she asks.

"Nope. Cash."

"Fuck. Well, that doesn't give you much to go on," she admits.

"I'll ask Mac about it tomorrow. But I'm pretty sure he wouldn't send some guy I've never met into my club without giving me the heads-up. He hasn't been shy about trying to get his friends VIP service in the past, anyway," I say.

"Well, I hope you find him one way or the other," she replies, tucking my last, soaked strand of hair under a cap. "Because at the very least I wouldn't mind the eye candy."

"You've only been married a year and a half. Ben not doing it for you anymore?" I tease her.

She pinches my arm as she goes around me to throw out her gloves and wash her hands. "I have no complaints in the bedroom, thank you very much," she replies haughtily. "But that doesn't mean I can't appreciate a big, fine man."

"You're incorrigible," I respond, removing the towel from around my shoulders.

She snaps the hand towel she was using at my ass as I exit the bathroom and it stings my cheeks through my thin leggings. "Less talking, more ordering pizza," she demands.

* * *

The food arrives right as my hair is ready to be rinsed, so it's a few minutes before we can get our hands on the hot, cheesy slices. By the time we do, we chow down quickly, both of us clearly starved.

When we've finished eating, Emma catches me up on all the latest salon gossip as she dries and styles my hair into long, loose waves. Most of it is about minor celebrities I couldn't care less about, but I know she enjoys it so I just let her talk. She doesn't stay long after, excusing herself as she needs to get home to "make dinner." Said with a wink that I didn't need, considering we'd just eaten.

Trying not to think about all the action Emma's getting that I'm not, I spend a while looking in the mirror. I barely recognize myself without a crazy hair color. It's been years since I was anywhere near my natural dark brown shade. Even with the nose piercing, numerous ear piercings, and

17

tattoos, it makes me look more businesslike. So, you know, there's that at least. But it's still going to take some getting used to. I'm still not sure why I did it, exactly. I just get impulses like that sometimes and completely switch directions.

I throw on a simple, tailored pair of black slacks and a shimmering, loose red halter with some red stilettos. And, of course, my signature red lip to match.

There's a charity function at the club tonight, so it won't be an extended affair, just a few hours, tops. Though it should be entertaining, with a burlesque show on stage and a silent auction, the proceeds of which will go to an Alzheimer's research fund. Nils has already told me he has it handled, but I figure it's best to put in an appearance anyway.

* * *

I arrive an hour ahead of the preshow cocktail hour, and everything is pretty much ready to go, Nils being the miracle worker that he is. I steal one of the canapés and disappear back to my office. On the way, Jess flags me down from the bar.

"Ms. Greco?" she says as she approaches, staring openly at my lack of pink hair. "Someone stopped by for you this afternoon."

My heart pounds in my chest. *Could it be him?* I clear my throat. "Oh? Did they leave a message?" I ask evenly.

Jess shakes her head, her blond curls bouncing. "No, it was the guy from last night. He said he wanted to apologize for something? But he didn't leave a name or a number or anything."

My stomach fills with butterflies. He did come back. But why leave in the first place then?

"Did he say if he'd come back?" I press.

She shrugs. "He saw there was something going on tonight. I told him it was a private event and he left."

A frown creases my face. "That's all?"

Jess shrugs. "Yeah. I was a little, uh, surprised. He's um ..." She trails off and blushes furiously.

"Yes, he's quite attractive, I'm aware," I reply drily. "Well, thank you for letting me know."

Jess nods and scurries off to continue prep. And I do my best to press on with my duties.

* * *

Four hours, a saucy burlesque show, and a smashing success of an auction later, I've seen the last employee out before I think about the mystery man again. I try not to feel disappointed at missing him stopping by as I lock up. Though knowing tracking him down will be nigh impossible leaves me feeling something I don't think I should be feeling. Especially not about a weird, overly familiar stranger that appears and disappears at the drop of a hat.

I climb into my cherry red convertible, a true American classic and one of the few luxuries I've allowed myself, and head home in the cool night air.

It takes me a while to get to sleep. And not just because I'm going to bed before four a.m. for once. My biggest problem is every time I close my eyes, I remember locking eyes with Mr. Mysterious and the shot of heat that ripped through me. Needless to say, it's not the kind of thing that's conducive to sleep.

Chapter 4 — Julian

My fuck-up didn't go over well with the boss. So here I stand, again, in front of the bombshell's club, *nervous*. Again. I don't do nervous. It makes me fucking angry. I'm the one who makes people nervous, not the other way around. But I have only myself to blame. And she's just a woman. Mesmerizing, hot, and tough as nails. Gah. *Get your shit together, you fucking pussy.*

My eyes flick up to the black dome over the door. Fuck all. I'm being recorded. Realizing I'm only making it worse the longer I stand here, I man up and push the service bell. And I say a prayer that nobody is here. Then I can go back and say I tried without having to put my big dumb foot in my mouth again. Or better still, without having to do what I was sent here to do.

Just when I'm about to give up and leave, the speaker above the button crackles to life.

"Can I help you?" a woman asks, barely cutting through static. I can't tell if it's the same blond dingbat bartender I got before or Frankie herself.

"Yeah, is Frankie Greco around?" I shove my hands in my pockets self-consciously.

"Do you have an appointment?" she asks.

I scrunch my eyebrows together. Seriously? It's Monday fucking morning. What, did I interrupt this broad doing her nails or something? I seriously hope this isn't the goddess I'd laid eyes on before, or the illusion is ruined. Or, maybe I *should* hope for that. It would definitely make this easier if she was a bitch.

"No," I reply, trying not to sound irritated.

"Then I'm afraid Ms. Greco won't be able to see you today."

"This is ridiculous," I spit out before I can stop myself. "I just need a minute."

Seconds later I hear the door unlatch. It swings out just enough for a dark head to pop through. I do a double take, realizing it's Frankie, pink hair replaced by a deep brown that doesn't make me want to grip it by the base of her neck as I fuck her any less. I banish the thought and fix my face to a neutral expression.

Reluctantly, she steps out. She's got a hand behind her back and I instinctively stiffen before I realize why. I'm freaking her out. It might be the middle of the day, but she's a woman. Possibly alone in a club in a neighborhood that's sketchy at best. And while she's a tall chick who clearly has enough attitude to handle herself, I get it.

And even if she's got a gun, I'm not particularly worried. So I do my best to put her at ease, leaning casually against the doorframe and shooting her my best disarming smile.

"You changed your hair," I remark. "And you're tall for a girl."

Her dark blue eyes that clearly miss nothing sweep over me, sending chills down my spine.

"And you're just tall," she replies impatiently. "What are you doing here?"

There's that attitude. I like it. A little too much. I push myself up so I'm hovering over her. She freezes, so I hold back a little, eyeing her carefully to determine whether its fear or attraction that has her rooted to the spot. My eyes trail down the shooting stars swirling down her shoulders, but I stop myself short of staring at her tits.

"I wanted to apologize for the other night," I reply with my carefully rehearsed line. "But maybe that was stupid. It just occurred to me that you probably see a million guys every night and you probably don't even remember me."

She glares at me shrewdly. "Then why would you bother coming back to apologize?" she challenges.

I can't help but laugh. This chick isn't about to fall for anything. I slide my hands into my pockets, feigning embarrassment. "I realized that night I might have been creeping you out, so I just left," I say honestly. "But then I felt like an asshole. I tried to just forget about it, but I couldn't. So yeah. I'm sorry if I creeped you out, and I'm sorry that I left so quickly. And now I'm rambling." I snap my mouth shut and she rewards me with a smile. Those full fucking lips turning up wake the sleeping beast between my legs.

"That still doesn't explain why you were looking for me in the first place," she points out.

I consider her carefully for a moment. "I knew of a Frankie Greco once. I thought you might be her."

She stares back like she's waiting for something. After a few beats, she narrows her eyes at me.

"Well?" she prompts.

Fuck, she's a tough nut. Time to give her back the upper hand. I shake my head and start backing away.

"This was a mistake," I mutter. "I should go."

I start to turn, definitely not wanting to go, but needing to play this just right. I'm rewarded when I feel a cool, silken hand slide over my forearm. I turn back, my eyes locking on hers as she grabs me, and I swear to the fucking Almighty my heart jumps in my chest. Like she felt it, Frankie sucks in a sharp breath and pulls her hand back. I try to shake it off, and hurry to regain composure so I can reel her back in.

"Apology accepted," she says, beating me to it. "But I don't even know your name."

My eyes sweep over her beautiful, guarded face, and something inside me wants to spill my guts, to really know her and let her know me. But that's the last thing I should do, for so many reasons. Instead, I extend my hand and offer the simplest answer possible.

"I'm Julian."

She slides her soft hand into mine and squeezes. It does things to me. Primal things.

"It's nice to meet you, Julian," she replies somewhat breathlessly. "But just so you know, I prefer to be called Francesca."

I cock my head to the side. "Really?" I ask skeptically. And not just because I was sent after *Frankie* Greco, but because the nickname suits her. Francesca seems too stuffy for a chick like her.

She gives me a funny look. "Look, I don't know you. *Frankie* is just a little too familiar for me. I'm weird like that," she replies defensively. She pulls her hand out of mine. Her eyes blaze a path down my face, over my chest and arms, to the hand she just dropped. Her face is red and she's breathing heavily.

She fucking wants me. Dammit. Unfortunately for her, that works to my advantage.

I give her a knowing smirk that makes her blush deepen. "It's not weird," I reply soothingly. "I'm the nutjob who can't stop showing up. It's not like you know me at all."

She starts to chew on her lip, and my eyes can't help watching. I clench my jaw, willing the thoughts forming back.

"Then maybe I should get to know you," she offers encouragingly, her stance loosening.

I flinch at the vulnerability in her voice and her eyes. I can't do this to her.

"As much as I'd like that, I don't think it's a good idea," I reply. Fuck, fuck, fuck all. I'm going to be in trouble for this. What is it about this chick that makes me lose all sense? Fuck.

"Have it your way," she replies with a shrug that's so carefully indifferent it betrays her deep annoyance. "If we're done here, I'll be getting back to work. Thanks for the apology."

My mind scrambles, knowing I can't let her go that easily. But totally seeing how erratic my behavior is. Though I think it's obvious to both of us that I'm just as attracted to her as she is to me. I both want to stay and don't. Ultimately, I remember I don't have a choice.

She starts to open the heavy door, and I close the small gap between us and slam my hand against the door, blocking her retreat. She whirls around, and I stare down at her, her face so much closer to mine than I'd anticipated.

A primal heat passes between us. And she smells so fucking good. Like strawberries, and mint, and the salty ocean air. My fucking mouth is watering thinking about consuming every inch of her delectably curvy body.

"It's not a good idea," I repeat, "but I don't think I'm going to be able to stay away from you, either." As soon as I say it, I realize it's true. Fuck.

She takes a deep breath through her nose and looks down at her feet, and for a moment I think I've lost her.

"I'm surprisingly okay with that," she says softly. Her head tilts back up, her dark tresses tumbling back over her shoulders.

I. Am. So. Fucked.

I slip my free hand under her chin, looking deep into her eyes. I slide a thumb lightly across her luscious bottom lip.

"Okay." My voice is low and husky, betraying me. "Have dinner with me."

"That didn't sound like a question," she points out with a smile. "But all right. I'll meet you at the diner," she points to the one across the street, "at six."

I drop my arms back to my sides. "I'll see you soon, then," I promise, backing away slowly and keeping eye contact.

She makes a small noise of assent and slips back into the building quickly. I turn away to walk off whatever the fuck just happened. And I wonder how the fuck I'm going to handle what comes next.

Chapter 5 — Frankie

I'm back in my office, head in my hands, convinced I've made a huge mistake when Nils shows up. The moment he walks in the office and sees me, he turns around and leaves. He's only gone a minute, returning with two old-fashioned glasses and a chilled bottle of top-shelf vodka.

He sits across the desk from me and fills both glasses nearly halfway. He slides one across the desk to me.

"Drink," he commands. "And talk." Then he reclines his tall, lean frame in the chair, looking at me expectantly.

I look up at him for a moment before lifting the glass to my lips. The freezing liquid goes down with little sting. I would have preferred whiskey. There's nothing like its bold flavor and strong burn to remind you that you're alive. And then quickly dull that feeling.

Nils and I have shared a lot, but mostly only about work. That's not to say we don't get along personally — there just isn't usually a lot of time for it. I decide it's better to tell him what's going on, at least enough of it anyway so he doesn't think I'm hiding something about the business.

"It's not about the club," I assure him.

He leans forward, spinning his glass thoughtfully in his long, slender fingers. Finally, he looks up at me. "Francesca, I think you are an amazing woman. And I know you like to focus on things here, but we all have personal issues that we need to talk about sometimes," he says calmly. "And I'm here for you."

I roll my lips through my teeth. "Thanks, Nils," I reply. "I appreciate that. I feel the same way, you know."

He smiles vaguely and waves a hand, encouraging me to talk. And to my surprise, I don't just give him the high level. I completely spill my guts. I tell him about the first conversation with Julian after Nils had directed me to the bar. I tell him about the missed visit at the charity event. And finally about the conversation today. About the date I'm supposed to go on in just a couple of hours with the most confusing and alluring man I've ever met.

When I'm done Nils lets out a deep sigh. "Well, you're obviously into this guy, so you must have decided he's not crazy. And you have good judgement, Francesca. So why the deer-in-headlights look?" he asks bluntly.

"I just feel like he's not giving me the full story. And it's not like I have a lot of time for dating right now," I say with a sigh. I don't admit that I don't trust my assessment of this guy, as I'm far too distracted by him physically to think clearly. Even though he never out-and-out lied, he was all over the map, and I couldn't get a good read on why.

Nils laughs. "You're too hands-on here. You make my job too easy," he teases me. "Live a little. Go get laid. Nobody ever offers up their full story right away. Get to know him. See if you even care about his story. And even if you decide you don't, he's clearly got other things you need right now." He looks down into his drink momentarily before downing the remaining liquid and rising from his chair. The man can certainly hold his liquor. Another reason he makes an excellent nightclub manager.

"Thanks, Nils," I say to his retreating back. I'm flooded with gratefulness. This is one of the things I like best about Nils. He doesn't mince words, and I can always count on him for an honest opinion.

He stops at the door and turns back to look at me. "You're welcome," he says. "Stop thinking so much."

I snort a laugh as he closes the door behind him. And I take another sip of my drink. If nothing else, a little more liquid courage won't hurt.

* * *

A few minutes ahead of our date, I head out of the club and to the diner. As I stride purposefully across the road, I decide Nils is right. I need to stop thinking so much. I work way too damn hard, and this could be good for me. Even if it's just a physical release.

I stride into the diner and spot Julian at a booth in the back. He is staring intently down at his menu and doesn't notice my approach. He's still wearing the fitted navy polo shirt he had on earlier. The one that I couldn't stop ogling him in. But he's switched into nicer jeans and his hair also looks like it has been more carefully styled. The click of my heels on the linoleum alerts him to my approach and his dark eyes snap up.

He slides out of the booth, standing to greet me. It makes me blush, and I stop at the table, feeling like an awkward teenager rather than an experienced woman in her thirties.

"You cleaned up," I remark with a teasing note in my voice. And I notice the shirt is unbuttoned at the top, revealing more tattoos on his chest. My eyes lift back to his and he's raised an eyebrow, that look of near-laughter playing around his eyes and mouth.

"Sure, yeah, I guess. I live close by," he offers as explanation, gesturing for me to have a seat.

I self-consciously adjust my green tank top and slide into the booth as he reseats himself across from me. "Well, that's convenient," I murmur. "Do you come here often then?"

He smirks unreservedly now. "Is that your best line?" he teases in a husky voice that sends a shiver down my spine.

"I don't do lines," I reply honestly.

He bites his bottom lip, but it doesn't keep the smile from pulling at his mouth. "That's refreshing. I don't, either."

"So what do you do?" I ask curiously. "Since you already know I run a nightclub, it seems only fair that I know what you do for a living."

Julian's eyes tighten and he looks like he might not respond for a moment. "I'm a headhunter," he finally replies, albeit somewhat reluctantly.

"So you lure people away from their jobs to go work somewhere else?" I ask. My tone is slightly teasing. I've got nothing against the practice, but it's not really the kind of job I pictured him doing. Maybe a mechanic. Or a construction worker. Anything that uses those big, strong hands and muscles of his.

He tilts his head to the side and narrows his eyes slightly. "Is there something wrong with that line of work?"

"Of course not," I backtrack. "What kind of businesses do you work with?"

"The kind that like discretion," he replies, leaning back in his seat and looking away.

I press my lips together to disguise my annoyance at his non-answer. "That's vague," I respond.

He looks back at me and laughs, and it lights up his whole face. And I melt just a little bit.

Just then Heather, the perky blond waitress who always works weekday evenings, stops by our table, eyeing Julian a little too openly.

"Hi, what can I get for you?" she asks, chewing on the end of her pen in an attempt at seduction.

Julian's eyebrows scrunch together, and he gives me a look. "Ladies first," he says to me with a gesture.

The pen slides out of her mouth and she turns to me with a heavy sigh. *Geez, dramatic much, lady?*

I give her the sweetest smile I can muster. "I'll have a club sandwich and fries," I say, batting my eyelashes at her.

"Anything else?" she asks dully.

And I just can't help it. "Yes, how about a verse of 'Killing Me Softly'?" I joke.

She stares at me like I've grown a second head and Julian busts up laughing.

"Just some iced tea, please," I tell her.

She turns to Julian as fast as she can manage and her whole demeanor changes, the pen finding its way back between her lips.

"I'll have what she's having," he says as he catches his breath from laughing.

She looks a little disappointed she didn't get to engage him more. She leans in ever so slightly and drops her voice. "Okay, is there anything *else* I can get for you?"

Christ, even I can see her cleavage from here. Julian catches my eye and holds it.

"No, thanks," he says firmly, keeping his eyes on me until she leaves.

"Wow," I mutter as she walks away, letting her hips sway in a far too exaggerated way.

"Yeah," he agrees. "I think she was a little young to get your reference. And a little oblivious to get that she was being disrespectful."

"Oh, I think she knew, she just didn't care," I reply, referring to the latter. "But you got the reference. Two points."

"Oh, really? And what are points worth?" he asks curiously, with a hungry glint in his eye.

"I'm afraid you don't get to hear about the points system until the third date," I tease him, finally relaxing into the conversation.

"Third date, huh?" he asks with a wink and a cheeky grin.

"Mhm," I murmur, blushing.

He leans back into the blue upholstered bench and slings his arm over the back of it, his muscles rippling distractingly. He runs the tip of his tongue over the inside of his top lip. Distraction turns into a lump in my throat, and suddenly I have a deep-seated need to run my tongue over his mouth, his perfect fucking chest, those arms. I take a deep breath and still myself.

"You're something else, Greco," he murmurs, his eyes dancing with amusement.

"Yeah? Why's that?" I ask.

"I never know what you're going to say," he replies seriously.

"Is that a good thing?"

He considers me for a moment, scrubbing a hand over the stubble on his chin. "It's fascinating," he finally replies with a small, crooked smile.

I shift uncomfortably in my seat, staring at him for a moment trying to figure out why I feel so awkward, when it hits me. I'm torn between my intense attraction to him and waiting for him to drop a lie. I realize how unfair that is and refocus on getting to know him. Because that doesn't mean I have to trust him. But I won't ever get there if I don't give him a chance.

Even so, there is still a question I want to ask him. I can't bring myself to form the words, though.

"You look like you just got caught with your hand in the cookie jar," Julian teases, leaning forward. "Care to tell me why?"

I decide to go for it and ask him about what he said outside the club earlier today. "Why isn't it a good idea for me to get to know you? Are you married or something? Gay? Escaped from a mental institution?" I try to keep my tone light.

He runs a hand through the long hair slicked back on the top of his head and it musses it back toward the wild, sexy mess it was when I first saw him.

"See, that right there is exactly what I meant. I wasn't expecting that," he replies, sighing heavily. His eyes flick back up to mine. "Not married. No girlfriend, either. And I think we both know I'm not gay." He gives me a long look full of promise and desire.

I look down, blushing, focusing on the tattoos winding around his wrist, words that I can't quite make out at this angle. It makes me wonder how much of his gorgeous body the tattoos cover.

"So mental institution escapee," I murmur, imagining tracing the lines on his arms with my fingertips. Or my tongue.

He huffs a laugh that snaps me back to reality and I look back up into his face. "No. It's just given my commitments, I shouldn't be trying to date you."

"And yet here we are," I reply softly.

Julian stares at me thoughtfully and I stare back unflinchingly. The attraction hums between us again. It's like nothing I've ever experienced. I just want to touch the man. And it's not like I can fault him for being too busy to date. I'd just voiced the same reasoning to Nils.

Waitress Heather chooses that moment to appear with our food, breaking the tension of the moment. She flirts with Julian the whole time, continuing to ignore me as she asks what else she can do for him, with heavy undertones that suggest she'd suck his dick under the table if that's what he wanted. It's all I can do to keep my mouth shut, and he brushes her off politely until we're alone once more.

"You know, I don't exactly have a lot of time for this sort of thing, either," I finally admit after we've both started in on our meals in silence. I look down into my plate, playing with a fry. "So maybe we just keep this casual."

Julian wipes his mouth with a napkin and sets it down on the table. "Really? Or is that just one of those things women say when they're afraid a guy is going to dick them around?" he asks matter-of-factly.

It makes me laugh loudly enough to catch the attention of the few people in the restaurant. "Yes, probably," I agree.

He stares at me unflinchingly. "I don't want to do that," he says.

I push my plate away and lean back. No internal voice clueing me in on a lie. So he doesn't *intend* to do that. But that doesn't mean he won't. I decide it doesn't matter, and I say so. It makes him laugh, and if I wasn't so confused I'd appreciate once again how gorgeous he is when he laughs.

Either way, it breaks the tension that had been building and I take the opportunity to change the subject. We spend a good, long while talking about other, less serious things, ignoring the dirty looks our waitress shoots us as dinner turns into dessert, which turns into coffee, until it's getting so late that I finally notice it's pitch black outside. I glance at my phone finally, noting it's after ten p.m.

"Holy shit," I gasp, showing Julian the time. "I didn't mean to keep you so long."

He laughs, his deep, rumbly laugh that shoots straight to my core and curls my toes. "I can't say I mind," he replies. "But I should get home. I do have to work tomorrow. You know, in the morning. We don't all run nightclubs." He winks at me and rises out of the booth, extending his hand to me. "I'll walk you to your car."

I suck my bottom lip between my teeth to suppress the huge grin threatening to break across my face. Despite my initial reservations, it was an amazing date. And we click on so much more than just a physical level. He's funny, in a dry, sarcastic way, and we have similar tastes. He almost seems too good to be true as I slip my hand in his and let him lead me out of the diner into the cool October night.

Walking alongside him quietly and comfortably feels so natural. I'm acutely aware of his huge, strong frame beside me. It's a short walk, though, and when we reach my car in the lot next to the club, I don't want to let go of his hand.

"That's your ride?" he asks in surprise.

I shrug. "Yep."

He lets out a long, low whistle and swings me around so I'm in front of him, my ass pressed against the driver's side door. My breathing accelerates as he steps into me, sliding his arms around my waist and dropping his mouth to my ear. His hot breath tickles me, sending shivers down my spine.

"It's almost as beautiful as you are," he murmurs into my ear. He pulls back to look into my eyes. "When can I see you again?"

This time I can't stop my smile. "Mondays and Wednesdays are technically my days off," I reply, realizing how that sounds as I'd worked today anyway. "Or most days in the early afternoon could work too."

"Wednesday then," he murmurs, looking down at me intently.

I can't say I'm sorry he picked the next time I'm available. The thought of waiting even two days seems too long.

I run my hands down his strong arms, relishing the feeling of being held. It's been far too long. He lets out a small sigh of contentment and, looking up into his face, I think he's going to kiss me. My whole body tenses in anticipation. But he takes his dear sweet time, lifting a hand to run down my cheek. I press my face into his palm, closing my eyes. His touch is electric, lighting up every nerve ending along its path.

"Open your eyes," he demands.

When I do I can see that his full lips are slightly parted, his massive chest heaving slightly under my hand. My eyes trail up his face. When our gazes meet, my breath stops for a moment.

"I'm not sure I want to kiss you." His words stop me cold, like a bucket of ice water on my libido.

"Excuse me?" I demand, slamming my hand into his chest to push him away. But it's like trying to move a brick wall.

He laughs, grabbing my wrists and spreading them apart easily like I'm a rag doll. I struggle anyway, trying to wrench myself from his grasp, but he tucks my arms behind my back, pulling me into his chest once more. I glare up at him, furious at his manhandling me.

"Easy there," he says soothingly. "Damn, you're feisty."

I scrunch my brow and pout at him defiantly. "And you're an ass," I retort.

The sexy smirk he's oh-so-fucking-good-at reappears. "Well, I can't deny that," he replies teasingly. "But I meant I'm not sure I want to kiss you, because I don't know that I'd trust myself to stop. And I really need to sleep tonight."

The fight drains out of me at his words, so he releases my wrists and I slump back against the car. "Oh," I say in a small voice.

He doesn't move. He just looks down at me, still smirking. "Are you always this spunky?" he teases.

"Only when someone provokes me," I grouse.

He brings out a lot of things I'm not used to feeling. I turn around, open the car door, and bend over to toss my purse into the passenger seat, forgetting for a moment that Julian's eyes are on me.

But I hear his sharp intake of breath. Then I feel his hands pulling at my hips, yanking me out of the doorframe, spinning me around.

His eyes are nearly black, his pupils dilated. "Fuck it," he huffs, and his lips are on mine.

He takes what he wants roughly, covering my lips with his, suckling at my bottom lip with his teeth before running his tongue across the seam of my lips, pressing for entry. Which I eagerly allow, meeting his tongue fiercely with my own, gliding my hands up his arms, across his chest, then wrapping them around his neck to pull myself into him.

The heat rises in my core as our bodies meld together, as I feel every inch of his hard body pressed against me. With his warmth, his smell, his body wrapped around me, I'm consumed by the intense explosion of our attraction. It overrides my senses, my logic, my whole body. His hands knead the soft flesh of my backside through my jeans, desperately trying to pull me closer. But there's no more space, and I can't tell where I end and Julian begins.

Until he pulls away abruptly, panting. The heat slowly fades to a simmer as he strokes his long fingers up and down my arms.

"You're something else," he murmurs, looking intently into my eyes. "But you'd better get out of here before I bend you over the back of this car and fuck you silly."

Holy shit. I gasp, my core tightening in response to his dirty, sexy threat. Part of me wants to call his bluff. But I'm not that easy. I press him away with one hand.

"You should get home," I respond, opening the car door and carefully sliding in on unsteady legs. I roll down the window and he leans his arms on the door, his face inches from mine.

"I'll see you Wednesday, Francesca," he says.

"Thanks for dinner," I reply, unable to keep the shit-eating grin off my face.

He leans in through the window and kisses me gently. "You're welcome," he whispers in my ear seductively.

We say our goodnights and I head home, knowing it'll be a long while before I sleep. And that even once I do, I'll probably dream about him fucking me over the back of my car.

Chapter 6 — Julian

"So you're seeing her tomorrow?" Sal asks again. The old man runs a hand back over the few greasy strands of hair he has left on his head.

I shift in his uncomfortable office chair, totally over this fucking conversation.

"For the third time, yes," I reiterate. "Want me to draw you a fucking picture?"

Sal's sharp eyes narrow, and he points a ringed finger at me.

"Watch your mouth, kid. Remember who you're talking to," he says ominously. He drops his hand to the ashtray in front of him, grabbing his cigarette and taking a drag like he's gearing up to rip me a new one.

I clench my jaw. Here comes the "I made you" and "you owe me everything" part of his speech. Old fucking news.

"Sorry, boss," I reply sarcastically.

And to my surprise, the bastard laughs. "You've always been a bold little shit," he scoffs, shaking his head and crushing the butt of his cigarette into the ashtray. "Whatever. This time, don't fuck it up, just get the goddamn information I'm sending you in there for."

I raise an eyebrow but don't fire back a snarky response. He's in a good mood. I don't know why, considering that his business is tanking and I don't fucking care, but I'll take it.

"I assume that means you still won't tell me what your plans are for this chick?" I ask, casually leaning back in the chair.

Sal snorts. "You ask a lot of questions. No, not yet. Just stick with her until you see how deep she's in."

"And if she's clean?" I ask. Because I'm pretty sure she is. I don't think Frankie would have accepted help to get where she is. At least, not the kind Sal is thinking. And I may not know exactly what he wants from her, but I don't think she's going to work for him, if that's what he's after. He may need her, but she sure as hell doesn't need this dirtbag. But, unfortunately, I do. At least for now.

Sal leans back in his chair, rocking dangerously far back in the piece of junk with a self-satisfied smirk.

"You like her," he accuses me in a taunting tone. If I didn't know him better, I'd say he was genuinely interested in my happiness. But thirteen years' experience tells me otherwise.

I don't break eye contact as I shrug. "She's cool," I allow. "But she's a job."

He allows his chair to settle back forward and leans toward me. "Good," he says with a manic glint in his eye. "Just remember to keep it in your fucking pants. We don't want this to blow up in our faces."

As if I needed the reminder that she's off limits. That it wasn't better for her if she never saw me again. That I shouldn't be having these endless thoughts of touching her, tasting her, making her mine in every fucking way possible.

So. Fucked.

* * *

As we arranged, I find myself at Frankie's door at five p.m. the next day. I tug at my black henley, smooth my dark jeans, and hope I don't look as fucking nervous as I feel. I tuck the surprise I have for her behind my back and knock.

When she opens the door, she looks good enough to make a guy forget just about everything else. Her high-waisted black pants fit her like they were spray painted on. The white top she wears bands over her gorgeous tits, a sliver of her soft, feminine stomach showing. Her lips are, as usual, as cherry red as her ride. Her hair is loose and wild, and I just want to wind my fingers into it.

But she's looking at me like I might be holding a murder weapon behind my back.

"Hi," she says cautiously. "Whatcha got there?"

"Hey," I reply. I let a mischievous smile creep across my face as I produce the pinwheel from behind my back and present it to her.

She takes it, not looking any less confused. "I'll just go put this in water?" she jokes.

I suppress a smile, instead leaning in and giving her a brief, but no less stimulating, kiss.

"It's a clue," I explain. "About our date."

"We're going to a kids birthday party?" she teases, stepping out and closing the door behind her.

"Something like that," I respond, trying to maintain the mystery.

She tries to wheedle it out of me the whole way to the car, but I won't budge. She'll see soon enough. When we get to my car, I open the passenger door and gesture for her to get in. But she's stopped on the sidewalk, gaping at my ride.

"You drive a sedan?" she asks incredulously.

I raise an eyebrow, hoping she's not as judgmental as that sounded. It's no classic American convertible, but it's a pretty nice fucking car. "Is that a bad thing?"

"No, sorry, not at all," she responds. "I'm just a little surprised. It's so practical." She slides into the seat and I close the door behind her. As I walk around the car and climb into the driver seat, I weigh my response.

"What did you expect?" I ask curiously as I start the engine.

She ponders that for a moment. "A motorcycle maybe?" she finally replies as I ease into traffic.

I give a short, derisive laugh and shake my head. "Assumptions, assumptions," I scold her. "You look beautiful, by the way." I glance over at her gorgeous profile, trying not to salivate and reveal just how hot I find her.

"Thanks," she says. "You're not so bad yourself."

I wave a hand dismissively. "What, this old thing? Pshh."

She laughs and we banter back and forth for the few minutes it takes us to get to our destination. As we pull into a parking lot at the Santa Monica Pier, I see her head whipping around to take in her surroundings in shock.

"You're taking me to the amusement park?" she asks, laughing.

I flash her a grin. "Can't get anything past you," I reply with a wink. "It closes in a couple hours. I figured we could play a little before grabbing some dinner. Is that okay?" I look over at her as I park, suddenly worried that this was a bad idea.

To my relief, she shakes her head and laughs. "It's totally okay, I love this place," she replies. "I just wouldn't have guessed it was your sort of date."

There she goes again with the assumptions. Part of me is glad I can surprise her as much as she surprises me. Part of me doesn't want to enjoy this as much as I am. In any case, I can't help teasing her a little.

"Do you always stereotype so much?" I ask.

She opens her mouth, but closes it again quickly, seemingly thinking better of whatever snark she was about to lay down. Because she knows I'm right.

"Maybe? I don't know. I don't feel like I'm usually this judgmental," she replies, blushing.

I can't say I've ever seen a woman blush so much. I realize she must really be into me. And I could be a snarky ass in return. Or I could seize the opportunity.

I cock my head to the side, throwing some intensity at her.

"Just with guys who are interested in you, then?" I ask.

A sexy little smile blooms on her face. "So you're interested in me, huh?" she teases, dodging the question as she slides out of the car.

34

Fuck yes. I love a good chase. But I don't rush, taking my time getting out and following her to the park entrance. I catch up to her in a few long strides.

"I thought that was obvious after the other night," I remark, falling into step beside her, but staying a careful distance away.

She shrugs as we enter the park. "I didn't want to assume," she replies airily.

I laugh loudly. "Well, that's a first," I reply with a wink as we round the corner into the main stretch of the park. "Where to?"

She points to the mini-hoops booth to our right. "How's your game?" she asks.

I can't help letting an ironic smile slip over my features. "I guess we'll find out." I eye the plethora of stuffed critters lining the columns and eaves of the booth. "See something you like?"

I carefully turn my eyes to hers, letting the suggestiveness of my tone do its work.

She blushes furiously and turns toward the booth. Probably to hide. But she quickly points to a fluffy pink stuffed elephant hanging from the side of the booth. "I'm going to name her Juliana," she teases.

With a burst of laughter, I accept the challenge. "I'll see what I can do, but I make no promises," I respond. Again, with the double meaning. I swear I'm not even trying to.

I slap the requisite cash on the counter, and the teenager behind the counter gives me an I-don't-give-a-shit-about-my-job stare as he plops three tiny basketballs in front of me.

I line up for the first shot, trying to ignore Frankie's eyes on me. Fuck, that girl does things to my insides. Distracted, I let loose and it falls short, swiping the tiny net. Out of the corner of my eye I see Frankie cross her arms and lean into the pillar, her eyes flicking between me and the hoop. I notice that her tits are shoved together and peeking out the top of her shirt, unbalancing me even more. My second shot goes wide. I take a breath and try to shove the image of her out of my mind. It doesn't work, and my last shot misses as well, bouncing spectacularly off the backboard.

What-fucking-ever. It's not like I'm trying to impress her, anyway. I turn toward her and raise my arms in an exaggerated shrug. I did warn her.

Her face is a mask as she pushes up from her leaning position.

"Nice try, champ," she says, looking up at me.

Well, shit. She surprises me once again with her chill response.

"You want a try?" I challenge her.

"No, I suck at basketball," she admits. "That's why I asked you to do it."

The honesty makes me laugh. "Fair enough." I stare back at her for a minute. I can't get a read on her. Is she the tough chick or the sweetheart? She can't really seem to make up her mind. I kind of dig it.

"What do you like to do here?" she asks curiously.

Well, that's a huge fucking can of worms. I suppress a sigh and lead her down a couple of booths to the water gun race. "I used to play this for hours when I was a kid," I admit, taking a seat on one of the black stools that are cracked with age and use.

She slips onto the stool next to me, her eyes following my movements as I play absentmindedly with the long, metal tube affixing the toy to its pedestal. There's still one empty stool, so we're asked to wait a few minutes before they give up on having a full lineup.

"So you came here a lot growing up?" she asks shrewdly while we wait.

I turn to face her, unsure of how much to tell her. She slides her legs between mine unexpectedly and leans in, waiting for a reply. I look down into her eyes. Her long lashes frame her dark blue eyes, her bright red lips begging to be ravished. But being this close to her, I'm moved in a way that's so much more than the primal reaction I seem to have to her. She's looking at me like she wants to reach down inside and pull out all the good stuff. If only there were any of that to give her. But something about this moment makes me wish I had something to give.

"Yeah," I finally respond. "You're a local — you didn't come here when you were a kid?"

"Not really," she replies, the corners of her full lips dipping. "I grew up in East L.A. so it wasn't like a regular thing."

"So what was your thing? Were you a daddy's girl or a rebel?" I ask, keeping the attention on her.

"Can't a girl be both?" she asks with a sly grin.

I'm intrigued, but I'm not going to let her off the hook that easily. So, I just stare at her with a raised eyebrow, waiting for a real response.

She lets out a sigh. And I get it. I don't like getting serious either. "My dad died before I was born. So no, not a daddy's girl. And my mom worked all the time, so I was pretty much raised by my grandma. She's a fucking saint, and as much as I wanted to rebel, I couldn't bring myself to do anything to upset her."

Raised by her *grandmother?* Again, she surprises me. And I can see how uncomfortable she is sharing. "I'm sorry, I didn't know," I say softly, leaning forward and taking her hand, hoping the reassurance keeps her from bolting.

Her eyes are locked on our entwined fingers and she seems frozen in place. I disentangle a hand and tilt her face up to look me in the eyes. Her vulnerability is on full display. This is the moment I would usually bolt. And regardless of why I have to be here, right now, I just want her to look at me and know that she's not just beautiful because of the strength she tries to project, but also because of the things she thinks make her look weak. Of all people, I get how hard it is to share that part of yourself. It takes more guts than most people have. Including me.

Our intimate moment is broken by the attendant calling everyone to the ready. Simultaneously annoyed and thankful for the distraction, I turn to my ready position. Frankie does the same with a determination on her face that is adorable. I can tell she really wants to kick my ass.

Not even a minute later, the race is over, and Frankie wins. Coming in a close second doesn't matter. By an inch or a mile, I fucking lost. To a girl.

"Fuck. I *never* lose at that game. I think your gun worked better," I grouse jokingly as we step away from the booth.

She elbows me lightly in the side. "Mhm, that must've been it," she agrees, obviously humoring me.

I shoot her a mock dirty look as we get to the end of the row of games, still keeping a careful distance. Because I know if I don't, I'm going to lose control of this situation and what I need to be doing.

"So you grew up in Santa Monica?" she asks, playing with the edge of her blouse as I step up to do the ring toss. Her awkwardness tells me she notices the physical and emotional distance I'm trying to create.

I pay and take the stack of rings I'm given, weighing one in my right palm while I also weigh how to answer her. Silently, I gently lob the ring in a graceful arc toward the mass of glass bottles pressed together. It slides neatly around the neck of the bottle I'd aimed at. Frankie looks at me incredulously as the attendant congratulates me. I shut them both out and weigh up the next shot as I find my words. I decide she showed me hers, so I should show her mine.

"Not really," I reply, eyeing the remaining bottles and looking for my next target. "I was in the system until I was fourteen. I was all over the place before then." I can't remember the last time I told someone that. Because you tell someone you were a foster kid and they automatically label you: Reject. Troublemaker. Loser. I fling the second ring a little too hard and miss the toss. The ring goes bouncing around, pinging with the sound of failure.

Frankie's hand snakes over my forearm. Reluctantly, I turn to look at her. Just as I saw her, she sees me. Before I can stop her, she slides into me, her soft hands wrapping around the back of my neck to pull my lips to hers. It doesn't last long, but it feels like her telling me I'm wrong. That I do have the guts to share. The acceptance in her kiss is reassuring in a way it shouldn't be.

But as she moves away, I react without a thought. I fling my final ring aside and reach to pull her back in. To taste her again. Just for a moment I let everything out in that kiss, dipping my tongue into her mouth, sliding mine against hers as if the connection could save us both from haunted memories. Despite its depth, there's purity and innocence in the kiss that stirs something inside of me.

Someone clears their throat. I pull away to find the booth attendant holding a generously sized stuffed unicorn in offering. We both look at the last ring, nestled neatly around the neck of a small bottle, and burst out laughing. I accept the prize, offering the fluffy creature in Frankie's direction.

"You should keep it," she says. "You earned it, after all."

I scrunch my eyebrows together. What the fuck am I going to do with a stuffed unicorn? But I bite that back, opting not to completely ruin the moment. Instead, I shrug and tuck it under my arm, wandering to a bench across from the ring toss. We settle onto it without a word.

"What happened when you were fourteen?" she asks after a bit.

I pull at the unicorn's mane, separating the rainbow of colors, then smoothing them back together, over and over again. Order. Chaos. Order. Chaos. It's a good metaphor for life.

"I decided I was over it," I reply carefully, not making eye contact. "Over hopping houses. Shitty foster parents just looking to collect checks. My fucked up 'brothers and sisters' always looking for a fight. I just wanted to be left alone."

She takes a minute to absorb that, but thankfully doesn't offer any token expressions of pity. I fucking hate when people do that. Her atypical reaction makes me want to tell her more. Or maybe it's just her. Either way, I do. I try to start slowly, but before long the words are tumbling out of me as if they've been waiting years to come out. Which I guess they have.

I tell her about my years in the system, then living on the streets until I was nineteen, when I met Sal. I don't mention him by name, since he'd fucking kill me, but I do reminisce that he helped me clean up my act, gave me a job, and took me under his wing, ultimately helping me become the man I am today. If only she could really understand what that means. The things he asks me to do. And how, despite my gratitude for being saved from the streets, I'm finally old enough to know I need to get the fuck out. When I'm done talking, we sit in silence for a few moments before she says anything.

"Wow, I'm impressed," she says plainly.

I look up at her in shock. She looks like she means it. I shake my head morosely.

"You shouldn't be," I reply. "There's a lot you don't know about me."

She huffs a small laugh. "True," she allows. "But there's a lot I do know about you. You're considerate. Respectful. Oddly conservative in your vehicle choices. You love classic cars, hard rock, and cheap beer." That elicits a laugh from me, but she keeps going. "And despite a rough start, you let someone help you, you learned, and grew, and now it seems like you're doing pretty good for yourself. Oh, and you have excellent taste in women." She gives me a teasing poke in the side.

"You forgot my *other* skills," I reply suggestively, still smiling.

She raises an eyebrow at me. "Must have slipped my mind," she responds sarcastically. The fucking minx.

"Is that so?" I ask huskily, leaning toward her. "Maybe I need to remind you then."

Her pupils dilate and she sinks her upper teeth into her bottom lip, drawing my eyes back to her mouth. It flips that fucking primal switch, and I need to get her someplace. Fast. My eyes flick up to the photo booth behind us.

Her eyes follow mine, and as I grab her hand it clicks. She lets me pull her into the curtained alcove, closing it behind us. I don't waste time. I don't have a choice. I need a fix of those fucking lips. I press her into the wall, urgently claiming them with mine. The stuffed unicorn falls to the floor, forgotten as I taste her.

There's nothing innocent about this kiss. I wrap my hand around her neck, trying to plunder her as deeply as I can, our lips working fervently together. My other hand grabs at her, needing to feel her responding to me. It lands on her perfectly round ass, pulling her hips against mine in a grind that causes her to moan against me.

I feel her wrap her arms around my neck, pulling herself up to slip her leg behind my ass, pulling me in. My cock hardens at the thought of fucking her right here. And I know this has to stop. I slide my hands to her hips and gently keep her in place while I pull away.

She stares up at me, panting and bewildered.

I try to play off that I'm just as lost to this as she is. "Well?" I ask as calmly as I can, scooping up the unicorn from the floor and stuffing it in my back pocket.

She's clearly worked up, and it takes her a minute to understand.

"Yes, your *other* skills are amazing too," she allows with a roll of her eyes. Seemingly having gathered her wits, she straightens out her clothes and pushes me out of the booth until she can get by me. She's clearly annoyed, and I don't get it. It seemed like she wanted me to kiss her before, and by the way she was responding I know I didn't cross any lines she wasn't perfectly happy to blow to smithereens. So what the fuck?

"Fuck, what did I do now?" I let slip. And instantly regret it as she turns on her heel to face me, her nostrils flaring, her gorgeous lips pursed.

"Try groping me to prove a point," she snaps. She makes to move away, but I'm not going to let that go without setting her straight, so I grab her before she can get away and turn her around to face me.

She's already gone from angry to hurt, so I slide my hands around her heart-shaped face, willing her to understand.

"For fuck's sake Francesca, that's not why I did it," I try to explain. But I can't think of any way to tell her why. So I show her, leaning down and capturing her lips with mine once more.

But different this time. Slower, more deliberately. I've always been better at show than tell, and I can feel her respond as her body softens into mine. I take the opportunity to slip my hands around her back, gently cradling her as I say with a kiss what I can't put into words.

The desire, the connection, the acceptance of each other is all spelled out mutely as we gently explore each other's mouths with our tongues. She tastes, and smells, like heaven. It's the silent primal bond that's between us made tangible in the perfect fit of our mouths and our bodies as she melts into me.

When we break apart, she puts her hands on my chest and looks up at me. The intensity of emotion is overwhelming, and I just can't deal with this right now. I'm all over the fucking map.

I lace my fingers through hers with one hand. "Come on," I say, pulling her to the ticket booth at the Ferris wheel. I'm hoping we can just enjoy the scenery and get a break from the intensity of the evening.

After we've climbed into one of the gondolas, spinning slowly to the top, I ask her more about her family, as nonchalantly as I can. I don't want to scare her off.

It's obviously a tough topic for her to discuss. She talks about her contentious relationship with her mother, that her grandmother always has to be their referee, but since the arrival of her younger brother twelve years ago they've managed to be more civil with each other for his sake. But that there's always an undercurrent of tension. I can tell there's a lot she's not telling me, but I know pushing the issue wouldn't help, so I just let her talk.

I try to put physical distance between us again, but I'm so wrapped up in what she's saying that every time I think to notice, I'm touching her. Holding her hand, stroking her thigh, wrapping my arm behind her shoulders. It's all too easy to fall into.

When she goes silent, finally, neither of us tries to fill the void. On our second circuit, as we flip oceanside we can see the sun setting in brilliant oranges and pinks reflecting off the dark ocean. It's always been one of my favorite sights.

"Did you plan this?" she asks, gesturing to the setting sun and nestling closer, leaning her head on my chest. It feels so fucking good to be close to her.

I let out a small laugh. "Maybe," I admit.

"You're smooth, I'll give you that," she replies.

If she only knew. A nagging feeling tugs at my gut. It takes me a minute to name it.

Guilt.

Here's this complex, smart, feisty, and gorgeous creature opening up to me. I'm such a fucking asshole.

I shake my head at my own thoughts, causing her to look up at me questioningly.

"Thank you," I say softly. I said it because I didn't know what to say, but I suddenly feel it, and more. "For opening up to me. And for not pitying me. The few people I've told did, or worse. It's why I don't usually say anything."

She nods. I can tell she understands, at least more than most people do. "I can't pity something that made you the man you are," she explains. "Because I like that man. A lot more than I want to admit."

There's that feeling again. Fuck. Sal was concerned about me fucking her. But now I'm concerned about something so much worse. "How much more?" I ask. Even though I think I know the answer, because I'm in the same fucking boat.

Her eyes rake over my face, and she's clearly unsure of what to say. But I'm not sure she needs to. I think we've both been hit harder by whatever this is than we expected. It takes a whole lot to scare me, but this might just do it. This situation is already too fraught with bullshit. I can't let this girl fall for me. She deserves so fucking much better.

"We've only been on two dates," she finally replies. "I don't know what to say."

I shake my head, withdrawing into myself, looking out over the water as the wind whips through our hair. As we descend to the bottom, the operator opens the gate and ushers us out, telling us the park is closing in a few minutes.

We wander silently to the exit, to my car. I open the door and turn to find Francesca looking at me with an expression between sad and scared.

41

"I freaked you out and now you're thinking this was a mistake." Her voice is low, but she's close enough for me to hear. And it's not a question.

We stare at each other in silence. What can I say to that? I do think this was a mistake, but not in the way she thinks. I want to punch something. I want to beat the ever-loving shit out of the forces of the universe that made us meet now. Under these circumstances. Because there's no way in hell I can be loyal to both Sal and Frankie. And I refuse to do that to her. Sal can get his intel some other way. But that doesn't mean I don't have to stay away from Frankie. There's no winning for me in this situation. And the why doesn't matter. No explanation is going to make this easier.

"I don't think we should see each other again," I reply sadly, avoiding admitting that I don't think she is a mistake at all. I'm the fucking mistake.

But if I've seen anything in my fucked-up life, it's the face of a woman determined not to cry. The face she's wearing right now.

"I'm not usually …" she trails off, clearly not sure what to say. "I didn't expect this."

I shut the car door and close the distance between us. I pull her face up so I can look her in the eyes.

"Me, neither," I respond. "I'm sorry, Francesca."

She blinks hard and nods. And her tough girl mask drops in, just like that. I'm almost thankful for it. Anything to make this easier.

She takes a step back. "Goodbye, Julian." She backs away.

"Let me drive you home," I plead. I want to reach out to her, but on some level, I know it's best to just let her leave.

She makes the choice, shaking her head and giving me a sad smile. "Take care," she says. And with a wave, she turns and walks away.

Chapter 7 — Frankie

I don't walk all the way home. It may only be a couple of miles, but that would be murder in heels. Instead, I stop in a coffee shop a few blocks away on the Third Street Promenade and grab a latte, sitting at a table outside to people watch. Wondering how the hell things went so fast.

Before the water race, in that out-of-nowhere intimate moment we shared, I realized there was a sincerity about Julian that made me like him more than I'd let myself like anyone in a long time. Chalk it up to all the lying jerks I've encountered. But Julian seemed different. Or so I thought. Though I'm an intense person. I don't hide who I am. If he can't take it, best that he figures that out now.

Though the disappointment on his face as we parted is going to haunt me. But it's for the best. The man affects me in ways that are not normal. I can't even figure out why.

I need Emma. As I place the call, I know she's going to kill me for not calling her last night or earlier today.

* * *

"Three fucking days, Frankie. I can't leave you alone for three fucking days," Emma says, shaking her head and grabbing a breadstick from the center of the table.

"A little louder, babe, I don't think the chef quite heard you," Ben remarks drily, taking a huge gulp of his beer and shaking his head.

"If you wanted quiet you shouldn't have married her," I point out. I note that I sound as tired as I feel.

Ben, totally oblivious, laughs behind another sip of beer.

Emma points a finger at me. "Deflecting," she accuses me. "So that's it? It's just over?"

I shrug. What else is there to say? I've already relayed everything to her that's happened since she left my apartment on Sunday.

"You know if he hadn't ended it, I would've gone home, freaked out, and never called him again," I reply.

Emma snorts a laugh. "At least you know yourself," she allows. "Damn, I really wish I would've gotten a look at this guy."

Ben scoffs. "I'm sitting *right here*," he points out, annoyed, running a meaty hand over his short brown hair.

"So you didn't even get to ..." Emma trails off, opening her mouth wide and gently inserting a breadstick into her mouth, sucking it suggestively.

Ben drops his head into his hands, groaning in embarrassment. They've cracked my pity party, and I laugh until I'm choking. I take a sip of water to calm down, then shake my head, wiping tears of laughter from my eyes.

"No!" I protest, still chuckling.

Emma grins widely, takes an enthusiastic bite of the breadstick and nudges Ben's arm, knocking his hand away from his face.

"You can look up, I'm done fellating the appetizers," she teases him. "And girl talk is over. For now anyway. Tell her about your promotion." Emma smiles encouragingly at Ben.

"Hey, you got a promotion? Congratulations," I offer with as much enthusiasm as I can muster. "What's the position?"

Ben shrugs his wide shoulders in a bad impression of modesty. "It's no big deal. They made me foreman." *Lie.*

Oh, boy. Here we go again. I suppress a sigh. I glance over at Emma. She looks extremely happy. I put on my practiced poker face.

"That's great," I reply, flicking my eyes back to Ben's sturdy frame. "Does that come with a raise?"

"Sure does," Ben says proudly. *Lie.*

"God, we'll *finally* be able to take a proper honeymoon," Emma gushes.

This is one of the things I hate most about my gift. Lying to people I love about the people they love who are lying to them. Because Emma specifically asked we never tell Ben about my ability for times like this. She thinks she wants to know. And while I've always known Ben is a compulsive liar, I learned long ago to keep my mouth shut about Emma's boyfriends. It just drives a wedge between us. And after all, everybody lies anyway. Though I just wish Ben didn't lie quite so much. Normally, I let it go. But this one is kind of big. And I know I'll have to say something next time I get her alone.

"That's exciting," I respond as sincerely as I can. But I don't ask questions, subtly discouraging continuing the conversation, saving Ben from digging himself deeper.

Thankfully, our meals arrive and there's silence as we tuck in. Well, as they tuck in. I pick at my food, realizing I don't have much of an appetite after all. I'm still yearning to really talk this out with Emma. Giving her an overview of what happened was fine with Ben around, but I left out a lot of the details. Especially the steamy ones, and we totally skipped a full dissection of the date. So now there are two things I need to talk to Emma about.

* * *

I dreamt of Julian that night. And every night thereafter. His eyes. His body. His vulnerability. The terrifying realization that I was already falling for him after only two dates. By Sunday, the daily emotional dream rollercoaster on top of three crazy nights at the club in a row has me wiped and ready to take a couple of days off completely to regroup.

Unfortunately, life moves on, and I have to drag ass out of bed at ten-thirty to get showered and ready to go to my mom's for lunch at noon. Despite knowing I often need to work until six a.m. on Sundays, she insists on the monthly routine. At least it's not every week.

The drive takes thirty minutes, about the same as it usually takes me to get to and from the club. It reminds me of that saying that everywhere you go in L.A. takes only thirty minutes. If only. I'm lucky I rarely have to drive during rush hour.

Pulling into my mom's driveway, the modest rambler looks the same as it always does with its peeling yellow paint and white trim. Mom's tank of a classic German automobile, still solid despite its obvious age, sits in the spot closest to the front door. Tony's bicycle leans against the bushes under the front window. And as soon as I pull in I can smell melted cheese. It doesn't matter what meal it is at Mom's house, it always smells like melted cheese.

Before I've even made it halfway up the path, the front door springs open and Tony comes flying out, nearly knocking me over with his tall, gangly, twelve-year-old body.

"Frankie," he greets me with a squeeze.

"Geez, Tony, you're huge," I groan. "What'd you grow, like a foot since last month?"

He pulls back, shoving me playfully. "Yeah, and I bet I can kick your ass now too," he teases, balling his fists in front of his face.

"Hey, watch your language, kid," I tease back, slipping a punch in under his defenses.

He rolls his eyes and allows me to drag him inside. I drop my purse and keys on the coffee table in the living room, my hand instinctively reaching behind my back to put down the handgun that's usually nestled there. But I stop short, remembering where I am. I never wear it to Mom's. She hates guns, so I don't ever bring them here, much less discuss my affinity for them.

I go through to the kitchen, where I know I'll find the women and sure enough, they're busy stuffing pasta shells when I walk in. Tony bounds in behind me, sneaking a finger into the ricotta mix they're spooning from. Mom slaps his hand away and looks up.

"Frankie, you're early," she says, her eyes tight and unwelcoming.

45

"Nice to see you too, Mom," I reply sweetly, walking over to the older of the two women. "Hi, Nonna."

My grandmother turns her papery cheek toward me and I plant a kiss on it. "Hello, dear, how are you doing?" Nonna asks, her rhythm unbroken as she fills the casserole dish.

"Tired but good," I reply. "Need help?"

Mom nods at a cutting board piled with a loaf of bread, a stick of butter, a head of garlic, and a bunch of spices.

"You can make the garlic bread," she directs.

I huff a laugh. Mom is all business in the kitchen. Wait. Scratch that. Mom is just all business. Everywhere. At least around me.

I watch her for a moment, her greying head bent over, her slim, strong fingers deftly working. She's always been a little too serious and focused for her own good. Unlike Nonna. Watching Nonna is like watching a dance. She floats through the kitchen, spinning and preparing the food in a graceful rhythm, always with a smile on her ancient, wrinkled face.

With a chuckle, I turn to the bread and get to work.

"How's work, Ma?" I ask without looking up.

"Busy," she says crisply.

I snort. My mother runs the cleaning business her father started decades ago. She busted her ass to prove herself to Grandpa so she could take it over. I'd say it's the reason I barely saw her as a child, but I can't blame it entirely on that. Though I think it was a good excuse for her to avoid me, as she very purposely has never involved me in any of it, even as the business has seemingly grown and taken off.

"That's good?" I reply questioningly.

"It keeps food on the table," she replies in a curt tone.

Nonna looks askance at her and shakes her head.

"Hey, Tony," I call, over trying to make conversation with my mother.

He pops up on the other side of the counter I'm working on. "What's up, Sis?"

"How's school?" I prompt.

He grins and slides onto one of the bar stools and proceeds to catch me up on his last month. I don't miss that, for the first time, he mentions a *girl*. Twice. I give Nonna a look and she just smiles beatifically.

I've long since finished preparing the bread, but Tony keeps me captive, talking until the food is all in the oven. He's still quite possibly the sweetest kid on the planet with his enthusiastic positivity, and the fact that he's still not too cool to hang out with his big sister. I always forget how much I miss him until I'm here, away from the distractions of the club.

Mom leaves the kitchen once she's finished cleaning to go do God only knows what. Heaven forbid she actually have a conversation with her only daughter. But then, there hasn't been much mother-daughter bonding my whole life. Why start now?

In any case, Tony pulls me into the living room to show me his newest video games, and Nonna settles happily into her favorite armchair. She crochets quietly until Tony is contentedly playing his game solo. I take the opportunity to slide onto the couch next to her.

"How are you doing, Nonna?" I ask her loudly enough so she can hear me.

Her hearing has been declining for years, but she refuses to acknowledge it. I think she's just too vain to wear hearing aids. It drives everyone nuts.

"Oh, just peachy," she assures me without looking up from her work. "How are you, *really*? You look sad."

"I'm just tired," I respond.

Now she stops. And gives me The Look. "Frankie, I've raised you from a babe. I know the difference. Who is he?"

Dammit, how does she *do* that?

"Nobody, Nonna. Just a blip on the radar," I grumble.

Nonna cackles. "Anyone who can stir up the imperturbable Frankie Greco isn't a nobody. What did he lie about?"

I sigh and shake my head. "It's not that."

"Then what is it?" she asks simply.

"It was just going too fast. It wasn't right." It sounds lame even to me. I expect her to chastise me, to encourage me to give it a chance despite my reluctance to let people in, to get in a serious relationship.

But Nonna always surprises me.

"You know what's best for you," she replies with a shrug, returning to the blanket she's making.

I look at her skeptically. "Is this a trap?" I ask.

Nonna smiles widely. "Allow an old woman to plead the fifth when her lie detector of a granddaughter asks a question to which she already knows the answer."

Before I can respond, my mom walks in.

"What's the question?" she asks curiously.

Tony calls out in a singsong voice, "Frankie's got a boyfriend."

Fucking kids. They're always listening.

"Oh?" my mother asks, suddenly very interested as she sits next to me on the couch. "Why didn't you bring him?"

I reach over and slap Tony on the back of the head, but he just grins and keeps playing his game.

"I do *not* have a boyfriend," I grumble.

"Methinks the lady doth protest too much," Nonna teases.

I clench my jaw, knowing the more they get a rise, the more they'll keep going. So I just cross my arms and sullenly sink back into the couch cushions.

My mother stares at me for a minute before rising to head back to the kitchen. Probably to clean something that's already been cleaned six times. Any excuse to avoid direct conversation.

"I'm sure, like every man in her life, it'll pass," my mother says archly as she walks away.

"Geez, that was low, even for her," I snipe after she's disappeared.

Nonna finally puts her crocheting down. "Now, Frankie, darling, you know she's just projecting."

As if I needed the reminder that Mom has never been married, or even able to keep a man around for very long. But for very different reasons. She's unbearable and frigid. My relationships usually end over whoppers. Except with Julian who, ironically, only lied to me once, the first time we met, in an attempt not to seem like a stalker.

"I know," I respond. "But she's not wrong."

A weathered, frail hand slips over mine. "I love you, you know that," she says forcefully. "So I'm going to give it to you straight between the eyes. Learn to stop trying to make things go how you think they should, and go with what is. Even if it doesn't end up where you want, at least you let it run its course. But your expectations are stopping you from being happy, Frankie."

"Even if I wanted to go with it, I'm pretty sure I scared him off," I explain. "We hadn't even known each other a week and I was spilling my guts to him." I stop myself short of saying I was also ready to rip the man's clothes off in public and do naughty things to him. I shudder lightly at the memory of his lips and his hands on me in that photo booth. Some things you just don't discuss with your grandmother.

The old woman smiles knowingly. "That's how it *should* be, Francesca."

I open my mouth to protest, closing it again rapidly. The truth of her words is like a smack in the face. I was so scared of it because it was like nothing I'd ever experienced before. It was so fast. That is, compared to my previous relationships. But those didn't work out. So what if how I feel around Julian really *is* how it should be? The real deal? I suddenly feel nauseous.

"Mhm," Nonna mutters smugly, leaning back into her chair and picking up her crocheting again. "You let that man know you want to give it a go, and you'll see whether he's really too scared."

Needless to say I'm pretty quiet the rest of the visit as I process things. But by the time I'm passed around for hugs on my way out, my resolve is set.

As soon as I settle into the driver's seat of my car, I cradle my cellphone in my lap, a blank text message to Julian waiting for my words.

I'm sorry about the other night. I just got freaked out. Can we talk?

And before I can chicken out, I hit "send."

Chapter 8 — Julian

Fuck. Fuck, fuck, fuck, fuck. I look at Frankie's text message again for the hundredth time and run a hand through my hair, tugging roughly as if that'll help me forget it. Right now, I need to focus on finding the words to tell Sal I've blown it.

No, no, no. That's not gonna cut it. I've got to spin it. After all, I learned most of what he wanted to know, right? I just have to hope it'll be enough.

I take a deep breath, fix the hair I mussed back into place, and smooth a hand down the black shirt and pants I'm wearing. Why the old man wants me to dress like the motherfucking grim reaper I'll never know. It's cliché and obnoxious in the still-way-too-fucking-warm Southern California autumn.

Focus. I have to focus. I lift a hand and rap my knuckles on Sal's solid wood office door. The dull thud reverberates through my tired brain.

"'Bout damn time, get your ass in here, son," he calls.

I get in one last eye roll and open the door. Sal sits behind his desk, his reading glasses low on his nose as he peruses a stack of ledgers on the desk.

"Christ, Sal, why don't you go digital already? Join the twenty-first fucking century," I say blandly as I drop into the chair across from him.

"Are you fucking kidding me?" Sal shoots back, tossing his reading glasses on the desk and leaning back in his chair. "I can burn all this shit and it's like it never happened. Put it on the computer, the FBI will be charging in here before the day is over." He looks at me sharply. "Now enough of that shit. Where are we with the Greco girl?"

"Like I told you she probably was, she's clean," I insist.

Sal shifts, looking deceptively patient. "I'll be the judge of that. Tell me what you've got," he directs thinly.

With a sigh, I relay everything she told me that was relevant. And just enough of what wasn't to make him happy. When I'm done, he leans forward onto his arms, tapping the sides of his face as he considers things.

After a few eerily silent minutes, he leans back once more and considers me thoughtfully. "You're even more into this chick than you were the last time you came in my office. I think you've done enough here," he states.

I clench my jaw, unsure of how not to rise to the bait.

"I'm a professional," I assure him. "And she's a job. But whatever the fuck you want, Sal."

Sal smirks knowingly. I forget sometimes that he's known me for so long. And I fucking hate that I didn't learn not to trust him until it was too late. I also hate not knowing what he's got planned for Frankie. It's one of the only things keeping me from walking away right now.

"Good. Because what I want is to make my move. So, stay the fuck out of it until further notice," he directs. "I'm serious, Julian. Deadly serious."

I shrug, feigning indifference to the sincerity of his threat. The exact opposite of what I'm feeling. Because I know Sal, and whatever he's going to do will hurt Frankie. If I thought I could get away with dealing with him myself, I would. But even in his downfall, he's still far too connected for that. And I'm just a little fly on a big fucking dung heap.

So instead of going straight to Frankie to spill my guts and warn her, like my instincts are telling me, I hit the gym to work out my frustration. Like a fucking coward. And I can't help thinking, again, Francesca Greco deserves so much more than I can offer her. So why can't I get her out of my fucking head?

Chapter 9 — Frankie

By Monday afternoon I still haven't heard anything from Julian. Instead, I'm sat at my desk in the club, with Nils and Jess sitting across from me, both awkwardly silent. I don't think I've ever seen Nils so uncomfortable.

"So is someone going to tell me why we're here?" I ask.

Jess shifts in her seat and shoots Nils a look.

"Ms. Wilson would like to lodge a sexual harassment complaint against Mr. Kelly," Nils relays calmly.

He goes to continue but I hold a hand up. "That's very concerning," I say, directly to Jess. "As you know we have a zero-tolerance policy for sexual harassment. Are you comfortable sharing the details with both Mr. Larssen and I?"

Jess tugs at one of her blond curls nervously. "I already told Nils," she says softly.

So he's Nils to her. Interesting. A little less formal than I like to be, but okay.

"All the same, I'd like you to tell me as well, so I can make notes," I explain. "We will, of course, keep what you say in confidence."

"Like, all of it?" Jess asks, clearly nervous.

I consider my response for a moment. "Well, as much as you want us to. Though if you want us to look into it, we may need to talk to Dave about it. But we won't share anything specific."

She shifts in her chair, weighing my words. "Fine," she sighs. "But like, he's totally going to deny it."

I shoot Nils a quick look and he shrugs imperceptibly. "Let us worry about that," I assure her. "Please, tell me what happened."

"It's just that we've been dating for a while," she starts. *Lie.* "But he changed, and I told him it was over, but he, like, clearly didn't get it." *Lie.* "He won't stop following me now, and he keeps trying to touch me even though I tell him to stay away from me." *Lie.*

I roll my lips through my teeth while I regroup on how to tease out some sort of truth that will help me figure out where this is coming from.

"So you and Dave dated?" I ask.

Jess's eyes widen. "That's not against the rules is it?"

"No," I reply, "I just want to make sure I have this straight."

She glances nervously at Nils. His expression is inscrutable.

"Yes," she finally replies to me.

After a beat, I conclude at least that much is true. "For how long, exactly?"

"I don't know," she hedges. "A month?" *Lie.*

Ooookay. "When did you tell him you wanted to stop seeing him?" I ask.

"Last weekend," she replies quickly. *Lie.*

I suppress a sigh. At least I got one truth. I continue to question her, but every detail after is a lie. That he's followed her home from work. That he's followed her around the bar, trying to touch her, kiss her, fondle her, to get her to get back together with him.

Fifteen minutes later I have a massive headache and only theories about why she's bald-faced lying. "Okay, I've documented it all," I say. "We'll look into this as quickly and discreetly as we can. If we aren't able to resolve this by your next shifts, which are ..." I look at Nils.

"Thursday," he supplies.

"Thursday," I reiterate. "Then we'll adjust the schedule so you're working different shifts. Is there anything else you'd like us to do in the meantime?"

I look at Jess expectantly, and I haven't missed her growing frustration.

"So you can't, like, just fire him or whatever?" she asks, clearly irritated as she tugs on her curls again.

"No, but as I said we do take this very seriously, and we will look into it right away," I reaffirm. "If anything else happens, please let us know. I'll check in with you on Wednesday to let you know where we are." I stand, indicating I'm done. Mostly because my pounding head can't take anymore lies.

"Okay," she sighs. "Um. Thanks." She sounds anything but thankful. Irritated is more like it.

Jess stands reluctantly, followed by Nils. I suspect he realizes I'm feeling less than stellar by the softness of his manner as he quietly opens the door and gestures for Jess to precede him out.

"I'll walk Ms. Wilson to her car," he says softly.

I nod my thanks as he disappears behind her. Collapsing back into my chair, I dive into my stash of ibuprofen, downing a few with a full bottle of water.

I'm rubbing my temples firmly in circles, eyes closed, when I hear Nils's designer shoes tapping down the hall. The door clicks shut and a gentle swish of fabric tells me he's waiting patiently in the chair across from me to discuss this.

I take a deep breath and open my eyes. Nils is looking at me with deep concern. I'm not sure if it's for me, or the situation.

"Did you know they were dating?" I ask quietly.

Nils shakes his head. "No," he admits. "I've never even noticed them talking more with each other than they do with anyone else. If anything, I see Dave and Peter chatting together more."

"Did she give you any information she didn't share here today?" I ask.

Nils shrugs. "She was a little more graphic with her language, but it was more or less the same story," he replies.

I raise an eyebrow at him. "She calls you Nils and is comfortable telling you the sordid details of how someone has allegedly harassed her?"

His nostrils flare, which is the closest Nils ever gets to annoyed. "Is that the question you really want to ask?"

"Come on, Nils, give it to me straight," I insist.

He smiles grimly and leans forward. "She flirts. A lot. With everyone. Myself included," he admits. "But she's a bartender. It's how she makes the best tips, so I usually let it go."

"Seriously? That's bullshit, Nils, and you know it. You can't let our female employees flirt with you. It's totally unprofessional," I press.

Nils sighs and shrugs but doesn't offer any response. For all his talents, confrontation is not his thing. And I know that. I'm sure it's why he brought Jess to me rather than handling it himself if her flirtations make him uncomfortable. Though it suddenly occurs to me it could be the exact opposite.

"You don't have a thing for her, do you?" I blurt.

Nils barks out a sharp laugh. "Oh, Francesca, please," he scoffs. "She's only twenty-two."

I cross my arms over my chest. "And you're only thirty-one. You're not *that* much older than her. I don't have anything to worry about here, do I?"

The smile drops off his face as quickly as it came. "No, you don't," he replies firmly. "I may put up with her advances, but I don't encourage them. Nor do I have any interest in her that way."

"Good," I respond, leaning toward him. "Would you like to review the security camera files, or shall I?"

"I can take care of it," he assures me. "I'll let you know tomorrow what I find. I'll also call Mr. Kelly in so we can speak to him tomorrow."

"Thanks," I say. "Call Johnny, Peter, and Ace in too. We should talk to all of them. Not just to get as much insight as we can, but to make it seem like we're talking to everyone generally about the topic and anything they may have seen. It'll keep the heat off Jess."

Nils nods in agreement. "Good thinking," he replies. He pauses, considering me for a moment. "You think she's lying, don't you?"

I look at him, surprised. Given years of experience hiding my ability, I could swear my poker face is ironclad. "What makes you say that?"

"You said he 'allegedly' harassed her," he points out. "And you chewed on your lips while she was talking."

"You're observant, I'll give you that," I allow with a smile. "No. I don't believe her. But it's getting a full investigation regardless."

"Indeed. Our hands are rather tied, aren't they?" he muses. Shaking his head lightly, he switches gears, leaning back in his chair. "There's something else we need to discuss. That new Latin club two blocks away is opening this Friday."

I grimace, leaning back in my own chair. "I know. Their launch promos have been stellar." I heave a deep sigh. I've enjoyed making this club successful again, but in this business it's like balancing on the edge of a knife. During a knife fight. "I plan to go to the opening, of course."

"Of course. I'll go the following Thursday if that works for you," he offers.

I nod. "Sounds like a good plan."

Nils stands up to leave, turning back to me from the doorway. "Everything okay, Francesca?"

"Just super," I reply drily. "Why?" I cock my head to the side, taking in the tension in his tall, lean frame, the expression of concern on his face.

"You just seemed out of sorts this weekend. And you still are today," he replies vaguely.

I can tell he wants to ask more. I suspect about Julian. But I'm not ready to talk about it yet. "I've just been having headaches," I lie. Well, sort of lie. I still do have one at the moment. "I'll be fine, but thank you."

He huffs a breath through his nose, clearly not totally buying it. But I've got enough on my mind already without having to placate Nils. I turn back to the work on my desk in clear indication that I'm done.

He takes the hint and leaves. As soon as he does I pick up my phone, checking my texts for the millionth time today. This time Julian has responded. My heart leaps into my throat.

I meant it when I said I can't. I'm sorry.

At first, I don't feel anything. But slowly the numbness is replaced by anger, which is then replaced by pain. It was one thing for him to reject me when I'd rejected him first. But this? This just sucks.

Then I'm angry again that I care so much. I barely know this guy. And somehow he's managed to creep through my defenses. As scared as I was by the sudden onslaught of feeling, I'm just as upset that his rejection clearly wasn't because he found himself, like me, caring too much too fast.

So here I am, out on a limb by myself, and it's just cracked under the weight of unrequited feelings. Fucking bullshit.

I go home that evening and I drink. A lot. Something I don't do much these days, as it's not conducive to running a successful club, ironically. But I make up for it in spades, finally passing out in the wee hours of the morning.

Chapter 10 — Frankie

I barely make it into the club on Tuesday afternoon, in large part thanks to about a gallon of water and a fistful of aspirin. But I still look like hell.

Thankfully, Nils doesn't say a word about my bedraggled appearance, he just takes me through his findings ahead of our staff interviews.

Unsurprisingly, his research demonstrated the exact opposite of Jess's claims. In several instances over the week, the footage clearly shows Jess aggressively pursuing conversation and contact with a retreating Dave. At least once, he's clearly forced to dodge her and disappear to avoid her advances.

Nils finds it baffling, which I find hilarious. I'm almost positive I know why, but I want to hear it from the staff.

We use the story that we're individually checking in with each employee to make sure they've read the employee handbook. So we go over the sexual harassment policy with each of them, along with everything else. And it's funny what people will tell you given the opportunity.

Johnny whines at length about how slow Peter is. Ace whines about what a hard-ass Johnny is because he sticks to the employee limit of two free drinks a night.

Peter is our first to say anything about inappropriate behavior. And it's specifically about Jess. He doesn't go on at length, but he basically says that Jess is crazy. That she doesn't have any boundaries. But after that he just keeps saying, "Ask Dave, dude, just ask Dave."

So Nils and I do just that. When we've finished going over the handbook and give Dave his chance, he doesn't complain about anyone. So we ask. Through some subtle coaxing we get him to finally admit that Jess pursued him for months, finally getting him to go out for coffee with her. When that went okay, they went out on a real date. After that Dave decided he really wasn't interested in her, and told her so. That was this past Sunday afternoon.

Then all evening Sunday, apparently, she went apeshit, calling him every five minutes. Texting him constantly. Showing up at his place, when he didn't even know she knew where he lived. And she didn't go away until he finally threatened to call the cops. Well, the second time he threatened and one of his neighbors echoed the sentiment, having been listening to the insanity all night.

57

Thankfully, Dave kept the texts. We assured him, of course, that he wasn't in any trouble, and that we'd deal with Jess. But once he was gone Nils and I were absolutely baffled why Jess thought she could get away with trying to report Dave.

I'd call her crazy, but the fact that she knew she was lying indicates something much worse. Something I don't encounter all that often. I try not to even think the word, because I hope I'm wrong. Because if Jess really is a sociopath, this could all go from bad to worse quickly.

* * *

I see Jess by myself on Wednesday. Though there are cameras in my office, I leave the door open while Nils works down the hall. But as far as Jess is concerned, we are alone.

She sits confidently in the chair, clearly believing she's about to complete her revenge for Dave's rejecting her.

"So we talked to the staff yesterday," I open, pulling out the employee handbook and laying it so it faces her. "We simply went through this and gave everyone an opportunity to talk about how things are going here. It occurred to me that we should probably do the same."

Jess gives me a funny look, clearly unsure of where I'm going with this. But I know I'd best have this conversation equally with all employees, and I know as soon as we get to the next part, she's not going to like what happens.

She listens attentively and doesn't have any additional concerns or questions when I'm done.

"So you understood the parts on sexual harassment?" I ask clearly.

Jess nods, clearly still very confused. "Duh, obvs, that's what started this whole thing," she responds sarcastically, rolling her eyes.

"Yes, about that," I reply, steeling myself. "Unfortunately, video surveillance of the club contradicts statements you made when you reported your issue with Mr. Kelly on Monday."

I watch carefully as she goes from looking like a deer in headlights to looking like a woman scorned. And I brace myself for the fury of hell.

"I want to see the footage," she demands. "You must not have seen the right part. Or I bet you couldn't see it at all. Those cameras are at a bad angle, and it's so dark."

"They're state of the art, perfectly positioned, with night-vision capabilities," I assure her. "But unfortunately we have additional information that suggests you were, in fact, harassing Mr. Kelly."

I purposely keep it vague and as unaccusatory as I can, but she's obviously furious anyway.

"I don't know what he told you, but he's lying," she screeches, red faced and near tears. *Lie.*

I know whatever she says and does now is just to save face and will only dig her in deeper, so I attempt to cut that off at the pass. "It's not about what he said," I say as calmly as I can, "it's about the video feed *and* the text messages. They are irrefutable proof that you acted inappropriately."

Her mouth drops open, clearly flabbergasted. "You said you wouldn't tell him what I told you."

Yeah, that fixes it. I have to work not to roll my eyes. "And I didn't. The discussion came about as an extension of the same conversation we just had about the rules. I'm sorry, Jess, I know this situation is difficult for you. But unfortunately, we have to let you go."

"I didn't do anything wrong," she insists. *Lie.* "It's all his fault." *Lie.* "I've been a bartender for three years, in tons of different clubs and I've never had any problems before." *Lie.* "He's doing all of this to get back at me for dumping him." *Lie.*

I'm ridiculously troubled that she knows she's lying. Because if she didn't my internal lie detector wouldn't work. That she continues to blame it on him tells me that she's likely not capable of taking enough responsibility for her behavior to change it.

I decide against using logic with her any further. "I'm afraid it doesn't matter," I insist. "You've egregiously violated our policies and blatantly harassed a coworker both at work and at their home. You'll receive your final paycheck via direct deposit within the week."

I'm forced to repeat myself several times before I can get her to leave. But as she leaves my office angry and in tears, I know this isn't over.

* * *

Thursday night goes without incident, even though we're short-staffed. Given that, however, on Friday I'm reluctant to go the opening of Los Jardines, the new Latin club down the road. After repeated reassurance that they'll call if they need me, I leave and I'm able to just make meeting Emma at the corner of Hollywood and Vine at ten-thirty.

Her pale blond hair is piled artfully on her head, her chest spilling out of a tight, red tube dress with chunky red heels to match.

"You look ready to salsa," I tease her as I approach.

She eyes my black halter dress with a cross-body ruffle. "And you look bo-ring," she sing-songs.

I hold up a finger, then twist my right leg to reveal a thigh-slit that would make a stripper blush. Okay, maybe not, but it's still sexy as hell.

Emma laughs appreciatively. "All right, you get a pass," she allows. "So we're checking this club out and going to find you some man-meat, right?"

I roll my eyes. "Because that's been working out so well for me lately," I grumble.

She tugs my hand, propelling me down the road for the few blocks to the club. I catch her up on my not-inconsiderably shitty week on the way, but I still can't quite bring myself to tell her about Ben's lying last weekend. Or exactly how much I was falling for Julian. I'm not sure why I hold that back. It would be like admitting what he and I had really could have been more than just an intense, physical attraction. And at this point I'd just rather forget about it.

As we approach our destination, all the usual stops have been pulled out, with spotlights and strobes visible practically the whole way. A huge line extends out from under the covered entrance, wrapping around the front of the building and down the block away from us.

We get to the red-roped side of the door and I pull us up to the massive bouncer holding the list. I give him my name and he opens the rope while making eyes at Emma. She winks and blows him a kiss on her way by. At that exact moment she is also unceremoniously shoved forward as someone pushes us from behind, causing Emma to press into my backside just as the door opens and a group starts to stream out. It sandwiches me behind the open door, Emma's generous curves keeping me from escaping back the way I came.

"Hey, watch it," Emma sneers, flinging her elbow back to dislodge the giant body pressing her into me.

"Ow, fuck, lady, what's your problem?" the guy she elbows cries out.

The bouncer presses him and his buddies backward, pointing at one of them in the back. "You gotta finish your cigarette out here, man," he says irritably.

The three huge men relent and take a step back, allowing me to squeeze out from behind the door as Emma steps up to tell off the asshole that pushed her.

But I'm distracted by the smoker, who now has his back turned to us. Because I'd know that ass anywhere.

Julian.

Panic grips me, and I turn to Emma to pull her away from the guy she's trading not-so-nice words with. It takes me a minute to get her attention.

"Emma, let it go," I hiss at her.

She finally turns and sees the look of sheer terror on my face. "Frankie, what the hell is wrong with you?"

She says it loud. And I groan, knowing I'm fucked.

"Francesca."

God. Fucking. Damn it. I glare daggers at Emma before turning around.

In fitted black jeans, with a tight black V-neck tee to match, and ridiculously sexy mussed hair, Julian looks as panty-droppingly gorgeous as ever. The shirt shows the hint of tattoos winding up his torso, the sleeves exposing the ones that cover both arms to his wrists. He'd be beyond ridiculously hot but for the cigarette hanging from his lip.

"Julian. I didn't know you smoked," I respond, trying to sound as bored as possible.

One of his buddies elbows him. "Who's your friend, *Julian*?"

Julian takes a drag of his cigarette, then grinds it into the ashtray of the trash can sitting on the curb.

"Just some chick," he responds with a shrug, looking as bored as I tried to sound. My heart drops into my stomach and it takes everything I have not to slap him. What the actual fuck?

Emma is frozen next to me, and I can see the realization dawn on her face. It's quickly replaced by anger.

"Fuck all of you losers," she spits, tugging my arm. She glares at Julian. And if looks could kill, he'd be six feet under. "Especially you, asshole."

Julian smirks, putting his hands up in mock surrender. His blasé attitude is beyond maddening.

And it gets worse as three of the most classless bimbos I've ever laid eyes on sidle up and latch on to Julian and his friends, eyeing us angrily.

It takes all my effort to close down my expression and walk away. Emma scrambles to follow me through the velvet rope, only catching up once we're inside. But Julian and his friends aren't far behind us.

I fume as we push through the crowd, making for the small, roped-off VIP section to the right of the massive dance floor. Once inside its confines, we collapse into a small, black leather sofa.

"Do you want to go?" Emma asks loudly into my ear.

I shake my head. "I'm working," I reply back into her ear. "Let's have a drink. I'll look around. Then we can go."

She nods her agreement, patting me reassuringly on the thigh. I lean into the sofa, allowing myself to recover before I think about anything else. I don't want to let this ruin my evening, but I don't see how I can just let it go.

One of the VIP area guards approaches us, leaning in to speak to me.

"Mr. Rivera has invited you to his private table," he says.

Carlos Rivera is the owner of Los Jardines and the reason I was on the VIP list in the first place. So I can hardly refuse him, though perhaps it'll be just the distraction I need.

I stand up and straighten my dress, swinging my hips so my leg slips through the slit as I strut out of the VIP area and across the dance floor to a set of tables just off the bar. In case Julian is watching, I might as well remind the bastard what he's missing out on.

Carlos turns out to be a pleasant, upbeat man in his mid-forties. He's energetic and charismatic, and he buys us margaritas, wishing us a pleasant time at his club.

After downing the drink, I feel distinctly calmer as I sit at the bar with Emma absorbing my surroundings. The club's design is basic, the Latin décor fairly subtle. But the music is high energy with Latin flair, and the packed dance floor pulses with the energy of the crowd. It's the multicolor strobe lights hung from the ceiling, however, that really give the place its atmosphere. All in all it looks like it's going to be pretty successful, but offers a different enough experience not to be direct competition, exactly.

I spot Julian and his crowd on the dance floor. One of the bimbos is wrapped around Julian, but he looks just as bored as he did outside. I huff a laugh and excuse myself to go to the bathroom.

As I'm coming out, however, Julian's bimbo is going in. I plan to ignore her, but she clearly has other ideas.

"Hey, you're one of the bitches that was messing with my boys," she snarks at me.

I don't even plan to respond. Her tiny tube top and barely there miniskirt are as cheap and trashy as she is, and I know no good will come of opening my mouth. Plus, it disgusts me to see what kind of woman Julian is really interested in.

But as I go to walk by, she throws an arm up to block me. I deftly duck under it without a word. It enrages her in a way that would make me laugh if I even cared that much.

Unfortunately she doesn't give up easily, and as I make to walk out of the bathroom hall back into the main area, she grabs my arm.

I whirl around and wrench my arm out of her grasp. "Don't. Fucking. Touch me," I say loudly and firmly.

And the dumb bitch finally seems to realize I've got a good six inches on her. This close to her I realize how tiny she is. I have to give her credit for being ballsy enough to start something.

"Whatever, bitch, stay away from J.C. — he's mine," she spits, turning back down the hall.

I blanch at her words, the memory of him telling me his last name at some point during one of our dates coming to the forefront. Charles. J.C. — Julian Charles. That's why his friends teased him when I called him Julian. I shouldn't feel offended that he clearly didn't even like me enough to have me call him what his friends do. Because I didn't let him call me Frankie either. Nonetheless, it stings a little.

And I'm not sure what to make of her claiming him either. He hadn't lied when he told me he didn't have a girlfriend. But maybe they don't use that label. My stomach turns at the realization that the little I thought I knew about him probably isn't even true.

Suddenly, the hair on the back of my neck stands up and my eyes involuntarily flick up to the dance floor to find Julian watching me. He towers over everyone around him, and his expression is dark with anger. I'm certain he saw the exchange. But I'm not going to give him the satisfaction of thinking I give a shit.

Disgusted, I turn and head back to the bar, sticking close to the wall to avoid the crowd, but I don't get far when a rough, warm hand closes over my forearm. I once again find myself ripping my arm away from unwanted contact and whipping around to face the person making it.

"Don't worry, I left your piece of ass alone."

My eyes lock on Julian's brooding face. I try to contain the anger seething from my pores, but I can tell by his expression, his body language, that he knows. And he's every bit as riled as I am.

"She's not my piece of ass."

I snort. "Whatever you call her then. You two deserve each other."

"Fine, have it your way. Gina and I are a thing." *Lie.* "That's why I can't keep seeing you." *Lie.*

"Liar," I gasp before I can stop myself, disgusted by the whole situation.

He arches an eyebrow. "I don't like being called a liar."

"Then don't fucking lie."

I try to step around him, but he locks his strong hands around my waist. It pisses me off to no end and I move to execute a defensive maneuver with my arm, but with lightning reflexes he grabs it and uses it to pin me against the wall. I struggle uselessly against him as he presses me into the brick with his arms and torso.

"Still feisty, I see," he murmurs in my ear.

And I hate myself for the shivers it sends down my spine. "Still an asshole, I see," I retort hotly.

He chuckles and loosens his grip so he can back off. But he doesn't let me go.

"What's your damage *J.C.*?" I press mockingly.

He frowns. "Don't call me that."

"Sure thing. Of all people I get it. Only your actual friends call you that," I reply scathingly. "Clearly, I don't know you at all. And I'm not sure what you're doing right now, because I thought that's the way you wanted it. Do you just like making random women fall for you then going total dickhead on them? Does it get you hot so you can go back to that skank and fuck her cheap ass?"

"You've got a foul mouth, Greco," he replies calmly, still not letting me go.

"Go fuck yourself," I spit back. I can't remember the last time I was this angry. I thrash under his hold, but he still doesn't release me.

But he finally looks furious, his thick eyebrows drawing together in a scowl. And I'm sure I've crossed a line.

"I'd rather fuck you," he replies huskily, surprising me. And his mouth is on mine, his tongue angrily plunging into my mouth, his hands sliding to my hips and pulling me to him.

I was expecting anger, not lust, and the physical response I have to him is as strong as ever. I'm unable to resist, melting into him, lacing my fingers into his hair. I have enough of my wits left to hope his girlfriend sees and that it pisses her off.

And I also have regathered my wits enough so that when he lets me go, I slap him as hard as I can. "Keep dreaming, asshole." I turn on my heel and walk away.

When I get closer to the bar and spot Emma, I'm stopped short, totally thrown out of the anger from my conflict with Julian and his girlfriend. Emma is pale, with tears streaming down her face. She can't have seen or heard what happened, but I know instinctively it has nothing to do with me.

I close the distance between us nervously. "Emma, what's wrong?" I ask.

She looks up at me, fury written all over her face, and shows me her phone screen.

Text messages from Ben admitting he lied about his promotion. My heart drops into my stomach.

"You knew," she spits at me. "Didn't you?"

Fuuuuuuuuuuck.

"Yes," I admit. "I was going to tell you tonight, I swear."

Emma laughs. And I've known her long enough to know it's her "bitch, please" laugh. But she doesn't say anything. She just gets up and walks away from me.

Desperate to explain, I follow her across the dance floor, through the entryway, and out the front door.

"Emma, wait, please," I call after her uselessly. The club is way too loud for her to hear me from any distance, much less the twenty-foot lead she's got on me.

Damn, if she isn't fast when she's mad. She's already at the curb and is hailing a cab that's gliding up next to her. As she gets in, she pauses.

"No wonder Julian doesn't want you," she spits, tears streaming down her face. "You've got nothing to give, Frankie. You can't even be a good friend."

I'm too stunned to respond. And then she's gone.

I clench my fists and squeeze my eyes shut, fighting back the anger. The tears. The outrage. I dig deep and steady myself enough to walk back to Baltia.

But when I turn around, the three cheap bitches stand around me, closing in to pin me to the curb.

Julian's girl, Gina, is in the middle. "I told you not to mess with J.C. He's *mine*," she screeches, shoving me in the chest. And I understand suddenly why she was so bold. They outnumber me, even more than they did before Emma hightailed it out of here. While I'm decent in a fight, I don't like the odds. Especially with my back to traffic.

"I have no interest in messing with him," I reply calmly, trying to keep from getting pushed into the stream of vehicles that I can feel whipping by behind me. But I knew it wouldn't do much, and I was right.

She gets right up in my face. "Oh, yeah? Then why were you kissing him?" she spits.

"He kissed me." It's my own fucking fault. I *wished* for it to piss her off. Why am I so fucking stupid when it comes to this guy?

She laughs. "Please, why would he do that?"

I look down at her. "You really think I could force myself on him?"

That gives her pause. But not for long. Logic clearly isn't her strong suit. "Whatever, bitch, I told you not to touch him — now you're gonna pay."

"I'm really not interested in fighting over Julian," I say, putting my hands up.

The girls on my sides close in.

"Then you should have gone home when you had the chance," the one on the left says.

I don't look at her. I know it's a trap. And lo and behold, Gina swings at me, anticipating that I was going to look. But I see the blow coming a mile away and dodge it. She spins past me, and I'm no longer trapped against the curb. *Thank you, boxing lessons*, I think to myself.

I can feel the crowd watching behind us. Annoyed that the bouncers clearly don't give a shit, I back up slowly. But the bitches advance.

"Carmen, Gina, Tammy," an angry voice barks from behind me.

The brute that ran into Emma earlier comes around my right side. And that distracts me into looking. Rookie move.

Gina comes at me and *grabs my hair* like the bitch that she is.

Fighting the pain, I wrap my hands around her forearm and bring my right knee sharply up into her midsection. It knocks the breath out of her and she lets go. But I take no chances. As she gathers her wits, I land a right hook to the left side of her face. She falls back, landing flat on the pavement.

Her two friends scramble to her side as she pushes herself up on her elbows, holding her jaw, clearly in pain.

Julian and his other friend appear next to the brute.

I drop my guard, backing off. "He's all yours," I spit at the stupid bitch as she picks herself up from the ground. "For what that's worth."

The onlookers let out gasps and jeers, but I block it all out, spin on my heel, and walk away. Fuck them all.

Chapter 11 — Julian

I make it outside in time to see Frankie land a punch on Gina. What a fucking mess. I should've left as soon as I laid eyes on Frankie. Because before I know what I'm doing, I tell Paul to get the girls the fuck home before they get us arrested, and I'm down the sidewalk after her.

I don't stop to ask myself what I'm doing. I know what needs to be done. Thankfully, she's slow enough in heels that I catch up to her before she gets to Vine.

"Wait up," I call as I close in.

She walks faster and I have to try not to laugh. In a couple more steps, I put myself in front of her.

"What?" she snaps, crossing her arms over her chest and glaring up at me. And goddamn it if she isn't even more beautiful when she's angry. It softens me in a way that I'd take the piss out of my friends for.

"That's some right hook you've got there. You okay?" I ask softly, resisting the urge to take her hand in mine and check her over.

She tightens her arms around her body defensively. "Oh, so now you give a shit again?" she seethes.

I take a deep breath. My usual ability to keep up the careful pretense of indifference melts under her anger. And I just want to make it right. "Who said I stopped giving a shit?"

She laughs angrily. "I can't handle this."

She makes to step around me, but I mirror her, stopping her advance.

"Please, don't go yet," I beg. "I'm sorry. This is why I said I can't."

"You're not making any sense," she grouses.

I clench my jaw and stare at the sky, trying to figure out how to explain this to her without telling her anything that could put her in danger. Or me, for that matter.

When I look back at her, she's resolutely glaring into traffic, arms still crossed tightly over her chest. So fucking stubborn, but goddamn she's beautiful. And if she's as riled as I am, she feels this. It gives me hope and I can't help but smile.

I reach out and turn her face toward me so I can give her the only truth that matters right now. "I'm falling for you," I admit. "But those guys back there can't know that. That's why I can't do this."

She stares at me, like she's waiting again. "I still don't get it," she insists.

"It's complicated."

"I'm pretty smart."

I laugh. "Yeah, you are."

She looks at me expectantly.

"I'm sorry, Frankie, it would take a lot more of an explanation than I can give you right now. And when you got freaked out, it was a good reason to put a stop to whatever this is. But then you wanted to try anyway, and I knew I couldn't expect you to trust me if I couldn't tell you everything. And there's just a lot going on I can't even begin to …" I drop my hands to my sides, curling them into fists in my frustration. I'm fucking this all up. "Look, I'm sorry I was such an asshole tonight. I thought it would be easier that way, but I was wrong. I fucked up."

"You're right. I don't put up with secrets and lies," she replies, ignoring my apology.

Lies. That reminds me. "How'd you even know I was lying back there?"

Her eyes widen a fraction. "Good guess," she says. She uses the same fake I-don't-give-a-shit tone she tried to pull when we ran into each other outside the club earlier tonight. And my BS radar is going off.

"Bullshit," I say. "I don't lie often. And both times I've lied to you, you've called me out on it. So let's try that again. How did you know I was lying?"

"It's complicated," she returns with a sneer. "And like you said, it's not like I can trust you to tell me everything either."

Something in her words feels like a threat. And I wonder how much she knows. If she really is dirty, and she's just been playing me this whole time, knowing who I work for. But I'm pretty fucking good at what I do, and I almost always know a con when I see one. Could she really be that good? Or are her words just a coincidence? The part of me that wants to fight for her takes a step back.

"Fine, have it your way," I reply, stepping aside to let her pass.

"None of this is my way," I hear her mutter as she walks away.

I don't stop her.

With a sigh, I check my phone, and there's nothing. If anyone was suspicious of my disappearing act, it doesn't seem to have raised enough flags for them to say anything. I decide to head home, beyond over tonight.

But every step I take just feels fucking wrong. And I know deep in my gut that Frankie isn't really dirty. That everyone has their secrets. Especially me.

She's the first person in a very long time who hasn't treated me like a piece of shit. One little comment and I ignore all of my instincts about her. Fuck, I'm a head case. I have to remind myself that not everyone lives in my world. And even though I'm supposed to stay the fuck away from hers, I find my feet rounding the block, heading back to Baltia. Back to Frankie.

When I get to the front doors, I realize I have no fucking clue what I can say to her that will fix this. I was telling her the truth: I don't like lying, and I try to avoid it. Life is complicated enough. But there's just too much I can't tell her.

I keep going, rounding the corner to the parking lot next to the club. I spot her ride toward the back of the lot. I approach it, admiring the gorgeous machine. I sink down next to it, leaning against the side, hoping her vibes will give me something. I tilt my head back and close my eyes, waiting for inspiration to strike.

* * *

I must have fallen asleep, because the next thing I know, I'm being nudged awake.

"You're lucky someone didn't mistake you for a dead body and rob you blind." Frankie's voice cuts sharply into my fogged brain.

I open my eyes to find her staring down at me with her arms crossed again. "They'd be getting more than they bargained for," I reply, as the hand that was resting on my belt pulls out the short blade I have hidden there. I palm it, spinning it once before sliding it back in place. She doesn't look impressed.

"What are you doing here, Julian?" she asks, slumping against the side of the car, clearly exhausted.

I climb to my feet, subtly checking the time on my way up. Four fucking a.m. Goddamn, I was asleep in the open in this neighborhood for hours. She's not wrong that I was lucky to avoid trouble.

As I stretch and settle against the car next to her, I don't miss her checking me out. But I don't let it go to my head, instead focusing on looking as contrite as possible. Because I still don't know what the fuck I'm going to say. But here goes.

"I tried to stay away," I explain. "But I can't. And I don't know if this will work, but I want it to."

She shifts uncomfortably. "I can't do this right now," she sighs.

With a frown, I push myself up off the car. I can't say I blame her after how I behaved earlier. "Okay," I reply. "I understand." I kiss her on the forehead. Not where I'd like, but at least I get to be close to her one last time. "Bye, Francesca."

I start to walk away, kicking myself for how this all went down when she grabs me around the wrist, pulling me back. I look up in surprise, and she looks beyond annoyed.

"No, asstwat, I mean I am literally too tired to stand. Can we talk later today?" she clarifies.

"Fuck, I'm sorry," I say hastily, realizing she looks like she's about to collapse. "Do you want me to drive you home?"

She swoons a little against the side of the car, and I decide no matter what she says I'm getting her home safely.

"That might not be the worst idea. It's been a night." She unfolds her hand, revealing her car keys.

A knot in my chest I hadn't realized was there unravels at her invitation. And it might make me a little giddy, because the next thing I do is scoop her up in my arms and carry her around the car to the passenger side.

"Geez, Julian, I can walk to the other side of the car, you know," she protests. While she sounds annoyed, she looks impressed. But still tired.

I don't bother to respond, I simply jiggle the keys into the lock, open the door, and place her in the passenger seat as gently as I can. Then I walk back around to the other side, get in, and start the car.

"But that was so much more fun, wasn't it?" I finally reply with a teasing smirk.

Rolling her eyes, she buckles herself in and sinks into the seat, clearly too tired to banter. And it's a good thing I know where she lives, because she almost immediately falls asleep.

It makes getting her up to her apartment and into bed interesting. But I finally manage it, removing only her shoes and lying her on top of her covers. By the time it's done I realize I'm beyond tired too, and I'd have to call a car to get home. Staying it is.

I contemplate lying down next to her but decide to go back to the living room couch instead. And staying was a good decision, because as soon as I lie down, I'm out.

* * *

I only get a few hours of shut-eye before the morning sun streaming through the living room windows makes it impossible to sleep. I peek in at Frankie, and she's still out cold. And so fucking beautiful it hurts.

And I suddenly have an idea to win her over. I rush out the door, bringing her keys with me, and hope I have enough time before she wakes.

I get a car home, pick up a few things, change my shirt, and drive back to Frankie's, picking up coffee and donuts on the way.

When I quietly reenter her apartment, I'm relieved to find that she's still asleep. Producing the stuffed unicorn from our last date, I place it on the pillow next to her with a note, then return to the living room.

About fifteen minutes later, I'm about to have a second donut when I hear laughter. Rising, I cross the living room and the short hallway to stand in her door.

She's holding the unicorn in one hand, the note in the other. The smile on her face tells me my plan is working.

"Good morning, beautiful," I say, and her eyes meet mine. And I swear I lose my damn senses every time. "I hope it's okay that I crashed on the couch. I tired myself out getting you to bed." I wink at her suggestively. "I went home this morning, picked up some breakfast and brought it back, though."

"That's really thoughtful, thank you," she replies sincerely, climbing out of bed. "I have to get to the club soon so I need to rinse off and get changed." She stops in front of me and points nervously at the door to the left of where I'm standing.

Fuck, she did not say that. Now I'm picturing her naked and wet. I raise an eyebrow at her, but I say nothing. I don't trust myself, and I don't think that was an invitation. So I return to the living room without a word.

I try to concentrate on eating a donut. It takes all of my fucking focus. I'm already semi-hard from knowing she's in the shower mere feet away. I eat a glazed donut wondering if she tastes as good. Who am I kidding? Of course she fucking does. The next fifteen minutes creep by. Finally, Frankie emerges.

And if I thought that would help, well, it doesn't. She's wearing a spaghetti-strapped fitted black top and tight pink cropped pants. Her damp hair reminds me of the water that was just running down her huge tits, ample hips, and round ass. I shift forward to hide the bulge in my pants.

"Donuts? That's what you call breakfast?" she asks, grabbing the second cup from the coffee table and sitting down in the chair across from me. Too fucking far.

I level a look at her. "I don't bite," I tease patting the couch cushion next to me and thinking, *Well, not unless you want me to.* The thought does nothing to abate my erection.

She scoffs at me. "Says you. I'm still not convinced you're not a complete asshole," she replies honestly.

I cross my legs so I can lean back, and I laugh. "Fair enough," I admit. "So how do I make it up to you?"

She leans forward and grabs a cake donut with chocolate glaze out of the box on the table. "I don't know."

I realize what a bad idea the donuts were as I watch her eat. I swear I try not to fucking stare, but it's impossible not to with the delicate way she nibbles off a piece, her pink tongue darting out to lick the crumbs off her lips. Fuck me.

It also doesn't help that she seems to be just as aware of me watching her. And it doesn't stop her. By the time she's done eating, we're both squirming in our seats.

I stand up, round the coffee table, and drop to my knees in front of her. I focus on breathing, keeping control, as I take the hand she was eating with and raise her long, slender fingers to my lips. Then, without ceremony, I suck the fucking sugar crystals off of her fingers. She stares at me, transfixed, as my tongue caresses her fingertips. Her lips part and her pupils dilate, and I have all the invitation I need.

I smirk at her, pulling back and licking the last of the sugar off my lips. She stares just as hard as I stared at her eating that fucking donut like a saucy, sugary vixen.

She searches my face for something. I don't know what.

"How old are you?" she asks curiously.

I raise any eyebrow. Really? That's what she wants to ask right now? "Thirty-two. Why?"

She smiles. "You're a little young to have wrinkles," she teases me.

I narrow my eyes. She's stalling. I must be making her nervous. With a predatory grin, I lean toward her. But she throws her leg up between us before I can get too close, using it to push me back.

She's unsure. I get it. I haven't exactly been reassuring. But my primal brain is in the driver's seat right now, and I need to taste this woman. I look down at her shapely leg, sliding my hand under her pink pants, running my fingers up her smooth, soft calf.

"You think that's going to stop me?" I ask in a low, husky voice.

I can see the shiver roll through her body. She tries to hide it by taking a sip of coffee. It doesn't work.

"No, but a good kick to the head might," she replies.

"You're still mad. I get it," I reply, dropping my eyes to her leg as I continue to stroke it. "But if you can't think of a way I can make it up to you, I will."

I slide my hand to her ankle, gently holding her and lifting her foot away from my chest. I bring her toes to my mouth, placing gentle kisses as I rub circles into the sole of her foot with my hands. I look back up at her as I kiss further up her foot, to her leg. She's panting and I can see her hard nipples through her shirt. Fuck. Breathe in. Breathe out. Focus. Control.

I set her foot slowly and deliberately on the ground and run my hands up her legs, moving into her until I'm settled between them. When she doesn't protest, I slide my hands up her thighs, rubbing slow, firm circles into her hips.

"God-fucking-damn it, if I don't want to make it up to you right now," I breathe, struggling not to pounce. I lean in to kiss her, but she stops me with a hand this time. Fuck.

"Julian." She says my name as if in protest, but the sexy sigh to her voice, the tension in her curves says she wants me.

My lips part as I say her name with a sigh. "Frankie."

It's the first time I've called her that since the night we met. I can see the fire blazing in her eyes. She slowly sets her coffee cup down on the end table next to her.

And I can't tell if she's going to slap me or jump my bones. Fuck, at this point, either would send me over the edge.

She slowly takes my hand, brings it to her lips, and kisses it gently. And the need for her takes over. I pounce, our lips clashing fiercely, my teeth pulling at her lip, my tongue thrusting into her mouth. She presses away, gasping for air, and I know it's not a protest this time, it's catching her breath from the ferocity of my need. Of our need.

I move to her neck, trying not to bite too hard as my animal instincts take over. I slip my hands under her ass, pulling at her pants.

"Julian, I don't think we should —"

I step up my game for just a moment, closing my mouth on her nipple, over her shirt, pulling at it with my teeth and growling into her chest.

"You think too much," I say roughly. But I pull slightly away, waiting for permission once more. She whimpers at my words, arching her back and pulling me back to her breast.

With a wicked grin, I oblige, biting at her hard nipple while simultaneously dropping a hand between her legs, stroking her roughly through the fabric. Helping clear her mind. Because I can tell we both need this.

I know I'm right when she lifts her backside up. I let out a low, eager moan and relieve her of her bottoms until her dripping pussy is fully exposed to my hot, eager mouth.

Breathe in. Breathe out. Focus. Back in complete control, I run my thumb down the length of her, starting at her clit, over her slick lips, dipping slightly between her folds.

I sigh softly. "Beautiful," I murmur. I take a moment to appreciate the work of art before me. Then I use my tongue to trace back the path my thumb just made, ending at the hot, tight bundle of nerves with a flick. Frankie cries out, her hands gripping the arms of the chair, her legs trembling. So, I do it again. And again. Until her hips are grinding against my mouth, tilting her clit toward the rapid movements of my tongue. But I need to let it build if I'm going to take her over the edge like nobody ever has before.

That's my plan at least, until she slips her hands under her shirt, tweaking her nipples hard. It might just be the sexiest thing I've ever seen, and all I can do is stare up at her from between her thighs. Our eyes meet, and the lust and desperation in her gaze rips through me. It spurs me back to action as I'm overtaken by the need to watch her come apart. I run my thumb in circles over her clit, staring hungrily for her response. I'm not disappointed. She throws her head back, arching her back, pressing into my hand.

My fingers find their way into her, and she gasps, crying out with pleasure. This. This is the moment I wanted. Her, open to me, under my control, giving her the pleasure I get just from looking at her. Being with her.

I pump my fingers into her, changing up the angle I'm stroking her clit at as I go, watching for what pleases her most. When her breathing accelerates, I rotate my wrist, taking my fingers deep until I find her G-spot. And I press it toward her clit with my middle finger at the same time my thumb works her on the outside. In an instant she's screaming her impending release.

"Oh, fuck yes," she cries, closing her eyes as her body tightens. "Right there."

Sweet fucking lord, she's like my own personal porno. "Come for me, beautiful," I groan.

My words are like a match thrown on gasoline, igniting her. Her breath quickens, her body tightens hard around my fist. I keep going. When I think she can ascend no further, I flex both fingers deeply, sending her over the edge. She screams her release, her hands closing over her breasts hard as she pushes into my palm, prolonging the sensation.

As she slowly comes down the wave, I wipe my face with my other hand and slowly ease my hand out of her. I slide up to cover her mouth with mine, giving her back her delicious taste while getting a dose of the trembling intensity of her mouth.

She laughs, licking at my lips. "If that's how you're going to make it up to me, we might have a deal."

That makes me laugh. "Seriously?" I ask.

She uses her foot to push me away again, which I don't resist this time, and swipes her pants off the floor. "No," she laughs, pulling her clothes back on. "But it sure didn't hurt your chances."

I sink back into the couch, shaking my head and laughing. I'd do that every fucking day if she'd let me, even if it didn't fix anything between us.

Her taste, the noises she makes, giving this amazing woman equally amazing orgasms. Fucking fantastic. I can't even begin to imagine what sex with her will be like. My already hard dick twitches in my pants at the thought.

She swipes another donut and sinks back into her chair, totally blissed out. She eyes me over the pastry in her hand. "Aren't you going to wash your hands?"

"Hell, no," I reply, bringing the hand I used to fuck her to my mouth and slowly licking my fingers. "At least not yet." Maybe not ever.

"You're a dirty boy, J.C.," she teases. She sets the rest of the donut she was eating down on the table.

"Had your fill?" I ask suggestively.

"Yep. You?" she shoots back, raising an eyebrow.

"Not even close," I reply, not breaking eye contact.

"You're confident, I'll give you that," she says, leaning back in the chair and crossing her legs.

"Not really. I've just made up my mind. I want you, Frankie, and I know you want me too." I smirk at her like the arrogant bastard I am. I can't help it if I'm used to getting my way.

"Oh really? And what about the things that are too *complicated* to talk about right now?" she presses.

"How did you know I was lying?" I counter.

She purses her lips. And I know I've got her on the ropes.

"We both have things we don't want to tell each other yet," I point out. "That doesn't mean this can't work."

I can tell she's trying to come up with a counterargument, but she stays silent.

"Mhm," I murmur. "That's what I thought." I rise from the sofa. "Think about it. I've gotta go."

I saunter over to her, plant my hands on the chair arms, and lean in so my face is inches from hers.

"I'll call you," I say lowly. My lips find hers in a brief but intense kiss before I pull away.

She looks completely dumbstruck as I walk to the door. And as it clicks shut behind me, I know I've won. Even though that opens a whole new world of complicated, right now, I don't fucking care. All I want, all I can think about right now, is Frankie.

Chapter 12 — Frankie

As mind blowing as my time with Julian was, unfortunately there's little time to parse through what happened and how I feel about it. I wasn't lying. I really did need to get into the club for an early event that's going to be a shit-ton of work.

When I get there, I find Nils helping Ace work with the lighting guys to get everything down for tonight's show. I take Nils aside and we check in. Everything has been quiet since I got here, though, so it's a struggle to stay on task. But once the club opens at ten, I don't have time to worry anymore even if I wanted to. The show sold out before the doors even opened, so we knew it was going to be insanity. With having let Jess go, I find myself behind the bar most of the night helping Dave, Peter, and Johnny keep up with the crowd.

I'm already pissed off for having to pick up the slack Jess's absence has created when it goes from bad to worse just after midnight as a huge fight breaks out at the bar. Some asshole comes crashing onto the counter, sending a row of pitchers waiting to go out flying everywhere and spraying everyone in the vicinity with beer.

Now I'm overworked, tired, *and* wet. So when Nils frantically flags me down it takes all my strength to keep from screaming. He pulls me into the security room, looking more panicked than I've ever seen him.

"We have a problem," he says, pacing behind the door to the bar. "I was on the balcony when I spotted Jess in the crowd. But by the time I got downstairs, I couldn't find her anymore."

"Are you serious?" I ask furiously. "What the fuck made her think coming here, especially while Dave is working, is in any way okay?"

Nils shrugs, agitated. "I should have warned Chris not to let her in," he mumbles.

I shake my head and sigh. "I didn't think of it, either. Let's just find her and get her out before it becomes a problem."

We exit, and Nils heads back into the crowd to alert the bouncers and search for Jess. As I scan the bar, two things become immediately apparent: Dave is no longer behind the counter. And Julian is standing there, looking around expectantly.

He looks so fucking good in his tight jeans and white T-shirt, his hair doing that sexy mussed thing, I want to go to him and run my hands through it and fold myself into him until everything else disappears. I'm a little surprised at the reaction, and part of me is still unsure if I really want to give in. Not to mention the Jess-sized problem wandering around the club, especially now with Dave MIA.

I stay there, frozen in my indecision long enough for Julian to spot me. And when he does his whole face lights up. A wave of mixed feelings washes over me. Happiness that he's here. Annoyance that he's here when things are so crazy between us. And at the club. Aggravation that things are so crazy. Anger at Jess. It's too much, and I think he sees the war of emotions on my face.

In two long strides, he's in front of me, wrapping me in his arms. It feels good to surrender for just a moment, but he pushes away when he feels the sticky wetness from the beer still on my black halter top.

"Looks like I missed something," he says in my ear.

I nod. "Sorry. I have to go look for someone," I say back in his. "Wait here?"

Julian agrees, so I flag down Johnny. It takes him a minute to work his way over to me.

"Where'd Dave go?" I ask loudly enough to be heard.

"Supply closet for napkins," Johnny yells back, pointing to the door on the opposite end of the bar.

I nod my thanks and point at Julian. "Give him whatever he wants, no charge."

Johnny raises an eyebrow but wisely doesn't respond. I head to the other end of the bar, toward our secondary supply closet, down the hallway marked "Employees Only."

The first door on the club side is just a buffer for the noise and in case anyone mistakes it for the public bathrooms. I step through that one and make sure it closes fully behind me before using my key to access the actual supply closet door to my right. It concerns me that it isn't open if Dave is supposed to be here.

And throwing the door open, I see the light is off, no Dave in sight. I close and lock the door again.

"Dave?" I call down the hall loudly.

A woman's scream echoes off the white tile walls. Panic rushing through my veins, I run toward the only other place it can be coming from. The employee bathrooms.

The first door is unlocked, the room empty. The other, however, is locked. I bang on the door with my fist.

I don't even have time to ask questions, or warn them that I'm going to come in if I don't get a response, before the door springs open and a half-dressed Jess tumbles out into my arms. She's sobbing hysterically, tears streaming down her face.

I look behind her to see Dave standing by the sink, his clothes disheveled, and a look of horror on his scratched and bloodied face.

* * *

If Nils hadn't found me immediately after I found Jess and Dave, all hell surely would have broken loose. As it was, we were able to deal with everything via the side door, which was closest anyway, without much disruption to the show happening inside the club.

With some terse instructions we were able to get one of the bouncers who'd previously bartended to help Johnny and Peter, and Julian unbelievably volunteered to pinch hit for security. With the adjustments, we managed to keep the front of the house running while Nils stayed with Dave and I with Jess until, at her request, an ambulance came for her. And, also at Jess's request, the police came for Dave.

Jess was too hysterical to say much besides he'd attacked her. And to call the police. So I hadn't much choice, even though the little voice told me she was lying. It killed me to say nothing, to watch them both taken away. To promise the police officers that I'd be down in the afternoon to provide all of our video footage, employee files, and other data pertaining to "the case."

Once they are all gone and everyone is back to their usual posts, I find myself standing in the employee hallway alone, listening as the stragglers are shown out, the after-party having been cancelled.

Knowing I can't hide any longer, I return to bar area to find the cleaning crew has already started. Nils sits at one of the bar tables looking as sad and tired as I feel.

Julian stands awkwardly by the stairs to the stage pit.

Sullenly shuffling around the tables, I approach him. "Thank you," I say. "I'm sure this wasn't what you came here for tonight."

He shakes his head, and reaches out to lace his fingers with mine. "I came here to see you," he replies. "But what you just went through … just tell me what you need, and I'll do it."

I chew on my lips, overwhelmed. "I need to talk to Nils," I reply. "But if you can wait a bit longer, I'd like it if you took me home."

He pulls my fingers to his mouth, kissing them sweetly. "Of course." He lets my hand go and I turn to head to Nils's table, but he's already making his way toward me.

"So you *did* go for it," he observes with a glance at Julian. "I wasn't sure there for a while."

I huff an ironic laugh. "Neither was I," I admit. I look around gloomily. "So that was a shit show."

Nils gives me a dim smile. "Never a dull moment. I'll meet you here tomorrow to go to the police station?"

I heave a sigh and nod. "I'll be in as soon as I'm up to get everything together. I'm too angry and tired to do it right now," I reply.

"God, of course, Francesca," Nils says with a wave of his long fingers. "Go home, get some rest. Text me tomorrow when you want me to meet you." He reaches out and squeezes my shoulder reassuringly. He gives another glance at Julian and leans in close. "Be careful."

I shoot Nils a sharp look and he backs up, raising his hands with a smirk.

When I turn back to Julian he's glaring daggers at Nils. I'm too tired to deal with a jealous Julian, so I choose to ignore it, instead gesturing for him to join me.

"Ready?" I ask tentatively as he approaches.

Julian's dark eyes flick to mine. "Yeah," he says shortly, winding his arm around my waist. "Let's get out of here."

But as soon as we're outside he lets me go, as if he no longer needs to mark his territory. Since I'm already worked up by the events of the evening it annoys me more than it probably should.

"You don't have to worry about Nils," I snap. "He's just my club manager."

Julian huffs. "Yeah, okay."

How two short words can be so laced with contempt and sarcasm is beyond me.

"Seriously, Julian," I say, grabbing his arm so he has to stop and look at me. "I don't deal well with possessive bullshit. And I've had a fucking awful night, so if you're going to have attitude, just go home."

He sighs and shakes his head. "I'm sorry," he replies, slipping his hands around my backside and pulling me into him. "I know. I'll drop it."

"There's nothing to drop," I insist angrily.

"If you pick a fight right now, nobody is gonna win," Julian murmurs, looking down at me, his dark eyes smoldering intensely.

I realize he likes it when I'm feisty. Even if it does make me into a total bitch at times. Either way, his words, his touch, and the small smile pulling at his full lips defuses the anger in me.

"You're right, I'm sorry. Take me home, please," I reply, going on my toes to bring my face to his.

Julian leans in to kiss me, softly and sensually, but he pulls away far sooner than I'd like. "You're sexy when you're giving in," he teases, unleashing his full panty-melting smile.

I disentangle myself from him and pull him toward the car. "Don't push your luck," I grouse back as seriously as I can.

He laughs as I hand him the keys. "I wouldn't dream of it," he promises with a devilish glint in his eyes.

* * *

When we get back to my place, I stand at the door, unsure of what I expected to do at this point as Julian looks at me like he's wondering the same thing.

"You should get some sleep," he tells me, his rough hand stroking down my face.

I consider him in the dark hall for a moment. He bears the usual signs of club work. Sweat, grime, and the smell of alcohol. Normally, I deal with a rough night by isolating myself and sleeping it off, but the thought of him leaving makes me feel miserably lonely.

"You look like you could use a shower and a nice, soft bed," I reply, opening the door and pulling him in behind me.

"So we're doing this, huh?" he teases as he drops the keys on the counter.

I set my purse next to it. "I don't know," I admit. "Do I really have to decide tonight? I really just want a hot shower and some sleep."

"Is that all you want?" he asks huskily, stepping into me.

"I want you to stay," I reply honestly, pressing my hands against the firm muscles of his chest. "That's all I know right now."

His thick eyebrows pull together as he studies my face, as if he's trying to figure me out through sheer willpower.

I tap him on the forehead, laughing. "Stop thinking. Start undressing." I point to the laundry closet on the other side of the living room. "You can put your clothes in the wash. I'm getting in the shower."

I turn on my heel and head into the bedroom, leaving a dumbfounded Julian in my wake.

I undress with a smile while the hot water of the shower starts to fog up the room. I wind my long hair up, tying it at the top of my head before getting in. I'm too tired to dry it after it's washed, and I can't sleep with wet hair, so it'll just have to wait until tomorrow.

As I slip under the stream of scalding water, I gasp at the sudden change. But I'm thankful for the heat, the cleansing of not just the physical evidence of the night — sweat, beer, and tears — but the emotional weight too. The heat wears at the tense muscles of my back from all the anger and frustration of the evening, until I feel myself mellowing out and winding down.

I hear the bathroom door open and I smile, glad Julian didn't wait until I was done. I don't know what I want with Julian, but I do know I want him with me tonight.

He taps on the glass. "Mind if I join you?" His voice is low and tired, but still sexy enough to stir me just a little. And that's saying something, given my level of exhaustion.

I open the door a crack in answer. As he steps into the not-quite-big-enough-for-two space, I only briefly register the satisfied smile before his massive chest fills the space in front of me. I realize I'm finally going to get a good look at his body, his tattoos, and … other things. The sudden thought perks me up considerably.

I scoot him around in a circle, so his back is under the water. The hot stream slips around his broad, muscled shoulders and he groans in relief.

"God, that feels good," he murmurs, closing his eyes and tipping his head back to let the water flow over the sharp angles of his face.

I slide my hands up his chest, tracing the designs on his pecs. He tilts his head back down and opens his eyes to watch me. Most of his ink is obviously religious. Hands clasped in prayer hold a rosary under my left hand. A large, ornate cross under my right. Dark angels adorn his arm on the side with the praying hands from the top of his shoulder to his wrist. The angel on top is inked darker than the rest, a look of wrath on his beautiful face. The others are surrounded by fire and crushed under his feet in apparent supplication.

"Lucifer," Julian supplies as my finger traces the angry features of the fallen angel. He watches intently as my fingers slip down the figures to trace the words at his wrist.

"Pride," I whisper.

"It was their sin," he explains. He shifts to expose his other arm to me, pointing at the top figure. "Michael," he names the angel on his other shoulder, "and his army of angels."

The angels on the other arm are surrounded by pristine, white clouds and heavenly light, have an air of serenity, and are breathtakingly beautiful. I tear my eyes away to look up into his face, to find him still and vulnerable as he awaits my reaction. I smile at him reassuringly, letting my fingers slide down his arms. The intense attraction that always thrums between us is a mellow hum tonight, in our tired state, but tugs at me nonetheless. Shaking myself back to the present, I switch my fingers to his other wrist to read the word written there.

"Humility." He smiles when I read it aloud, tracing his hand down my back.

81

His last set of tattoos are twins, seven in roman numerals, on each side of his ribcage. I run my fingers over them and he giggles. The sound makes me smile again, and I look up at him coyly from under my eyelashes.

"That tickles," he tells me, leaning down to rub his nose against mine before planting a soft kiss on my lips.

"What do they mean?" I ask curiously.

His eyes sparkle in the fog of the shower and he looks like a dream with his rugged, striking features.

"It's a reminder that there are seven deadly sins," he explains once more. "But there are also seven virtues. Every day I have to choose between them."

"Every day?" I ask, confused.

He runs his thumb over my lips. "Every day, beautiful. We all do, really."

"I didn't realize you were religious," I reply with a smile.

His answering smile is sad. "I'm not. But that doesn't mean I don't have faith. That there's a better way to do things in this world. And the next."

I'm silenced by the depth of emotion behind his words. Unsure of what to say, I grab the bar of soap behind him and carefully wash him instead. He allows me access, patiently watching me with those dark, intense eyes.

When the hot water has rinsed all the soap away, he takes the bar from my hands and runs it over my back with one hand, the other trailing down the tattoos on my upper arm.

"What about yours?" he murmurs.

I shrug, self-conscious. "They're all variations on the night sky," I reply. "Nothing particularly meaningful, just beautiful pictures I like."

He moves to soaping my front, his rough hands gently working around my breasts in a way that's more relaxing than stimulating.

"You like the stars?" he asks contemplatively.

"Love," I whisper. It's not a story I want to share right now, so I go on my toes to close the large gap between our mouths, still needing to pull him down to me because he's that damn tall.

He kisses me softly. "You're short without your high heels," he says with a smile.

"I'm still tall," I grouse back. "You're just a freak of nature. What are you, six-five?"

"Six-six," he says with a smirk.

"Freak," I mutter jokingly.

That gets a full smile and throaty laugh from him. Like everything else about him, his smile and his laugh do things to me that defy logic. I almost forget about the little voice inside when I'm with him. Somehow, he never triggers it, even though I know he's not completely honest with me. But like he's pointed out, it's not like I'm completely honest with him, either. Nils made a good point the day I decided to go out with Julian for the first time. Maybe I need to decide whether he's worth getting past whatever bullshit is holding us back to stop, well, holding back.

"Come on, I think we're clean enough now," Julian says, breaking into my reverie. "And I'm sure we could both use some sleep."

I raise an eyebrow at him. It's what I'd intended in the first place, but I'm a little surprised he's so willing to go along with it. Though admittedly I am tired enough that the intense heat I usually feel between us is still a low simmer. I'm more relaxed than anything in his presence at the moment. As he steps out of the shower, I get the full visual of his well-muscled frame and realize that considering how fucking amazing he looks naked, that's once again saying something about how exhausted I must be.

"You're right," I admit. "But ..." I trail my eyes over the perfect tautness of his chest, arms, and abs. And I finally let my gaze drop lower. *Good lord.* Now I know I'm tired because his semi-hard, generous package barely stirs the sleeping fire between my legs.

When my eyes move back up to his, he's tolerantly smirking at me. "Like what you see?"

I shrug nonchalantly. "Sure, I guess. What's not to like?"

His booming laugh echoes through the bathroom. "Damn, woman, you're stubborn."

I bite my lip, but it can't stop the smile and subsequent laugh that escapes me. "Come on, let's go to bed."

We finish drying off, stealing glances at each other all the while. Julian follows me into the bedroom, where I slip on a short, silky nightgown.

"Hmmm, I might have a pair of shorts or something around here you can wear," I murmur, flipping through my drawers. When I turn around Julian's already in bed.

"It's okay, I sleep naked anyway," he says, leaning against the cushioned headboard.

I take a deep breath. "Of course you do," I laugh, climbing into bed beside him.

"What does that mean?" he asks with an answering laugh as he slides down next to me.

I snuggle into my pillow with a yawn. "It means you're already practically irresistible and you know it," I murmur sleepily.

"Mmmm," he murmurs. "And you are much more relaxed than you were."

I look up at him from under my heavy eyelids. "Hm. You're right. I can go back to being in a foul mood, if you'd prefer."

Julian leans over me and turns off the light on my nightstand, plunging us into near darkness. I feel his large, warm frame slide back down next to me, followed by one strong arm sliding around my waist, pulling me against him in the dark.

I snuggle happily into his chest, his scent filling me, calming me, lulling me to sleep.

He brushes my hair away from my face gently. "No," he says softly. "All I wanted was to make sure you were okay. I'm glad you're feeling better, beautiful. Now get some rest." His warm lips kiss my jawline under my ear.

A small happy noise escapes me as I drift off to sleep.

Chapter 13 — Frankie

The blackout shades in my room are drawn, so when I wake I have no idea what time it is. But I'm definitely alone in bed. I sit up sleepily, twisting to look at the clock and gain my bearings.

Before my eyes can even adjust, the bedroom door opens and a sliver of light expands across the bedspread as Julian comes back into the room. In the light I can see that he's still fully naked. And still fully gorgeous, his toned body flexing as he tries to quietly navigate in the darkness.

"Whatcha creeping around for?" I whisper.

"Gaaaahhhh," Julian shouts, jumping about a foot in the air.

I cackle delightfully.

"Geez, Frankie, don't do that," he grumbles. "I had to use the bathroom so I figured I'd switch my laundry. It's still early, you should go back to sleep." He slides back under the covers and his cool skin meets mine. "Mmm you're nice and warm."

"How early?" I ask.

Julian's hands skim over my backside as he wriggles into me. "Just after seven."

"Fuck, that is early," I mumble into his chest. "Wait, *I* should go back to sleep? Aren't you?"

He buries his face in my hair, inhaling deeply. "Not likely while I'm lying here naked next to you," he whispers seductively in my ear.

It has an immediate effect, and I can feel my body tightening in response. And so can he. His hand runs down my nightgown and over my hardened nipple appreciatively.

"Goddamn it, Frankie, you are so fucking sexy," he murmurs before pressing his lips to my neck as his hands continue to roam.

I push my hand against his chest, which I'd meant as a gesture of uncertainty, but when it hits the wall of muscle that is his body, it takes my breath away.

Honestly, what did I expect climbing into bed with him? That we'd wake up, shake hands, and go our separate ways? No. I have to admit to myself that this is exactly what I'd wanted.

If only I wasn't so damn worried about what he isn't telling me. But right now, as his lips stroke the sensitive skin on my neck and his hands work my breasts, my mind is blissfully blank.

Surrendering to the moment, I push on his chest again until he lets me roll him onto his back. As I rise to my knees I can just make out him watching me as I place myself between his legs. I stroke his thighs lightly with my palms, lowering my lips to him. He lets out a low moan, realizing what I'm about to do.

I capture him just with my mouth until he's expanded to fill its wet warmth before slipping my hand around the wide base of his cock. The noises he makes as I slowly and firmly work him have me just as ready as he is. I relent with my mouth, sitting back to take him in as I slide my hand up and down his length.

His hands are locked behind his head, his chin tipped up and eyes closed as he groans with pleasure. His body is so fucking perfect in every way that I can't take it anymore. I let him go long enough to get protection out of the nightstand, then roll it down his hard length as quickly as I can, my whole body trembling with the anticipation of having him inside of me.

"Oh, fuck, Frankie, yes," he gasps as I finish readying him. "Goddamn it, I want you on top of me so fucking bad." His husky rasp has me so wet it's all I can do to calmly slide up his body and meet his lips with mine.

His tongue plunges hungrily into my mouth, his hands closing around my face. I grab his wrists and free myself, slipping one hand between us to guide him into me. I then slide back mercilessly, and he fills me with an intensely pleasurable pain, our moans synchronized with the thrust.

"Shit, you're so tight," he groans. "And so wet. You feel so fucking good."

I don't tell him how amazing he feels, not trusting myself to speak. I'm already so turned on that anything could tip me over the edge. So I concentrate, pushing myself up to a sitting position and removing my nightgown as he watches, his eyes heavily lidded, his breathing heavy. And then I start to move. Slowly at first.

His hands find my hips, tugging at them. "Faster, Frankie," he urges. "Give me that pussy, please, God, it feels so good."

"If you keep talking like that, this isn't going to last much longer," I promise, stilling myself as a shiver rolls through me. Just looking at him hurts, much less hearing him talk dirty while I fuck him.

Julian looks up at me and laughs. "You don't like it?" he asks huskily, with a sly smirk playing around his deliciously full lips.

I raise his hands to my breasts, and his thumbs work my nipples in tantalizingly rough circles.

"I think I like it a little too much," I admit, biting my bottom lip.

Julian's eyes darken and he sits up, pulling me into his chest, ravenously consuming my mouth with his. He pulls back and looks into my eyes, his thumbs and forefingers now closing over my nipples and tugging at them.

"Lie down," he commands. "My turn to have my way with you."

My insides pulse and tighten, and he smirks, feeling it around his cock. He raises an eyebrow and pushes me gently off him onto the bed. With one hand, he strokes himself firmly from root to tip and back down as he climbs to his knees between my legs.

His other hand slips over my dripping core. "Your problem," he says slowly, spreading my wetness, "is that you're always in charge." He leans forward, positioning himself to enter me. "I think you like having someone take control." He slides smoothly in, causing me to gasp at the sudden, insanely pleasurable sensation.

With one hand, he holds my leg against his shoulder. The other he uses to press against my clit as he starts to move.

"Tell me you like that, Frankie," he begs, his voice thick with need.

"Oh, yeah, I like that," I breathe.

"Good," he murmurs, his rhythm unbroken. "Now tell me you like it when I fuck your beautiful pussy."

My back arches off the bed, my core tightening as the eroticism of his words adds to the ache rolling through me. "Goddamn it, I love it when you fuck my pussy," I moan back as he continues to do exactly that, each thrust sending a new wave of ecstasy through me.

He lets loose a predatory grin and drops my leg back down, settling over me on his forearms. He glides mercilessly in and out, his breathing accelerating in my ear as he whispers a raunchy, explicit narrative about how good I feel, how much he's wanted to be inside of me, how hard he's going to make me come.

I've never had someone stimulate me this way during sex, and it has every part of my body clenching in anticipation. He doesn't even seem to mind that it has me so lust-fogged that I couldn't even form a sentence unless he told me what to say.

And rearing back while pulling me into his lap, he does exactly that.

"Tell me how to fuck you, Frankie," he instructs.

"Harder," I urge with a moan.

He thrusts harder, deeper. "You like it hard like that?"

"Yesss," I hiss as he pounds me just right. "Right there. Fuck, you're gonna make me come."

"Perfect," he says with a satisfied smile, "Now tell me how fast."

"Slower," I say, wanting to feel every inch as he pushes into my sensitive opening, then all the way deep down into the spot only the head of his long cock can reach. I want to climb to my orgasm as slowly as he brought me there with his hands and mouth, to feel that earth-shattering pleasure again.

He ratchets down accommodatingly until he's doing exactly that — hitting my G-spot with hard, slow thrusts. I feel the ache start to spread between my legs.

"Faster," I breathe.

He leans into me and picks up his speed just slightly. The ache builds and I throw my head back, unable to speak.

"Oh, damn, you just got so tight," he groans, closing his eyes.

I whimper at his words.

"I'm going to go faster. Hang on," he says breathlessly.

I nod mutely and grasp the sheets beneath me.

And he goes faster, asking over and over if I like the way he's fucking me. All I can do is writhe and moan in response.

And faster, now telling me how fucking good I feel. I have to grip the bed tightly to keep myself still enough to let the ache fill me as his words distract me to a whole new layered level of pleasure.

Sweat rolls off Julian's toned chest as he's finally silent, focusing on giving me all he's got. At the sight, I can feel my muscles contract, pulling him in deeper with each thrust. He shifts his weight to his left hand and slips his right one between my legs, stroking me in time with his rhythm, encouraging me with his sexy, dirty words once again. I throw my head back at the added stimulation, feeling the ache coil into a tight ball that threatens to explode through me at any moment.

"Come for me, beautiful," Julian says. It's his same plea as last time, but this time the tenderness in his voice undoes me completely.

"Ohhhhhh, yessss," I cry out as I tighten around him, riding up the wave, cresting, and still more until my body is shaking.

And just when I think I'm going to roll back down to earth he leans over me so he presses into my clit harder with every thrust and I'm riding even higher than before, screaming my release over and over.

Somewhere in the throes of passion I hear Julian loudly finding his own release. But I'm so racked by bliss that I don't come back down until he's slowed, then stopped completely.

He disentangles himself from my embrace and pulls out, leaning back on his haunches to catch his breath.

And now I'm the one who can't shut up, repeating "fuck" over and over as I try to catch my breath and wait for the shaking in my limbs to stop.

I watch Julian remove the condom and wrap it in a tissue before he lies down next to me, laughing.

"You okay?" he asks.

As the trembling of my arms and legs subsides, I lie, unmoving, on the bed next to him. "Beyond okay," I assure him when I can finally speak again.

Julian pulls the blanket back over us. "Good," he murmurs, curling up next to me and pulling me into a spooning position. "Now go back to sleep, beautiful."

I couldn't argue if I wanted to, as blissed out as I am, with his warm, strong body curled around mine, his abating erection pulsating on my backside, his lips resting against my hair. I drift peacefully to sleep, wrapped contentedly in Julian's ridiculously perfect arms.

* * *

When I wake again it's nearly noon and Julian isn't in bed. And a quick walk through the apartment tells me he's really gone. I check my phone and, lo and behold, he's texted me. *Figured I'd be a distraction, and you have things to do. I'll call you soon. x*

Shaking off the disappointment of waking up alone, I realize it was probably for the best. Because not only do I still not know if it's a good idea to agree to really give things with Julian the good old college try, he's also right — I have some serious shit to handle today.

* * *

It takes the afternoon and into the evening to put together the security footage and other data, go over it, and take it to the police station. To be fair, the time includes giving our own statements.

Jess isn't there, thankfully, and we aren't permitted to see Dave. Supposedly, he's in contact with an attorney, though, so we can only hope that everything will be okay. And guess at whatever details Jess provided to convince the police to hold Dave. Even without the advantage of knowing exactly when people are lying, Nils is absolutely in agreement with me that Jess set Dave up.

Disheartened and troubled, Nils and I are both famished, so we decide to head to the diner across the street from Baltia and talk things out.

As we finish our meal, I sit, picking at the last of my fries. I lean back in the booth, still trying to make sense of it all.

"So will there be any consequences for her when they prove she's lying?" Nils asks curiously, folding his long arms over his chest.

I huff a dry laugh. "How can they prove she's lying?" I point out. "At best we can hope they can't find enough evidence to support her story."

"Except we provided direct evidence that she lied to us," he counters.

I shake my head sadly and look up into his eyes. "That's not how it works, Nils, darling," I reply. "They weren't there. They won't take our word for it. For all they know we'd rather hush this all up to avoid bringing attention to the club." I shift in my seat, agitated. I hate when people get away with lying. Especially on something as damaging as this.

"Well, the video shows her following him into the bathroom," Nils says again for what feels like the thousandth time today. "She's going to be hard-pressed to prove she wasn't stalking him between that and the text messages he has."

I wave my hand dismissively. "There's nothing we can do about it, and I'm tired of talking in circles," I grouse, taking a sip of soda. "Can we talk about staffing? Because we were already short one bartender, and now there's no knowing when we'll get Dave back."

Nils leans forward on his arms. "I've thought about that," he admits. "And our situation in general. Even aside from this, business is a little too good for the coverage we've got all around. I think we need to make a few more additions as well."

I raise an eyebrow. I hadn't intended to increase staffing until after the first year, but I realize he's probably right. We've all been running ourselves ragged to keep up. And I, for one, could use a break.

"Okay," I agree.

Nils laughs. "I thought I'd have to fight a little harder," he replies with a smile.

"I've got no fight left," I reply, rubbing my temples.

Nils reaches across the table, uncharacteristically laying his hand over mine. "Hey, everything okay? It's not the brooder, is it?"

I laugh at his ridiculously accurate nickname for Julian. "I don't know," I admit. "I have reservations. But it's just everything. I think you're right, we need more help. It's all a bit overwhelming at the moment."

He studies my face carefully, still not withdrawing his hand. I turn my palm up and give him a reassuring squeeze.

"Really, let's do it," I reiterate.

He finally withdraws pensively with a nod. "I'll set up interviews as soon as I can manage. Two new bartenders and an assistant manager?"

"Sounds good. Thanks, Nils. For everything," I reply.

He runs a hand through his long blond hair, somehow seeming more bothered than before. "My pleasure, Francesca."

"Nils, is everything okay with you?"

He looks up warily, not responding right away. "Yes, no complaints here." *Lie.*

I suppress a sigh. "Come on, Nils, you can talk to me," I assure him. "You're important to me. To the club. If there's something going on, I want to know about it."

"I can't," he says, shaking his head. "Not after I encouraged you to go for it."

My eyebrows jump. "This is about Julian?"

He cringes and nods. "I don't trust him."

I smile widely and chuckle. "That makes two of us, Nils. But I appreciate your concern."

"Do you?" he asks, tilting his head to the side.

Suddenly, I'm not sure I like where this conversation is going. It feels too personal. Like there's something he's trying to tell me. Something I probably don't want to know.

"Yes," I say firmly. "As friends and coworkers, we should look out for each other."

He nods, and I hope he's read between the not-so-subtle lines. "Indeed," he says softly, holding my gaze. "Come on, let's get back to the club." He slides out of the booth.

But the walk back is silent and tense, and I wonder if I've heard the last of what's really on his mind.

* * *

On Monday afternoon Dave appears in my office door.

"Ms. Greco?"

"Dave," I reply, jumping out of my seat in surprise. "I'm glad to see you. Please come in and sit down."

He enters tentatively, and I note he looks exhausted and disheveled. I guess jail will do that to you.

"I was released this morning," he says by way of explanation as he settles into the chair across from me. "Everything happened so fast the other night. I wanted to come as soon as I could and tell you my side of the story."

I want to tell him there's no need, I know Jess set him up, but I know I shouldn't. "I'm all ears," I say instead, retaking my seat.

"I was going to the supply closet and decided to hit the head first," he says, nervously twisting his fingers in his lap. "But before I could lock the door, Jess came in and locked the door behind her."

He stops, shaking his head. I stay silent, not wanting to lead him one way or the other.

He looks up at me, brushing his shaggy brown hair out of his sad, grey-green eyes. He's a handsome kid, and it kills me to see him so miserable.

He's usually so laid-back, happy-go-lucky even. What a shit lesson to learn at only twenty-two.

"She said she missed me. That it wasn't fair you were keeping us apart," he finally continues. "I tried to tell her again that it wasn't just you, that I didn't like her like that, just like I've told her before." He chews on his bottom lip. "She told me she'd give me one last chance to make the right decision, or else."

"Or else what?" I ask softly.

He snorts. "She didn't say, and I didn't ask," he responds. "I told her it wasn't gonna happen." He looks down and blushes a deep red. "She took off her shirt, and tried to touch me. I pushed her away, and she went nuts."

"Went nuts how?" I ask, leaning forward.

"She was like an animal," he says. It comes out a hoarse whisper, and he clears his throat and looks up, gesturing at the faint scabs adorning his cheeks. "She scratched the shit out of me, tore at my shirt, pulled her own fucking hair. Then she heard you call my name and she just screamed like a fucking banshee." He stops himself. "I'm sorry, it's just hard to talk about it without getting mad. It sounds crazy. The police looked at me like I was crazy. Like, why would she do that? They didn't get it. Honestly, I don't get it, either."

And I just can't take it anymore. "Dave," I say sharply, bringing his eyes back to mine. "There's definitely some crazy happening here, but I can pretty much guarantee it's not you."

He looks immensely relieved. "You believe me? You think it's her?" he asks.

"I believe you. She has already proven that she's capable of serious deception," I insist.

"I'm glad, but I don't know how the cops are going to know who to believe," he replies despondently.

"There was no question in my mind once we reviewed the evidence. And I'm confident the same will be true this time," I assure him.

"I hope so," he sighs. He scratches the back of his head. "So what happens now? With my job and everything, I mean."

I let out a heavy sigh. "Unfortunately, while the investigation is pending I have no choice but to suspend you," I reply.

The look on his face is one of the things I hate the most about being the boss. Because my hands are tied, and I'm unwillingly complicit in Jess's scheme to fuck him over for rejecting her.

"That's just fucking perfect," he spits venomously. Then immediately looks like he regrets it. "I'm sorry, I know you have to. This just sucks."

"I get that. And I can't pay you until this is resolved, but once it is — and it will be — you'll get backpay for the days you would've worked," I assure him. He looks slightly less unhappy at that news. "We'll keep in touch through this. Try not to worry too much. This will all be over soon."

Dave shakes his head sadly. "I have a feeling it's only just beginning."

Chapter 14 — Frankie

By Wednesday the list of people I haven't heard from has grown. The police. Emma. Julian. If I'm being honest with myself, the last one stings the most. I'm not sure what his definition of "soon" is, but not calling a woman you've slept with more than three days later isn't okay in my book.

I've resolved to call him this evening, but first I need to go see Emma. I haven't tried to call her since the club five days ago because I know how stubborn she is. I have to get in her face, beg her forgiveness. Even though it's not like I wasn't going to tell her about Ben's lies.

As I pull up in front of their building in Mar Vista, I try to drop the attitude. On my fourth deep breath, I realize I'm not annoyed at Emma for assuming I wasn't going to tell her. I'm mad at Julian for not calling. The realization makes me sad, which sucks, but at least I feel less angry and more prepared to face Emma without escalating the situation.

With a sigh I put up the ragtop and amble out of the car to face the music. I take my time climbing the stairs in her building, noting every crack in the wall on the way. *Geez, don't want to face the music much?* I should probably be giving myself a pep talk, but I'm not in a peppy mood, I guess.

I stand in front of Emma and Ben's peeling beige door and heave a sigh before biting the bullet and knocking.

As if she knew I was coming, and was standing there expectantly, I've barely dropped my arm when the door opens forcefully to a disheveled Emma.

Her blond hair is pulled back, but far messier than usual, and she's still wearing her pajamas. I guess if I didn't have to work in the middle of the week I'd be wearing mine too. I don't even have time to register her mood when she grabs my hand and pulls me into a big hug.

"Oh, Frankie," she murmurs. "I'm so sorry."

Surprised, it takes me a moment to return the hug. Her reaction is the opposite of what I was expecting.

"Well, this is already going better than I'd expected," I tease as she squeezes me roughly.

She pushes away, but grabs my hand once more and pulls me into their tiny one-bedroom apartment. She flops dramatically on their old, cracked brown leather couch and pats the cushion next to her. I sit reluctantly, still not believing she's magically over it.

"Seriously," Emma insists. "I was a complete bitch, and I feel like shit for it. Even if you weren't going to tell me, it wasn't your fault. It was Ben I was mad at. Can you forgive me?"

I laugh drily. I know the feeling. Same as how I'm not mad at her either, though I can't say the same for Julian.

I reach over and give her hand a squeeze. "I know how you feel," I commiserate. "And of course I can. I *was* going to tell you, I promise. There was just so much going on, and I wanted to work up to it. But I fucked up. And I'm sorry too."

Emma leans over and pulls me in for another hug.

"So what's with all the hugging?" I tease her gently. "Are you and Ben okay?"

She sighs, pulling at her stretchy pajama top. "We will be," she finally replies, fidgeting in her seat.

"Did he say *why* he lied?" I ask. I don't even want to know how she found out. I'm just glad she did before she went into vacation planning mode.

Emma's lips press together in a deep frown. "I've been getting on his case a lot about getting a nicer place," she admits. "But it's not like we can exactly afford it."

"That still doesn't make any sense," I press.

Emma shrugs. "I don't think he thought too hard about it — he just wanted me off his back," she responds. "Who the fuck knows what goes on in a man's brain?"

I huff a dry laugh, shaking my head. "Preach," I grumble, looking at my hands in my lap, fighting a wave of unexpected tears. It makes me angry, and I let out a growl as I press my palms into my eyes. I don't fucking cry for anyone, and I'm not about to start.

"Frankie, what's wrong?" Emma asks, clearly alarmed.

I drop my hands to find her staring at me bewildered. I can see it's just as jarring for her to see me like this as it is for me. And last she knew Julian was on my shit list. Not that he isn't right back there.

"Oh fuck, it's the asshole, isn't it?" she demands. She pushes me hard. "Dammit, Frankie, you let him back in and he fucked with you again, didn't he?"

"No," I protest. "Well, yes, but …" I trail off, shaking my head in anger. But I'm less mad at Julian now. I'm starting to be angrier with myself. Emma is not wrong. I *knew*. I knew we were too similar. That it was going to be a fucking rollercoaster. I let myself be taken in by the attraction, by his promises, his words. I know I'm smarter than that.

In any case it's a burden I can't bear alone anymore, so I spill my guts to Emma. I tell her about what went down at the club while she was at the bar, and after she left, both with the fight with the bitches and with Julian following me. I tell her about our encounter the next day in my living room, and the mess at the club with Jess and Dave that night, and how Julian helped, cared for me, connected with me. How we fucked the next morning. And that when I woke up again, he was gone. And that I haven't heard from him since.

She's quiet for a moment, clearly incredulous. "Wow. You're really looking for trouble these days, aren't you?" she muses. She looks up at me suddenly with a wicked look on her face. "How was the sex?"

I laugh. "That's what you want to know?" I shake my head. "Fucking amazing."

"And everything else? I mean, do you really *like* this guy?"

I rub my thighs, irritated. "I guess? I mean, yes. Until we fucked and then he hasn't called for three days," I growl. "Part of me wants to write him off. But mostly I want to know why. Or maybe this is normal? Or am I supposed to call him?" I shake my head again, completely agitated and out of my element.

"Jesus H. Christ, Frankie, it hasn't been *that* long since you've dated," Emma replies, rolling her eyes. "You're totally right to be pissed. You guys fucked. He said he wants to be with you. He knows you're going through some shit. He said he'd call. He *should've* called."

I take a deep breath and lean back into the cushions. "You're right," I agree. "You're absolutely right. So what do I do now?"

"Say you call him, and he's an asshole. Do you really want to deal with that now?" she asks shrewdly.

I chew on my bottom lip, trying to be as objective as possible. I want to believe Julian isn't trying to be a dick, but let's face it, he's not doing himself any favors at the moment. And I've got enough on my plate.

"No," I admit.

Emma shrugs as if the answer should be obvious. And maybe it is. But she spells it out anyway. "Then don't call him. Deal with it when you're ready to."

"That's a strangely liberating way to look at it," I respond slowly. I roll the idea around in my head for a while. And the more I think about it, the better it sounds. He doesn't want to talk to me? Fine. I don't want to talk to him right now either. I sure as hell don't have the energy to get through that conversation.

* * *

I'm sitting in my office at Baltia on Thursday morning when the detective on Dave's case finally calls. He tells me they've dropped all charges. In combination with the pile of evidence against her story, apparently there have been two other restraining orders taken out against Jess in the last three years for stalking. He also shares that he's advised Dave to do the same, and for me to let him know if there are any further issues.

When I hang up, I'm relieved, but I still have an unsettled feeling. I sit, staring into the distance and stroking gentle circles into my desk while I try to pinpoint my disquiet.

It's how Nils finds me just before we're supposed to interview new bartending candidates. I fill him in on the latest and let him call Dave to confirm he can come back to work before we begin our interviews.

It takes the rest of the afternoon, pushing up into opening, before we've gotten through everyone, as I'd forgotten we were also interviewing for an assistant manager. We found the latter almost immediately, as Nils had a friend he'd worked with before whom he was itching to hire, so I just told him to go ahead. We also found one experienced bartender we hired on the spot — a stunning redhead in her mid-forties who didn't drop a single lie and whose no-nonsense attitude was immediately appealing — and had another few candidates to think on before we filled the second spot. All in all, not a bad place to be in.

But having been made to skip dinner, I'm in a pretty foul mood for the rest of the night. Though I can't blame it entirely on lack of food. Thankfully, one of the perks of the job is that it's hard to think about much else once the music starts.

* * *

Unfortunately, Friday does little to improve my mood. Nils and I make the decision on the second bartender and just as I have the phone in my hand to call, Jess walks into my office.

She beams at me as she enters, her blond curls bouncing innocently as she parks herself in the chair in front of my desk. "I'm here to ask for my job back. I realize what I did was wrong, and I think I deserve a second chance," she says cheerfully.

I'm completely dumbfounded. And just as quickly, extremely disturbed.

"Jess, you've been banned from being here. I'm not sure how you got in the door, but you need to leave, now, and not come back. Or I'm afraid I'll be forced to file an order of protection. You wouldn't want that, would you?" I prompt.

"But I'm a new Jess now," she replies, still chipper. "Dave got another chance. I should too."

It's not lost on me that she knows Dave has returned to work, and I wonder if she's been back to the club without our knowledge. The further this goes, the more disturbed I get.

"Yes, because the charges against him were dropped. I don't punish innocent people," I reply pointedly. "You were fired for provable misconduct."

Jess's mouth drops open stupidly, but the confusion on her face is rapidly replaced with rage. Red-faced and clearly beyond agitated, she springs from her chair and slams her hands on my desk.

"You can't do this," she seethes. "He got a second chance. If you don't give me one, I'll sue you for discrimination."

The absence of the voice tells me that it's not an empty threat. I take a deep breath through my nose and rise slowly from my chair, circling the desk to hold the door open in an obvious signal that I'm not interested in discussing this further. She folds her arms over her chest resolutely, glaring at me as she roots in place.

"In that case, I'm obligated to direct you to our attorney," I say firmly. "Now please leave or I will have you escorted from the building."

"Fine," she hisses. "But you're going to regret this."

And with that she stomps past me and out of the club. And I have an ugly feeling that she means to make good on her threat.

Nils slinks into my office.

"What the hell was that?" he asks.

I shake my head, not in the mood to discuss it.

"Can you call Rick, please? I didn't get the chance before Ms. Wilson's visit."

"Oh, I saw her coming, so I already called him. He'll start next Thursday. Really, Francesca, we should discuss this," he insists.

I sigh. He's right. But before I can, my phone buzzes distractingly on my desk.

"Fine, just let me check this," I grouse, circling my desk and grabbing my phone. It's Julian. The fucking bastard. I send it to voicemail without hesitation and shove my phone angrily into my back pocket. When I turn back to Nils, he's suppressing a smile. "What?"

He presses his lips together. "Sorry," he apologizes honestly. "I can guess who that was by the look on your face."

I narrow my eyes at him, and he puts his hands up, laughing. "I won't say a word against him," he promises. "I just hope you don't ever look like that when I call."

That throws me off and we stare at each other for a moment, tension hanging thick in the air. But before I can formulate a response, Ace appears and drags Nils away on some urgent sound-system-related business. Nils vows to return to discuss Jess, but I don't give a flying fuck either way right now. I bury myself in work to forget it all. Nils. Jess. Julian. Especially Julian.

Unfortunately, he doesn't take the hint, and over the next few hours until doors open, I feel my phone buzz several more times. I only glance at the screen long enough to confirm it's Julian and not some other, more urgent business, before going back to firmly ignoring him. But, if it's possible, it makes me even grouchier than I'd been the night before. Against my better judgment, I throw back a couple of drinks as I work the floor, trying to take the edge off the stress of the week. But the universe has the last laugh, as it's not enough to dull my internal turmoil, just enough to give me one big motherfucking headache.

* * *

Fortunately, late the next morning I meet Mac at the shooting range. And every target is Julian. I nail each one in the head *and* the heart for good measure. It improves my mood considerably. That is, until Mac looks at me with his wise, old eyes that see everything. Thankfully, he doesn't say anything. He just lets me go at it until our two hours are up, then buys me tacos as we shoot the shit about everything else.

I haven't even mentioned Julian to him, and I'm not about to start now. That's not the kind of stuff Mac and I discuss. And the catharsis of killing dummy targets and eating Mexican food is short lived, as I realize I really do need to talk about it.

But I'm just not ready yet, so I head back to the club to keep busy until tonight. What I don't expect is the strange old man waiting for me at the front door.

"Doors don't open until ten," I call out as I approach.

He turns toward me and smiles. He looks to be in his late sixties but based on the cigarette hanging out of his mouth that looks like it fits nicely in its well-worn groove, he could also be younger. A few strands of thin, greasy hair are slicked back on his head. He'd be average height if he didn't stoop a bit, and he looks like he was attacked by a pawn shop jewelry counter.

"I know. I was looking for *you*," he greets me, extending a weathered hand.

I look down at it and cross my arms over my chest. "Yeah? What for?" I ask defensively.

He cackles happily. "You've got spunk, Frankie," he says fondly. "I knew you would."

If I didn't already immediately dislike him, I do now. "You've got two seconds to tell me who the fuck you are and how you know me before I kick your ass off my property," I warn him.

He huffs one last laugh. "My name is Salvatore Moretti," he replies. "And I'm your father, Frankie."

Chapter 15 — Frankie

I stand there, completely speechless, staring at this old man who claims to be my father. And the little voice inside me says not a word. It's a full minute before I find my voice again.

"You must be mistaken. My father died before I was born," I assure him. I don't know if this guy is crazy or misinformed, but the fact that he believes it tells me I need to be very careful.

"Ah," he says. "So that's what Sam told you."

I mash my lips together. Okay, he also knows my mother's name. That just means he's more well informed than the average nutjob.

"Look, I don't know who you really are, but I can assure you that I know without a doubt that my father did die before I was born."

He smiles patiently. "She lied to me about you, too," he says softly. "I understand that this must all be very shocking for you, and I debated just leaving you alone. But I've already missed out on thirty-four years of your life. Allow me to prove it to you?"

I want to tell him my mother can't lie to me. But I stop myself. I know better than anyone that there are so many ways to hide the truth. And I have to ask myself if I remember when my mother told me my father was dead, and how.

"How did you find me, then?" I ask.

He gestures to the door. "Perhaps we should sit down and discuss this?" he asks politely.

But the thought of letting this man into my club doesn't sit well. I tuck my arms closer around myself and shake my head. He sighs deeply, leaning into the building.

"Okay, then. I saw a news piece on you. And the club." He gestures to the building. "You looked just like my mother, and I knew Sam had lied to me. See, I knew she had a little girl, years ago. But she lied about your age, said you weren't mine. You looked different enough then that I didn't see it. As soon as I saw you now, though, I knew. And when I saw how old you really are, well, it was more confirmation of something I already knew."

I shake my head again, finding it impossible to absorb. "How did you know my mom? How did you not know she was pregnant?"

The old man sighs and runs a hand over his greasy head. "That's your mother's story to tell."

I laugh. I might as well go ask my mother to get a mani-pedi with me and have some girl talk. In other words, not gonna happen.

He eyes me shrewdly. "She's a tough nut, your mom. I know," he says.

I raise an eyebrow. "So how exactly did you plan on proving this to me?"

His thin lips stretch in a smile. "If you have some time, there's a hospital four blocks away. Same-day paternity tests." He checks his watch. "So long as we're there in the next forty-five minutes."

I mull on that. I have the time. I don't really need to be at the club for another few hours. And I realize I both have nothing to lose, and if I don't find out, it'll bug the shit out of me. At least this way, if he's crazy, I'll know now. And if he isn't, well, that's a whole other thing I'm not ready to unpack yet.

"Can you walk it, or do you need me to drive?" I ask him bluntly.

He straightens up, gesturing to the sidewalk in front of him.

"I ain't dead yet, doll. After you."

The next hour was quite possibly the most awkward hour of my life. But I did exactly as he'd suggested, and we parted ways at the hospital. Despite the shock and my initial reservations, I recognize he did his best not to freak me out. In that vein, he gave me his number when we parted so that I could call once the results were in. If I wanted to.

Feeling like I'm living in a surreal version of my own life, I blindly trek the four blocks back to the club and sit in my office until things pick up for the night. I try to keep busy, to keep my mind off Salvatore Moretti and, of course, Julian.

But by an hour before doors open, I find myself feeling pretty damn useless. With our new, more experienced bartender working seamlessly with Johnny, and Nils having an eager new assistant manager whom he already has a rapport with, there's really not much for me to do.

I should be happy. But instead I do something I haven't done in ages. I grab a beer and a pack of cigarettes and head out the side door to wallow. Slinking against the building, I take a long pull off the bottle before I nestle it between my legs, so it's less obvious. And then I light up a cigarette, taking a disgusting drag. And feeling like a fucking hypocrite. But as the nicotine soothes my nerves, I find myself caring less.

"Frankie. I didn't know you smoked."

I nearly jump out of my skin at the voice. And lo and behold, I look up to find Julian sauntering toward me.

"I guess ignoring your calls was too subtle. Fuck off, Julian," I snap, trying to look anywhere but at him. So I look up at the sky. But I'm disappointed again. You can never see stars in the city. Not even when you need them the most.

I finish my cigarette and take a long sip of beer. I feel, rather than see, Julian take a seat next to me.

"I'm sorry I didn't call sooner," he says softly. "My boss sent me out of town this week."

I snort. "I wasn't aware L.A. is the only place with phone service."

"It's complicated, Frankie. I couldn't call you. I wish I could've. I didn't stop thinking about you the whole time."

When the voice stays silent, I look at him in surprise. Usually, when guys say shit like that it's total bull. A line to get in your pants. But the asshole *means* it. And he looks so damn good, his five o'clock shadow rough on his strong jaw, his dark eyes pleading with me to forgive him. Goddamn it, this *is* going to be complicated.

"I don't know what you want me to say," I reply honestly.

A small smile tugs at the corner of his full lips. He slides a hand up my thigh and it sends shivers down my back.

"Say you missed me," he replies, his voice husky and inviting, his eyes dancing in the dark.

I want to. I really do. But I'd be lying. "I did at first," I allow. "But then I was too busy being pissed off that you didn't call. Or, apparently, didn't bother telling me you'd be going out of town and couldn't call."

Julian pulls his hand back and looks up into the sky, clearly at a loss for what to say.

"Don't bother looking for stars," I say, standing up and brushing off my pants. "You can't see them from here."

He looks up at me thoughtfully. "Yeah? Where can you see them from?"

I shrug, tossing my empty bottle into the trash can on the other side of the door. "Griffith Park. Or drive out to the desert." I turn away from him. "I've got to get back."

"Don't go," he pleads, standing up. "Not yet."

I turn back to him without meaning to and our eyes meet. Dammit, how I want to say no. But my body has its own ideas when it comes to him. And he knows it.

He advances a couple of steps until he's standing in front of me. He slips his hand under my chin, forcing me to keep eye contact. His thumb grazes my lower lip and it's all I can do to stay still, to not jump his gorgeous fucking bones, despite myself.

Thankfully, inside I hear sound checks, indicating we're close to opening. It clears my head enough that I take a step back, out of his arms, and gain control.

"I really have to go," I whisper.

103

Julian scrubs a hand over his stubble. "Let me make it up to you tomorrow night," he asks. "Please, Frankie."

His soft tone seeps under my defenses and I close my eyes. "You can try." I turn and go back inside before he or I can say, or do, anything else. I've already had enough for one evening, and it's only just begun.

Chapter 16 — Frankie

The paternity tests results don't actually come in until Sunday morning, when I'm still fast asleep after another crazy night at the club. But it was the contained kind of crazy. The kind that helped me forget everything going on. So it's to an unfortunate dose of reality that I wake, in the form of a voicemail confirming that there is a 99.9% chance that Salvatore Moretti is my father.

To say I'm dumbfounded is an understatement. I get dressed faster than I ever have, and I'm in the car on the way to my mom's house before I can even begin to process what this all means. I force myself not to think on the way. The more I think, the madder I'll get.

Though by the time I pull into her driveway, I'm still pretty fucking mad. Tony is on the porch, sorting collector cards. His face lights up when he sees me, and I do my best not to look like hell's fury incarnate.

"Hey, Big T," I tease him. "Mom home?"

"Frankie!" he exclaims, jumping to his feet. "Yeah, she's in the kitchen with Nonna. As usual." He starts to follow me inside, but I put a hand on his chest.

"You might want to sit this one out, little dude," I say firmly.

Tony's eyes widen, and he nods, stepping back to his cards as he watches me go inside.

Just as Tony said, they're both in the kitchen. They look up in surprise as I enter. My mother considers me dully for a moment.

"Your schedule's off, Frankie — it's only been two weeks," she says, turning to go back to whatever she was chopping.

But Nonna needs only one look at me to know that I'm well aware of the date. "Everything okay, dear?" she asks.

"No," I reply shortly. "Can we please be alone?"

Nonna looks like she wants to ask what's going on but wisely says nothing. She simply nods, planting a kiss on my cheek as she passes. I wait for the click of her bedroom door shutting before turning back to my mother.

"Frankie, I don't know what's bothering you, but if you're upset, we should really do this another time," my mother preempts me. I almost laugh. It's such a typical response. If I'm at all emotional, there's no discussion. Over the years I learned she sees it as weakness. So I try a different tack.

"Oh, I'm not upset," I say cheerfully. She looks up and raises an eyebrow. "Confused, maybe? See, this guy showed up at the club yesterday claiming to be my father. Said his name was Salvatore Moretti. I told him that just couldn't be possible, since my dad is dead. But then ..." I hold up my cellphone and play the paternity results voicemail for my mother. In moments, she's white as a sheet. And I actually am less upset than I thought I'd be. The terrified look on her face makes me happy in a way I know it shouldn't. For once, I have power over my mother.

"Well," she says primly, trying to regain control. "Is there a question here? Because it sounds like you have all the information you need."

Not that I needed her confirmation, but that statement pretty much blows my whole childhood out of the water. Knowing about my ability, my mother agreed early on not to lie to me. Or I thought she had. But clearly the web of lies is much more subtle than I thought. And the thought of how far this could reach is staggering. I feel like the foundation of my whole life has been yanked out from under me.

"You played with my loopholes," I accuse her. "You've been playing with them my whole life."

My mother throws down her towel and rolls her eyes. "Of course, I did, silly girl. I'm your mother. It's my job to protect you from things that could hurt you," she snaps condescendingly.

"No, Mom," I correct her. "It was your job to prepare me to handle those things myself. If you can't trust your mother, who can you trust?"

"Exactly," she replies emphatically, slamming her hand on the counter. "I did what was best for you. Always. You should trust that that's true."

The voice is silent. I guess there's some comfort that she thought she was doing what was best for me.

"I've been an adult for a long time now," I press. "Why didn't you tell me? You knew he was still out there. You thought he'd just never find out about me?"

"That is a long and very personal story," she says tightly. "Suffice it to say that no, I didn't think he'd ever find out about you, and if he did, I didn't think he'd have the balls to come anywhere near this family again. Now. I'm done talking about this with you. You know as much as I'm willing to tell you, and I won't stand for you questioning my decisions when you have no idea what was going on."

And with that she waltzes out of the kitchen with her nose in the air. I hear the front door slam. And a moment later, the engine of the car roars to life, its puttering trailing off as my mother literally flees from the mess she created.

I sit down at the kitchen table and sink my head into my hands. It's not long before I feel Nonna's hand on my shoulder. She seats herself next to me, rubbing circles gently over my back.

"Salvatore Moretti was a very charming young man who worked for your grandfather," she starts quietly. I look up into her eyes. All the love I wanted to see in my mother's eyes is present there. "Your mother was only seventeen. We didn't even know they'd been seeing each other. Or whatever it was they were doing." Nonna sighs. "If you remember anything about your grandfather, surely it's his temper. But your mother didn't want your father to know about you, so he was simply fired. And told never to come near the family again. I'm sure it was very confusing for him at the time, and I believe he cared very much for your mother, but your grandfather's warning was enough. He was a very intimidating man."

I huff a laugh. Oh, I remember. He regularly lost his temper with me, at times becoming physical. I recall with a shudder one of the worst incidents, when he yelled at me for an hour straight the day I scratched his precious car. The same one Mom still drives to this day. When I refused to cry, he took a belt to me until I did. He was a sadistic hothead, and I can't say I miss him.

"But why? Why didn't she tell me once I was grown? Why keep up the lie?" I press. "And what else has she lied to me about?"

Nonna smiles indulgently. "Frankie, darling, surely you've learned by now that just because you know a lie when you hear one doesn't mean you know the truth," she says sagely. "Your mother has always been very self-contained. She doesn't explain herself to anyone, and she's not used to being questioned. You've always pushed her limits, and it's made her draw further away from you."

I blanch. "You're saying the way our relationship is is my fault?" I ask, insulted.

Her hand closes over mine. "No," she says emphatically. "It's just the way you both are. You push. She retreats. You quest for truth. She holds her secrets close. It's not your fault, it's fact. Don't ever forget that."

I examine my grandmother's face, grasping to understand something I can't quite pull from her words.

"If she'd just talk to me …" I trail off, not quite sure what I'm trying to say. "He's my father. But if she kept him from me, I want to know why. So I don't go into this blind."

"I can't tell you what you want to know," my grandmother says carefully. "But that's how life is, dear. Even when we think we know something, we're all really just flying blind. Things change. People change. You can never have all the facts. And even if you did, my darling granddaughter, you have always been stubborn, always had to learn things the hard way. I doubt anything your mother could tell you would change whatever it is you plan to do."

"You're wrong," I say with a twinkle in my eye. Nonna raises an eyebrow. "I don't *always* have to learn the hard way. Just most of the time." That gets a hearty laugh from her. "Thank you, Nonna."

She smiles brightly, and I lean in to hug her.

"You're welcome," she murmurs into my hair. Pressing me back at arm's length, she examines my face. "Now. How are things going with your young man?"

Picturing Julian, a smile creeps across my face. The joy of talking to Nonna is that her advice is almost always universal. And her words have not only helped me start to accept my new parental situation, but I also realize now that they apply to my feelings for Julian as well. I know he hasn't lied to me. I know he's got his secrets. But I don't need all the facts. I know how I feel about him.

"We're still getting to know each other," I admit. "But I think it's going somewhere. Somewhere really good."

Chapter 17 — Julian

"We're going somewhere really fucking good, that's all I'm going to say."

"Not even a little hint?" Frankie presses, twirling her dark hair around her perfectly manicured finger. Like that's going to sway me.

I fold my arms over my chest and smirk down at her. "Nope," I confirm. "And we're taking your car."

She levels a glare at me, but quickly thinks better of it as a devilish smile replaces it. "If you tell me where we're going, I'll let you drive."

I take a step forward, pressing her against the kitchen counter behind her. "Oh, I'm driving all right," I assure her. "But I'm still not telling." Her hands slip to the counter behind her for support, and her pupils dilate. And I know I've got the upper hand, which I fully intend to press.

In one swift movement, I lift her onto the counter and bury my face in her neck, running my tongue up the soft flesh. She groans beneath me, arching into my body. As I work her neck with my mouth, I slide a hand under her shirt, stroking and squeezing her gorgeous tits.

"You're driving me crazy is what you're doing," she says with a moan. The sound goes straight to my cock, and I swear if I hadn't just planned the perfect evening for her, I'd spend the rest of the night fucking her on this counter and any other surface she'd let me. It's been a full week since I've been inside her, and it's practically all I can fucking think about.

But I rein it in. That's not what tonight is about. It's about making it up to her. Again. Even if she is wearing a black skirt that floats around her in a way that's asking me to lift it and fuck her senseless.

With a sigh, I push back, letting her slide back down onto her feet.

After a few more unsuccessful attempts at not touching her, I finally manage to convince her to get into the car.

The whole hour-plus-long drive, she badgers me about where we're going, but I don't spill the beans.

As twilight descends and night sets in, we get farther out of the reach of civilization.

When we finally reach our destination, I pull into the small lot of a state park, lower the top and cut the engine.

"What are we doing here?" she asks, looking over at me, confused.

I simply smile and point up. She looks up, and watching her mouth drop open in awe at the unadulterated starry sky above us is just as rewarding as I thought it would be.

"Holy. Fucking. Shit," she whispers. She glances over at me, her eyes filled with tears. "This is amazing. Thank you, Julian." She reaches over and gives my hand a squeeze.

I tear my eyes from her to look up. And it is amazing. Beyond amazing, actually. The dark, velvety sky is dotted with all the stars you'd never see with the lights of the city drowning them out. Even the Milky Way is just visible, and the effect is un-fucking-believable.

I reach out and stroke her face. "I'm glad you like it," I reply. I lean my seat back as far as it'll go, and she does the same. Her hand slides back into mine and we lie watching the stars for a good long while without speaking. I glance over at her occasionally, watching her drink in the sight in blissful silence.

Eventually, I crack. I turn to her and trace a finger down the moon tattooed on her left shoulder. "So you gonna tell me why you like the night sky so much?"

"You'll make fun of me," she replies, keeping her eyes fixed stubbornly on the heavens.

I want to protest, but I can't make any promises. "Try me," I say.

She presses her lips together and finally looks over at me. She studies my face, so I study hers back. Her long, dark hair dangles over the headrest, putting her high cheekbones and full red lips on display. But it's her eyes that I can't stop looking at. Deeply, darkly sparkling blue, alive, and full of light, mystery, and emotion. If I could freeze a moment, it would be this one. To remember her like this forever.

Fuck. *Did I really just think of Frankie and forever in the same sentence? Am I that far gone?* I turn away from her and close my eyes. I realize I may just be getting carried away in the moment. Then again, maybe not.

"Okay," she says softly. My eyes open and snap back to hers. There's vulnerability there now. She props herself up on her elbow to look down at me. "When I was a kid, I didn't feel like I fit in with my family. My mom kept me at such a distance. My grandfather was a tyrant. And my grandmother spent most of her time buffering between my mom, my grandad, and me, that we didn't have the closeness we do now. I just felt alone." She breathes deeply in through her nose, then shakes her head. "I'm not explaining this very well. It's just complicated."

I sit up, popping my seat up, then climb into the back. I motion for her to follow suit, and she does. She settles onto the small bench seat in the back next to me, laying her head on my chest. I wrap my arms around her and plant a kiss on the top of her head. Her hair smells like strawberries, and she feels like fucking heaven in my arms. But I want her to open up to me, finally. I need her to. Even if I can't fully reciprocate.

"So uncomplicate it," I say simply. She strokes a hand over my chest, and fuck if it isn't the most relaxing thing I've ever felt.

"I used to run away. A lot. And nobody noticed," she admits with a sigh. "Eventually, I took to sleeping in the park near our house, trying to spot a star here or there in the darkness of the night while I told myself stories to make myself feel better. My favorite was that I was really an alien. And one of those stars was my real parents, trying to find me. To bring me home."

I can't help laughing. So much so, it shakes my whole body, and she sits up, glaring at me. I shake my head, wiping the tears from my eyes. "I'm sorry," I manage. "It's just too fucking cute."

"Cute?" she asks venomously. "My childhood trauma is cute?"

I shrug, trying to keep from laughing again. "No, baby, it's just that most kids would come up with something a hell of a lot more dangerous to get into than stargazing and making up stories about being an alien."

Her eyes glitter down at me, her face a mask suddenly. Self-consciously, I sit upright, worried I've seriously offended her. "I'm sorry, I —"

She puts her finger on my lips to shut me up. "You called me 'baby,'" she whispers.

I wrap my hand around hers, kissing her finger before drawing it away from my lips. "I did," I agree.

She sits up fully, drawing away. She looks nervous but determined. "Julian, the reason for my family trouble, the reason I had no friends growing up, that I didn't want any ..." she closes her eyes and takes a deep breath. "You asked me once how I knew when you were lying. That's why. Because I know. When people lie to me, I know."

Confusion and anxiety push away the extreme relaxation that had settled over me. My heart starts pounding in my chest. Maybe Sal was right about her after all. Fuck. If that's true, then she knows about me. And if *that's* true ... fuck. But I need her to tell me to my face. That she knows. That she's just been playing me.

"Like how? Someone gives you the dirt on anyone you ask about?" My voice comes out thin and scratchy. God-fucking-damn it, I need to pull it together.

"God, no," Frankie replies emphatically. She rubs her temples with both hands, frustrated. She looks up suddenly. "Have you ever played two truths and a lie?"

I give her a reticent look. While my initial panic has passed, I'm not sure I like where this is going. And all of my instincts are telling me to cut and run. "Yes," I say slowly, struggling to contain myself.

"Good," she replies, grabbing one of my hands with both of hers. "Tell me two truths and one lie. Things you wouldn't have ever told anyone. One at a time."

"I don't understand what this has to do with anything," I say shortly, quickly losing my patience. If she's fucking dirty we need to deal with this. Now. I'm already putting myself on the line even being here with her against Sal's direction. If she's just playing me, I'm the biggest fucking patsy ever. And like fucking hell I'm going to let that keep happening.

"Please, Julian," she begs, reaching for my face. I'm tempted to recoil, but instead, I stay as still as stone. Trying to wrap my heart in the same hardness. I'm usually so fucking good at it, but when she withdraws, sensing my aversion, the yearning on her face cuts through my resolve like a knife through warm butter.

I close my eyes. "I was born in a monastery." My chest tightens. "I love puppies." I bunch my hands into fists, struggling to keep my eyes closed. "And I've never been in love." As soon as the words are out of my mouth, my mind whispers, *Before now.* And I wonder if I just told two lies. But maybe not, if I didn't realize it until after I'd said it. After all, I never thought I'd find someone I could trust. Can't say I was wrong there. Or maybe I just never thought I had a heart to give someone. Much less one for someone to break. And because it feels like that's exactly what's happening…

I push the thought back and open my eyes. I stare at her, still stone-faced, waiting for whatever comes next.

Her hand slowly moves toward my face. I remain motionless while she wipes a tear from my cheek with her thumb, cupping my jaw when she's done.

"God, Julian, that's fucked up," she whispers. "Who doesn't love puppies?"

I blink. And despite myself, I start laughing. Hard. And the tears I didn't know were even there turn into tears of laughter. She sits back, biting her lip to restrain her smile, clearly unsure of what to make of my outburst.

"I'm sorry," I choke out, wiping my face with both hands. As I settle, I stare at her, still beyond confused.

"I know," she says. "It doesn't make sense. But I was being literal. Nobody's been giving me intel on you, Julian, if that's what you were worried about. Though don't think for a minute we're not going to unpack that one later." She raises an eyebrow sternly. "I just know when people lie. You can tell me another one if you don't believe me."

I give her a funny look. But okay. Let's fucking do this. It's as crazy as her claim, but I'll play along. "I put honey on pickles."

Her nose wrinkles. "Ewww."

"I cheat on my taxes."

"Lie."

Shit. "I cheat on my girlfriends."

"Pshh," she scoffs. "I don't even need the ability to know that's a lie."

I smirk at her, despite myself. "Fine," I allow. "I cheat at cards."

She smiles. "You're a dirty boy, Julian."

I lean back into the leather seat. Fuck. She *can* tell when I'm lying. Like, really. Like, really really. "How is this even possible?"

She shakes her head and splays out her hands. "I don't know," she says plainly. "I've been able to do it since I can remember."

I run a hand through my hair, still agitated, still finding it hard to absorb. "That's some fucked-up shit, Frankie."

A smile creeps across her lips. "Have I told you how much I love it when you call me that?" she asks, ignoring the mockery of my reply.

I huff a dry laugh. "Yeah, I caught that when you didn't bust my balls over it," I tease.

She shoves my shoulder. "Hey, I don't bust your balls," she protests. I raise an eyebrow at her pointedly. "Okay, okay, so I bust your balls a little. Sometimes."

I raise both eyebrows, giving her a skeptical look, and she blushes a deep crimson. It makes me laugh, melting the last of whatever negative emotions I'd been having.

"So how's it work?" I ask curiously.

"That's it? We're on to acceptance? You're not running for the hills?" she replies.

I run a hand over the budding beard on my jaw, considering that. "Guess not."

Frankie barks a laugh. "Loquacious as usual." She shakes her head.

"What's that supposed to mean?" I counter.

"You're a man of few words," she replies, then with a wicked grin, "except in bed."

"You're not going to distract me with sex," I deadpan.

Her grin widens. "Oh?" I shake my head and she laughs. "Maybe later then."

And I wasn't lying, but as we stare each other down, I have to admit, I'm a little distracted. Being in bed with her isn't something that's easy to forget.

113

Being with her period wouldn't be easy to forget. And I find I'm not of a mind to, even in light of this new, bizarre revelation. It suddenly occurs to me that Sal would kill to know about this. As I stare back into her beautiful, blue eyes, I decide here and now that he's never going to hear about it from me, no matter what happens between us.

"You don't have to explain it if you don't want to," I allow, touching my finger to her knee. "It's part of you. Freaky. But part of you." Now it's my turn to grin. "Besides, I don't mind a little freaky from time to time."

She scrunches her nose and shakes her head at me. "Trust me, it's almost never the good kind of freaky to know what I know about people." She pauses. "Though it's not a magic bullet. I got a pretty big fucking reminder of that yesterday."

The tension in her voice worries me, and I know I'm still in this, because I care.

"What happened?" I prompt.

She looks up at me, seemingly unsure. She brushes her hair back and brings her knees up to her chest, wrapping her arms around them. Going into her little cocoon. I allow it, for now.

"I met my father," she says blandly.

And I'm confused again. "Didn't you say your father was dead?"

Frankie snorts. "That I did. But apparently that whopper got past me." She presses her lips together, barely hiding her anger.

"So, it's not infallible, this ability of yours?" I ask.

"No," she admits grimly. "There are loopholes."

"And you're upset because your mom used them."

She shakes her head. "No. She's been doing it my whole life. I think I knew that on some level."

"Then what's bothering you?" I ask, finally reaching for her.

When I take her hands, she looks relieved. "I'm used to not having a real relationship with my mother because of how I am," she says, playing with our entwined fingers. "And I've been fine without a father. If anything, her hiding him from me successfully tells me I have no way of knowing who to trust. So how can I trust him? How can I even begin to get to know him? But then, how can I not?" She heaves a big sigh.

I tug at her fingers, pulling her until she's between my legs, our faces inches apart. "Welcome to how the rest of us have to go into relationships. Blind. I don't trust anyone either. But you're right about one thing," I say, my eyes locked on hers, "you'd probably regret not checking the guy out."

She responds with a dim smile, moving in and rubbing her nose gently against mine. At this distance I can see every fleck in those beautiful blue eyes. "Thank you," she says quietly. "For not only sticking around, but actually being here for me."

I trace a finger down her cheek, sliding over her jaw and cupping her chin. "Still can't seem to stay away," I murmur with a smile.

She closes the gap between us, her soft lips grazing mine. Even that small touch is enough to rile me. I make to deepen the kiss, but she pulls back and considers me.

"Mmm. So what dirt were you worried I had on you?" she asks out of the blue.

Thank fucking God I'm good at keeping a straight face. I consider my reply carefully. "Nothing I won't tell you in time," I assure her. "But not right now. I think the better question is, what are you going to do about your father?"

Frankie shudders. "I don't know. I guess I'll call him and see what happens. But I gotta say, it's weird even hearing you call him my father. This is going to take some getting used to."

"I doubt he expects you to call him dad," I point out. "If I found my long-lost daughter, I'd be pretty weirded out too. Just call him whatever you're comfortable with. You guys will figure it all out."

"That reminds me, he called me Frankie right off the bat," she says. "I spent the first few minutes ready to punch him just for that."

I laugh. "I remember being quickly corrected on that," I recall teasingly. "Did you want to punch me too?"

She smiles mysteriously. "Yes," she admits. "But I couldn't decide what I wanted to do more — punch you or fuck you."

I raise an eyebrow. Damn. "Really?"

"Really," she confirms, running her hands up my arms in a way that toys with the edges of my control. But tonight was supposed to be me showing her I'm here. And even through some intense stuff, I still am, and I want this to be whatever she wants.

"Punching me would have been almost as much of a turn on," I tell her.

She gasps and slaps me playfully on the arm. "You're a dirty boy, Julian."

Her suggestive tone takes my semi to a full-on, but I sit still. "Only if you want me to be," I taunt her with a grin.

Her eyes flick down to my pants. "Either way, looks like you're ready to be one," she says. Her voice is husky and filled with desire. It takes all of my control not to have her on her back crying out my name.

I lean toward her slightly, and her body unconsciously sways toward me. I take a deep whiff of her scent. I can smell her arousal. It's fucking heady. "Smells like you're ready," I murmur into her ear. She gasps, her hand clenching my arm. With her other hand, she moves aside her skirt, then guides my hand between her legs.

I slip a finger under her black, lacy thong. Fuck me, she's so goddamn wet.

"Fuck, Julian," she gasps, her eyes closing and her back arching so her dripping pussy pushes into my palm. And I do just that, sliding two fingers in and fucking her tight little cunt. She writhes under me, one of her hands still clutching at me. She snakes it toward my zipper as I pump my fingers into her, running her hand over my cock as it strains against my jeans.

"You want that cock in you?" I ask her, unleashing control.

She bites down on her lip and nods, looking desperately into my eyes. She grabs my cock full on, squeezing. I suck a sharp breath through my teeth, telling her how good it feels when she touches me, but I don't let her stop my rhythm. In fact, I twist my wrist, flipping my thumb toward her clit so I can bring her to orgasm before I fuck her.

"Not yet, baby," I breathe. "First, I'm going to make you come so hard you forget your own goddamn name."

It doesn't take long. A few hard circles over the sensitive spot, along with a simultaneous massage of her G-spot and she comes completely undone, bucking and screaming her release. As I watch her red cheeks, peaked nipples, and trembling body, I can't remember ever being so turned on by a woman. Everything she does, she does to the fullest. She's fucking intoxicating.

"Fuck, Frankie, you're so damn beautiful," I tell her, covering her mouth with mine. She desperately nips at my lips and tongue as her orgasm recedes. As she finishes her descent, I withdraw my hand, unleashing my hard-on and fishing in my pocket for a condom. It's only a moment before she's recovered and removing it from my hands. But she doesn't put it on. Instead, her sweet, gorgeous red lips hover over my twitching, red cock.

"You want it?" she prompts.

I clench my jaw against the surge of desire that rips through me. "Fuck, yes, baby, suck my fucking cock with that beautiful mouth," I urge her.

There's no prelude, no teasing, she buries me deep in her hot, wet mouth, her tongue violently swirling around my dick as she sucks and pumps my shaft with her mouth and her hand.

"Fuck, Frankie, that's amazing," I moan. "But I'm not coming until I've fucked another orgasm out of you."

When she hears that her suction goes up a notch, her grip tightening. She fucking loves the dirty talk. And I can't say I've ever loved it quite this much. But damn if she isn't working me in a way that's going to make me explode any second, and I tell her as much. Thank God she only does it a few more times, because even with my self-control still mostly in place, it'd be practically impossible not to come.

She finally relents, and I hear the foil rip.

"Fuck, baby, that's the best fucking sound in the world," I groan. Her eager hands roll it down my length before lifting her skirt to give me a view of the little triangle of hair between her legs. "Damn, you have a gorgeous pussy." The sight makes me fucking hard as a rock, so when her tight folds slide over me, I feel every fucking inch of her warm wetness.

She grins like she's won a fucking prize as she buries me fully in her. Tilting back and forth, she sets a rhythm so much slower than her frenzied sucking, using the head of my cock to rub her G-spot. I watch her tits tighten, her back arch, as she pleasures herself on me.

"I love watching you fuck me," I breathe. "But it's my turn, baby." If I let her get herself off, it won't be nearly as rewarding. For either of us. So, I take over.

As she tilts me back into her, I slam upward. She gasps, her hands dropping to my chest so she can absorb the impact. I reach up and roll one of her nipples through my fingers. "You like it when I pound you? When I sink my dick deep and hard into your hot pussy?" Her body sways toward me. That's my sign that it feels so fucking good she can't even sit up anymore. I slam into her again, and her nipple slides out of my hand as her chest meets mine.

"Keep pounding me," she begs into my ear. I slam into her again. "Aah, yes, just like that. Harder, please, Julian, fuck me so much harder."

My head dips back as electric bolts shoot through my entire fucking body at her words. "God, baby, you're fucking perfect, in every way." I grab her ass with my hands, lifting her each time I swing my hips so I can drive into her harder, faster. Soon, she's clutching on to me, just along for the ride. "And you feel," *slam*, "so," *slam*, "fucking," *slam*, "good." *Slam, slam, slam.*

My breath hitches as my orgasm starts to churn below my cock. The way she's tightening, I know just what to do. I grip her hard, her soft flesh on fire in my palms, and I lift her ass in the air, holding her in place as I unleash. I fuck her so hard there's no breath for more dirty talk. I'm afraid I'm going to hurt her, but her continuous scream of pleasure eggs me on.

"Omigod," she screams only moments later. "I'm coming, I'm coming, I'm coming." She seizes tightly, her velvet pussy clenching around my cock, milking my orgasm out of me in bursts of hot gratification. It ends with me buried inside her, my cock pulsating, her still spasming around me.

As the tremors subside, Frankie's mouth finds mine. And the languid, deep kiss spreads the feeling of satisfaction through my whole body until I feel like I'm floating, with only Frankie to anchor me.

As I bliss out with her in my arms, I thank the universe for this moment. This amazing fucking woman in my arms. Feisty, unapologetically honest, and fiercely loyal, she's not just a good fuck. Scratch that, an amazing, off-the-charts fuck. She challenges me in every way. Makes me want to be this guy who's worth being hers. And fuck all if I don't want her to be mine.

As she breaks the kiss, I look deeply into her eyes and try to figure out how to say something I've never said before. The words stick in my throat long enough for her to pull away and get dressed. With the moment passed, I clean up too.

We drive back to her place in comfortable silence. I'm not worried. I'll find a time, a way to say what I need to. To stake my claim on her, if she'll let me. As I kiss her goodnight at her door, it's all I can do to let her go. But I must.

"I'm traveling again this week," I tell her.

Her beautiful mouth droops. "Poop," she grumbles.

I laugh heartily. "Wow, watch the language there," I tease her. "But hey, I'm telling you ahead of time this time."

She smiles thinly. "True," she allows. "But I'll still miss you."

I look down at her, trying to bring the words, and failing once more. "I'll miss you too. But you'll have plenty to keep you busy. Especially if you plan to contact your …" I trail off, stopping short of calling him her father again. "What should I call him?"

Frankie wrinkles her adorable nose. "His name, I suppose," she sighs, looking up at me from under her dark lashes. "Salvatore Moretti. I wonder if he has a nickname, because that's a fucking mouthful."

My heart stops. "He probably goes by Sal," I say quietly.

"Huh," she says thoughtfully, chewing on that gorgeous bottom lip of hers. "That does fit his whole sleazy old guy vibe."

And if the name didn't confirm it, the description sure as hell does.

Fuck. Fuck, fuck, fuck, fuck, fuck, fuck, fuuuuuuuuuuck.

Sal is Frankie's fucking father. I've been fucking my boss's daughter. After he told me to stay away from her. No — threatened me if I didn't stay away from her.

I'm illicitly fucking the daughter of one of the most dangerous crime bosses in Los Angeles. Not only is there now no way in hell I can tell Frankie what I've been trying to find the words for all night, if I don't stop seeing her it could unleash hell. For both of us.

But then, maybe it's too late for that anyway.

Chapter 18 — Frankie

I lie awake that night, unable to sleep. I mean, how could I? I just discovered my mother has been lying to me my whole life. Something I didn't think was even possible. Because what she usually resorts to is feeding me bits of truth, pulling the mom card, or just plain pretending I don't exist. But this time she let me believe a lie I'd apparently heard before I had the ability to hear the little voice inside or before it was even there. A new loophole that blows the lid off of my already fucked-up childhood.

My biological father is not, in fact, dead. Something that became quite obvious when he showed up at my club two days ago.

But let's shelve that, shall we? Why, you ask? I mean, that's a pretty big thing. Even for a girl who's supposed to know when she is being lied to. But there's another truth that hit me unexpectedly in the face tonight. I wanted to chalk it up to post-orgasmic bliss, but there's just no denying that what passed between Julian and me in the back seat of the car, after the most amazing fuck in the most amazing place ever, was more than just physical.

I'm falling hard for Julian. And that's a big deal. Not just because I can't remember ever being with a guy that didn't straight-up lie to me constantly. But also, because despite his seeming just as into me, I still can't get past there being things he's not ready to tell me.

I have to wonder if it's that they're so bad he knows they'd scare me off, or if he's just reserved. Which let's face it, he is. Well, most of the time.

A sly smile spreads across my face. It's hard to deny that the dirty talk might be playing a big factor in this. I'm pretty sure even without it the sex would still be insane, but damned if it doesn't take it to a whole other level of hot I didn't even know existed. But then, he turns me on in just about every way possible, inside the bedroom and out. Not that our fuck under the stars was in a bedroom.

A sigh escapes me thinking about what a perfect date he'd planned. No frills, just stars and orgasms. Not every girl's dream date, but it's pretty much mine. Both are a scarcity for me living in L.A., running my club, avoiding dating. But Julian is different. I hope.

Eventually I drift off to sleep, with visions of Julian's face dancing behind my eyelids, then in my dreams.

* * *

The next day I decide to take my first real Monday off since buying the club. I'm tempted to tell Nils I won't be in, but as I pick up the phone, I realize how silly that is. I'm not *supposed* to be in, and every time he finds me there on one of my "days off" he laughs at me and tells me to get out. He really is a gem.

Part of me also wants to visit Emma at her salon, to get her input on all of this. And I will, but maybe not right now. Right now, I still need to know more, and I don't want her swaying me one way or the other.

Before I can talk myself out of it, I call Salvatore Moretti. My father. Ugh. Weird.

"Frankie," he answers. "Great to hear from ya, doll."

I smile wryly to myself at his cheesiness. "Hey," I respond. "So yeah. This is me. Calling."

He chuckles. "Glad you did. I take it you talked to your ma?"

I huff a breath sharply through my nose. "That's one way to put it. I didn't get much out of her," I admit.

"Ah," he replies. "So you were hoping I could tell you more." He's not stupid.

"Or anything," I respond with a sigh.

"Like I said, some of it isn't my story to tell," he hedges. "But how's about I take you to lunch, and I'll tell you what I can?"

"That depends," I reply.

"On?"

"Do you like tacos?"

* * *

"Okay, you know how I said tacos aren't my favorite? Well, I was wrong." Sal — having confirmed that to be his preferred nickname — laughs and polishes off his fourth, and final, taco.

I brush crumbs off my lap and laugh, tossing my crumpled napkin on the picnic table.

"There's a reason there's always a huge line. Can't beat this place," I reply. With our appetites satisfied, I shift nervously. "So."

Sal wipes his face, puts his napkin down, and leans forward on his arms. "So."

"My mom said she didn't think you'd have the balls to ever contact me," I throw out.

Sal bursts out laughing. "Well, your mom would know a lot about balls," he chortles. "She's got a bigger pair than most guys I know."

"Even back then, huh?" I ask with a smile. I have always admired my mother's tenacity, one of the few things I was thankful to inherit from her.

Nonna may be right that our differences push us apart, but then, I think, so do our similarities. It's a no-win situation.

Sal shifts. "Yeah, even back then," he agrees. "But I didn't know about you back then, either, so tough to say if I woulda had the balls to fight for you." He immediately looks sorry for saying it. "Not to say you aren't worth it, doll. You're obviously a hell of a lady." Sal pauses, fishing a cigarette out of his pocket. "But things were complicated. Luca, your grandpa, he wasn't someone to cross. And that kept me from even trying to talk to your ma."

I look up into the bright sky behind him, squinting into the sun. The biggest, brightest star in the sky, casting its revealing light.

"Can't say I blame you," I admit. "One at a time, they were bad enough. But damned if when they teamed up it wasn't hell." I don't pull my poker face on fast enough, and I can tell Sal sees the pain etched there.

"I'm sorry I left you to that, kiddo," he says sadly, taking a puff off his cigarette.

I don't miss the nasty looks of those around us, though I doubt Sal cares about things like how many feet away from an establishment he is when he lights up. And I don't bother pointing it out. Given my mental state, it's all I can do not to ask for a drag. It's not a habit I want to get sucked back in to, despite my recent lapse.

"I had Nonna," I finally say. "She helped a bit. And Nonno died when I was a teenager. It got better after that."

"Maria is a wonderful woman," he replies with a sincere look of love in his eyes as he talks about my grandmother. "How is she these days?"

"Full of quiet wisdom, same as ever," I respond. "But now that Nonno's gone you actually get to hear it. Works out better for Tony than me."

"Tony?" Sal raises an eyebrow.

"My younger brother," I clarify. "He's twelve. Great kid. Probably all thanks to Nonna. Mom still works as much as ever."

"She was born like that, I think. She was only a teenager when we were together, and even then she was a serious, driven young woman," he replies with a grimace, folding his hands together.

"Yeah," I agree. Something in my gut twists, and I know I need to stop thinking about my mother for a bit. She's always best taken in measured amounts, even in conversations she's not present for. "So what about you? What is it you do again?"

Sal's lips twitch. "Well, I have a business that caters to a specific clientele," he hedges. "I mostly deal with imports. You know, whatever goods they need help bringing into the country. I also help manage their business affairs, logistics, that sort of thing. But I'm doing less and less of that these days, the older I get."

I raise an eyebrow. I've heard enough hedging and roundabout talk in my day to know what that might mean. "Mhm," I murmur. "Are we talking legal imports here?"

Sal looks up at me with a leering grin. "You're a sharp cookie," he compliments me. He spreads his hands out. "I do what I'm asked. I let my clients worry about the legal aspects."

I'm not loving this. "Uh-huh," I grunt. "What other services do you provide?"

"Whatever my clients require," he reiterates simply with another smile. "Don't you worry about your old man. I'm not about to get myself in trouble with the law." *Lie.*

Oh, geez. I fold my arms over my chest with a frown, purposely letting my displeasure show.

"Ah, come on Frankie, don't be like that," he urges. "Not all of us can run a successful night club. Seems like you're doing really well with that place."

So. Many. Red. Flags. "Yeah, my investors are pretty happy," I say pointedly. "I may even start recouping all the cash they put into it someday." It's a partial truth. Some of the cash did come from other investors. Though I'm the biggest investor in the club, having put in more than seventy percent of the capital. But in case he's looking for a new benefactor, or client, or whatever, I'm not going to make myself an easy mark.

He nods. "Been there," he says. "You seem real smart. I'm sure you'll do great."

"Thanks," I reply with a thin smile, wondering if this lunch was a huge mistake. The things I really want to know, the why, well, I realize only my mother knows. I heave a sigh, knowing I'll probably never have the answers I'm looking for.

"Tell me more about yourself," Sal presses. "I hope you don't spend all your time at the club. You got friends? Maybe even a boyfriend?"

I shrug lightly, my poker face back in place. "I have a few friends. Nobody I'd call a boyfriend," I reply. *Even if there is someone I want to call that.* "But the club takes most of my time. It's not a bad thing. I enjoy it."

"Good, good," he says with a nod. "Maybe once that's all settled down you can find yourself a nice boy and have a family." I don't stop the incredulous look that settles on my face. He quickly moves to cover his tracks. "You know, if that's what you want."

I press my lips together and try to consider where he's coming from. And I know in his time those were the life choices that went with security and happiness. So maybe that's all he's saying. The thought calms my independent streak considerably. Because after living through my fucked-up childhood, I'd honestly never planned to have kids of my own. Which is good, because with my ability, even getting married is a dicey proposition.

"Look, I appreciate that you want me to be happy," I finally say carefully. "But I am. Really. I'm finally in the place I've been working toward."

Sal nods apologetically. "That's great, Frankie," he says with relief. "That's all I want."

He sounds so genuine that despite my reservations, I can't help feeling like his approval fills some kind of hole in my life and my heart. I'm almost disappointed at myself at the realization. But then, I've lived my life bereft of a father.

When we make plans to have lunch again next Wednesday, I wonder if there will be enough good that comes of allowing Sal into my life. Or if I'm just setting myself up for more heartbreak. I make a mental note to ask him more direct questions next week. Before I get in too deep.

* * *

I'm spared having to call Emma when she texts me on Monday night to remind me we're going to a Halloween party on Wednesday. It's one of those crazy ragers that, being on the actual holiday and on a weeknight, mostly only people with nontraditional jobs will attend. So it's bound to be insane, and a shit-ton of fun. Plus, it's been a while since Emma and I cut loose like this, and I find I'm actually looking forward to it.

Unfortunately, with everything going on I'd forgotten to line up a costume, so as I stand in my closet on Wednesday evening, I find my choices are limited. Thankfully, club wear can easily double as a costume in a pinch. I grab a black leather minidress and some fishnet tights. Paired with raging sky-high lace-up boots, some heavy goth-looking makeup, and a red lipstick trail of "blood" out of the corner of my mouth, I make a decent looking vampire. The dark hair works well and, possibly for the first time, I'm glad I went back to my natural color. I don't worry about the fact that I don't have fake fangs. I'll just have to wear my sharp wit instead.

In the cab on the way to the party, I have some time to catch Emma up on my new-found father, Julian, and a few other happenings of the week. Her advice is predictable. *Check out Sal, what have you got to lose? Go for it with Julian, what have you got to lose?* If only the answer to both questions wasn't, well, everything. Emma has always been a goer, not a thinker. Thankfully, she recovers from hurt and rejection quickly. Me, not so much.

As we arrive at the venue, though, everything slips from my mind. It's a private residence in the hills of Malibu, and swank would be an understatement. The huge, imposing modern structure is decorated to the nines with realistic cobwebs strung across the building, backlit terrifying silhouettes in each window, and even a group of skeletons made to look like they're climbing up one of the walls and into the house. Partygoers surround the house inside and out, drinking, laughing, and dancing. Emma looks pumped and more than ready for Halloween revelry in her sexy fairy costume, her ample bosom barely contained by the shimmery pink fabric, with tiny gold wings dancing enticingly behind her.

As soon as we're inside, Emma goes straight for the booze. Our unspoken rule is she drinks, and I make sure she doesn't get in trouble. It's not hard, actually, as she usually ends up dragging me around with her, dancing with whatever hotties she can get her hands on. Either Ben doesn't know, or he doesn't care, and I'm not about to tell him.

And after she's had a couple of shots, she does pretty much exactly that. She finds the hottest, most scantily clad man in the place. Dressed like Lucifer, with small horns on his head and some face makeup, he's naked but for a tattered pair of jeans hugging his tight ass, purposely burnt in places. I'd say it's because he's supposed to be the ruler of hell and all that, but it might also be because he's that smoking hot. So, of course, Emma is all over him. Before I know it, they're grinding to the music, and one of Lucifer's friends is behind me, trying to keep rhythm as my body presses into the back of Emma's.

Emma snakes a hand behind her, pulling me in for a drunken dance, or hug, or God knows what. It makes me laugh, though, and I feel myself loosening up. I give myself over to the beat, letting Emma's infallible rhythm set the pace. Before long, we're out of breath and sweaty, and heading to the makeshift bar for some water. And then more booze for Emma. Lucifer trails behind her, clearly liking the taste he's gotten.

I shake my head, laughing. Emma, while not as tall as me, has always been a curvy girl too. The guys definitely seem to love it. Her confidence doesn't hurt, either.

I chug a bottle of water and make her drink some too. When I'm satisfied she won't be a drunken mess, I gesture to the hall with the bathrooms, then point at the floor. *Stay here*, I mouth. She nods, so I slip away to relieve myself as quickly as possible.

Thankfully, it only takes a couple of minutes and I'm back. Only to spot Lucifer and Emma, making out like teenagers. His hand is up the back of her dress, fondling her ass, and her hands are thrown wantonly around his neck as their faces are practically merged.

My heart drops into my stomach, and I push my way through the crowd as quickly as I can. I didn't think she was *that* drunk. I kick myself for not paying better attention.

As soon as I get to them, I use all my strength to shove Lucifer off of her.

"What the hell?" I barely hear him over the music. And I don't fucking care. I give him a death glare and cage Emma behind me. When it's clear I'm not going to let him get back to her, he finally stalks off into the crowd to find his next victim.

A tug on my arm makes me turn around to face Emma. She looks pissed. With a sigh, I grab her hands and lead her out the front door. We have to get a good thirty feet from the building before I can hear her.

"What the fuck, Frankie?" she demands, her hands on her hips, sounding perfectly sober.

"What the fuck, *Frankie*?" I echo in disbelief. "How about what the fuck, *Emma*?"

"I was just having a little fun," she spits. "You don't have to be such a fucking prude."

Whoa. She did not just.

"Are you serious right now?" I spit back. "You're *married*, in case you forgot. And I'm here to keep you from doing anything stupid."

Emma folds her arms over her chest defensively. "I'm also a grownup," she says heatedly, "and if I want to make out with a hot guy, I'm going to."

The anger drains right out of me. This isn't my best friend. Something is up.

"What's going on, Emma?" I ask calmly.

My change in attitude leeches the sass out of her. But she still clams up, and tears fill her eyes. "Let's just go home," she grinds out, heading back to the street, presumably to hail a car.

I grab her arm and stop her. "Really? You're not going to talk to me?" I ask, hurt.

She turns, her face laden with sadness. "No," she says, the tears spilling over her round cheeks. "I really don't need the judgment right now."

She may as well have slapped me in the face. My first reaction is feeling hurt. But the feeling is quickly replaced by anger. Of the two of us, Emma judges me far more than I judge her. The hypocrisy doesn't sit well with me. Thankfully, of the two of us, I'm also the one who is least likely to say something I'll regret later, and I'm able to keep cool enough to respond.

"I don't want to judge you, for fuck's sake. I want to help, Emma," I respond evenly.

"Fine," she shouts, throwing her hands in the air dramatically. "You want to know what's up? I'm getting divorced is what's up. I'm a fucking failure, and you knew it before I did. Happy?"

I want to say I'm not happy, because I know she's miserable. But she's not wrong: I've always known Ben was a liar. That he wasn't good enough for her.

"You are *not* a failure," I say, latching on to the one piece I disagree with.

She huffs and rolls her eyes.

I grab her by the shoulders and lean in to be on her level. That I'm already a good deal taller doesn't help, but the boots make it a challenge. Still, I hold my ground. "You're not a failure," I repeat softly.

Her lower lip trembles, her big, round eyes filling with tears once more. She only holds out for a moment before bursting into sobs and burying her face in my chest. I wrap my arms tightly around her, and she does the same. I stroke her hair gently until she stops crying.

"Why didn't you tell me sooner?" I ask. "You let me go on and on about my shit. I love you, darlin', and I'm here for you no matter what."

With a sniff, Emma straightens up, wiping her nose with the back of her hand. "I know," she admits with a nod. "I just wasn't ready to talk about it yet, and if we talked about me, I knew I'd have to lie to you, and then you'd know. It's like I can't win." She looks at me sadly.

It crushes my heart hearing that my ability stopped her from talking to me. Not for the first time, I wish it wasn't a part of me.

"I'm sorry," I say sincerely. "You shouldn't ever feel like you have to lie to me or not tell me things. If you don't want to tell me something, don't, but I'm here for you and I'll do my best not to be judgmental." I bite my lip, knowing that I can be. But it's only because I care.

"Deep down I wanted to tell you," she replies. "But I remembered all the times you tried to tell me about him while we were dating, and all I did was shut you down. I was just so *in love* I didn't want to hear it. And now look at me. I'm such a fucking idiot."

I shake my head, grasping her free hand in mine. "You're not an idiot," I insist. "There's a whole expression for it, even. 'Love is blind.' Right? It makes fools of us all." And I can't keep my thoughts from flitting to Julian. And if I was unsure before, I know now. I love him. Even though I know he's withholding. Even though I know better. Whatever magic that happens between two people that makes you fall in love has hit me hard. And I can't blame Emma for being its victim, either.

"Yeah," she finally admits begrudgingly. "But it still fucking sucks."

I laugh, and she laughs with me. "Yeah," I agree. "But it won't always be that way."

Emma shakes her head. "I hope not," she says quietly. "Come on, let's go get something to eat and talk."

I fall into step beside her, wrapping my arm around her shoulders. "Now that sounds like a smart plan."

For the rest of the night I let Emma spill her guts about the whole situation. And I do my best to just listen. She's obviously had a lot pent up, and I know I just need to put my own problems, my own judgments aside and be there for her. I even spend the night at her place, as Ben has packed up and gone to stay with friends. Despite the horrible circumstances, or maybe because of them, it feels good to really reconnect with her. Because through a full night of heart-to-hearts, I start to see why she felt the way she did.

I often let my ability dictate a conversation, rather than my heart, or even my head. I never thought much about how that feels for other people. The irony isn't lost on me that it causes just as much trouble for the people I care about as it does for me. Because everybody lies. It's a necessary coping mechanism. That's easy for me to forget with the constant voice in my head reminding me of every little transgression, like it's something unnatural, wrong, and harmful. And sometimes it is. But sometimes, it's just what we need to do to protect ourselves.

Chapter 19 — Julian

As I drive back into the city on Friday night, all I can think of is Frankie. Her gorgeous face, her tight little pussy, the verbal sparring that makes me want to not just fuck her but keep her. I'm so twisted up with need for her that it takes all of my willpower to check in with Sal first as he requested instead of heading straight for Baltia and ravaging the shit out of her.

Especially since Sal is getting on my last nerve these days. Everything that was good about our arrangement has long since died. And I know it's time to break away, but that's easier said than done.

His first words as I enter his office don't help.

"It's done?"

No hello, no making sure I'm okay, nothing. Didn't even look up from whatever file he's poring over. All he cares about is what he wants. Never mind that I nearly died in the process. But I never bore him with those details. I know he's long since stopped caring.

"Yeah," I say shortly, wiping the disgust from my face. "That all you wanted to see me for?"

Sal points to a chair across from him, still not looking up. I sink into it, looking affectedly disinterested.

"No. I know I told you to stay away from Frankie Greco, but I need you to do something for me." He finally looks up, leans back in his chair, and crosses his legs.

My heart races. Does he know something? I shrug as nonchalantly as I can, inviting him to continue. And he does. But what he asks strains my ability to stay cool. And I know the time has come to choose.

* * *

With a heavier heart than earlier this evening, I leave Sal's office and head to Baltia. I try to push it out of my mind, because I don't have to decide tonight. But by Monday ... well, that's exactly what I don't need to think about right now. With no consequences now for going to do exactly what I would've done anyway, I go to the club. To Frankie.

As soon as I'm inside, I push through the noisy throng and spot her leaning over the balcony of the VIP section, scanning the crowd. Her long, dark hair is slicked back into a sexy-as-fuck ponytail, and she wears a pink halter top the same color as her hair used to be. Her tight leather pants look halfway between rocker and dominatrix. Both alternatives make me fucking hard for her.

As if she could hear my thoughts, her eyes lock on mine. Her expression doesn't change, but she straightens up and saunters casually down the stairs. My feet move before I'm even conscious of it, and I meet her as the gatekeeper opens the velvet rope for her.

Her black heels easily put her over six feet, evoking images of fucking her in nothing but those heels. She stops in front of me, still having to tilt her head up to look in my eyes. She's technically at work, so I refrain from pushing her up against the wall and showing her exactly how much I missed her. But the desire in her eyes matches the anticipation thrumming in my cock.

She slips her hand in mine and turns, leading me around the corner and down a hallway. At the end of the hall is a dark door that she leads me through and closes behind us. With a flick of the lights, I realize we're in her office.

She turns back around, leaning against her desk. "I missed you," she says evenly. Too calmly.

If I've learned anything about Frankie, it's that the calm is a mask for the ever-changing emotions underneath. I'm hoping the emotion she's suppressing is the same one I am.

I close the gap between us, stroking a finger down her cheek. "I missed you too."

She leans into the touch with a sigh, and in response my dick strains the limits of what my pants can take. She holds my hand in hers as it slides down to rest on her chin, lifting it to her lips and kissing it gently. She looks up at me from under her lashes.

"Show me how much," she says softly.

Desire shoots through me from head to toe, escalating the sensation between my legs. Calmly, I pull her up by her hands. I lean in, kissing her softly at first, letting everything I'm feeling flow through our lips as my tongue delicately plays with hers. She arches into me, her arms wrapping around my neck. I pull her into me as tightly as I can, deepening the kiss, letting it become more demanding.

I skim my hands down her sides, letting them rest on her gorgeous, plump ass. I knead her backside with increasing fervor, until she breaks away and moans into my chest.

"Say it, baby," I encourage her. "Say you like it when I touch you like that."

"Your hands feel amazing," she groans, tilting her chin up and offering her mouth to me.

I place a light kiss on her cherry red lips. "Tell me how you want to be fucked tonight," I whisper in her ear.

Her nails dig into my shoulders, and my cock twitches.

"From behind," she sighs.

I lick up her ear.

"Rough or gentle?"

She arches into me again. I love how turned on this makes her.

"However you want me," she whimpers.

"I want your skin against mine," I admit.

I'm happy to take her any way she wants, but I can't stop thinking of our naked bodies touching. I slide my hands under her shirt, peeling it upward. She lifts her arms like a good girl and lets me undress her. She starts to unzip her pants, but I grab her hands, lifting them above her head. I give her a stern look, and she bites into her lower lip and nods. She understands; I'm going to do it, and she'd better keep her hands over her head.

I slowly peel the leather over her gorgeous ass, trying to maintain control as the smell of her arousal fills my senses. She lifts her heels so I can slide each leg off, until she's fully naked, save the heels, just like I wanted her.

I continue to ignore my hard-as-rock dick as I stroke a hand back up her center, sampling her wetness, sliding over her round, feminine stomach, and pinching her nipples hard as my hands come to rest on her breasts. I give her a quick kiss, sweeping my tongue in her mouth possessively, and then I step back.

I hook my thumbs in the collar of my black T-shirt, pulling it over my head. She sighs happily, reaching out to run her hand down my pecs and stomach, fingering the tattoos, the grooves between my abs, and the trail of hair leading down to the top of my pants. I smooth my hair back, appreciating the desire on her face.

But when she goes to undo my belt, I stop her.

"Hands up," I command.

She complies readily, resting her arms on top of her head, panting for me. I undo my belt and kick off my pants. My long, hard cock stands to attention, dripping for her.

I make a motion with my finger for her to turn around. She complies, and I press down on her back, her extended arms draping over the desk as her chest comes to rest on the desktop.

I step back to admire the view. Her slightly spread legs display her damp, swollen pussy and her gorgeous ass. These are the moments I'm glad for my controlled nature. Otherwise, I'd come right here at the sight. Instead, I drop to my knees on the carpeted floor and lick her delicious pussy like a starving man.

"Fuck, Frankie, you taste like heaven," I moan into her.

She grips the desk beneath her, moaning her response, clearly unable to form words. I relent, only to let her catch her breath and say the words that will spur me on.

"Say it, baby."

"Fuck me," she pleads, looking back at me desperately.

I stand up, letting my erection graze her. Fire licks through me, and I clench my jaw against the pleasure. I slowly retrieve a condom from the pocket of my discarded pants and put it on.

"Mmmm," I mutter. "You sure you don't want me to lick you until you come in my mouth?"

She arches into the pleasure once more. Fuck, this woman is beyond beautiful.

"I need you inside me, Julian," she says with such intensity that I don't make her wait. I simply plunge into her fully, her tight, wet warmth pulling me in to the hilt.

"Fuuuuck," I moan, unable to form a full sentence. "Goddamn, I needed this pussy." I smack her right ass cheek. Hard. She cries out and clenches around me. "You like that?"

Looking back at me, she nods, all of her cheeks flushed. I pull back slightly, pumping while still deeply inside her, knowing it will stroke her into a dizzy heat. I'm not disappointed as she clutches hard at the desk, breathing heavily and moaning. I lean forward over her, gathering her ponytail in my hand. I give it a tug as I bury myself fully in her and she cries out.

"You want me to give it to you?" I prompt her, going back to gentle, deep thrusts.

She moans. "Fuck yes, please," she says.

I slam into her again as I pull her hair back, so she leans back toward me. Her breasts push out, taut and peaked. I reach around with my free hand, roughly grabbing one so her nipple presses between my fingers. I keep her pulled taut by her hair, roughly squeezing her nipple, and I unleash in a frenzy of thrusts, slamming deep and hard. My stomach muscles clench as I balance myself to make sure it's pleasurable for her. With less control it could end up doing the opposite of what I intend. But her body fits perfectly in my grasp, her hot nipple fully peaked under my touch, her beautiful body responding perfectly to the firm grasp I have on her hair, her tight pussy hungrily accepting my hard thrusts.

"You're fucking perfect, Frankie," I breathe as I fuck her. Her moans grow louder. "That's right, baby, let me hear you. I want to hear you when you come. Come for me now."

I slam into her with almost everything I've got, reserving only what I'll need for after. And like the sexy vixen that she is, one of her hands clamps over the one I have on her breast, while her other does the same job on her other nipple. With a jerk, she comes on my dick, screaming her release as she seizes around me. It's almost enough to make me explode inside her.

She slumps forward onto the desk, satisfied and panting. But I'm not done with her yet. I pull out gently, repositioning the rubber. I run a hand down her trembling legs, wrapping my other arm under her, and with one swift, gentle movement, I roll her onto her back, lifting her legs up. I slide her back onto the desk so her backside rests on the surface, with enough room to stand in front of her.

Rather than squat down, I lean in and mount her, wrapping her legs around me as I sink back into her delicious warmth. I lean all the way onto the desk, propping myself over her, so I can look into her eyes. Her hands come to rest on my face, and she pulls herself up to me for a kiss.

I give her a dangerous smile. "Starting to see how much I missed you?" I tease.

She feigns thinking about it, then smiles. "Maybe," she says. "But why don't you keep showing me, just in case?"

I flick an eyebrow up and smirk at her, tilting my pelvis so I slide out of her. And I gently slide back in. "Like that?"

She throws her head back and moans. "God, yes."

So I do it again, slowly, and ask again. She moans her agreement again. We do the same dance over and over, and the exchange speeds up. But before she crests, I back off to start over, to make the payoff that much more intense.

I focus on keeping rhythm, and telling her how good she feels, all the times I thought about fucking her this week, how much I missed her in every way possible. As I feel myself starting to build toward climax, I stand back up, lifting her ass with my hands and holding her in place. She rests her legs on my chest, her ankles on my shoulders.

Having her in this position, looking down on her wantonly splayed out on the desk, I know without question that I'll be true to her. Do anything for her. Do whatever it takes to be with her.

I slip my hand around the top of her thigh, using my thumb to circle her clit. Her eyes were closed, but snap open at my touch.

"Time to come again, beautiful," I groan.

Her hands fly to grip the desk's edge behind her, her eyes locked on mine and overflowing with desire. Still supporting her with one hand, I keep stroking her with the other, swinging my hips into her with increasing speed as I feel myself tighten, as she tightens around me. And in the last moments, as I watch her breath sharply speed up as her orgasm hits, I have to stop the words from tumbling out of me as I find my release.

I lie over her for longer than I probably should, unwilling to step out of this moment. But all good things must come to an end, and before I know it, we're getting dressed and slipping out of her office.

As if I fucked it out of her, Frankie's all-business demeanor is gone, and she keeps hold of my hand, leading me to the dance floor. The deejay is playing a sultry, heavy beat, and she steps into my arms. We move together just as flawlessly as we do naked, and I let myself sink into her smell, her warmth as she grinds against me. With the beast sated, it sleeps soundly for the moment, allowing me to enjoy being close to her without the need to fuck her silly.

She turns in my arms, her back against my chest, her hands on my thighs. I rock her in my arms to the beat, allowing the simple pleasure of touching her to fill me. But something causes me to look up at the balcony. And when I do, I lock eyes with her club manager, the Nordic bastard who clearly has a thing for her. He doesn't look happy. I offer no other challenge than returning his glare. I don't need to. Frankie is fucking mine.

* * *

Frankie asks to stay at my place after she closes down the club. It's nearby, after all, and we're both exhausted and sweaty. I don't even have to consider. I'm down with whatever will be the fastest way to get her naked again.

And not even fifteen minutes later, we're entering my apartment. The second we're in, I shove her up against the door. I get no protest. On the contrary, we help each other strip quickly so not even a minute after that, I'm entering her.

I fuck her hard against the door, and I couldn't give a shit about the noise or the hour. It's all over in minutes anyway, then she's screaming my name as I unleash an expletive-ridden orgasmic tirade in her ear. Completely exhausted from the volume of serious fucking, dancing that might as well have been fucking, and simply being awake for so long, it takes all my strength to make it through a quick shower with her before we collapse into bed, still slightly damp.

As I'm about to fall asleep, Frankie stirs next to me, clearly uncomfortable.

"Everything okay?" I ask sleepily. I turn to her to find her wide awake and looking terrified. It snaps me awake immediately. "What is it, baby?"

She looks askance at me and shakes her head. "It's nothing. I'm sorry, I don't want to keep you up," she replies softly.

I roll toward her, pulling her onto her side to face me, to look me in the eye. "Talk," I insist, kissing her collarbone along the line of small stars tattooed there.

She pulls a deep breath in. "I'm scared, Julian," she admits. I draw my face up to meet her gaze. "About the way I feel about you."

I prop my head up on my arm. "I'm not," I reply.

She gives me a confused look. "Yeah, well, I've already spilled my guts to you," she reminds me. "And that's what freaks me out. There are things you still won't tell me."

Ah. Fuck. And I may not be scared of what she's feeling for me, or I for her, but I am scared that telling her everything would ruin that. I just need time to disentangle myself from Sal. You know, without him killing me. And, as if that weren't enough, then I have to hope he never tells her he sent me after her in the first place. I realize that's hoping a lot, and that I may have to tell her someday. Fuck that, I know I *should* tell her. But there's something else I want to tell her more, and I know it's completely unfair.

"I get that," I admit. "Given the situation, things have been difficult for me too." I pause to take a deep breath. "But that hasn't stopped me from falling in love with you. I don't think there's anything that could've stopped that. You're fucking amazing, Frankie, and I want to be with you, even though we don't know everything about each other right now. Because I know we will, someday." As soon as the words are out of my mouth, I make a liar of myself. Because I've just laid it out there and I'm fucking scared shitless that she'll leave.

Tears spring to her eyes and she presses her lips together in a thin line. I go to reach for her, and she shakes her head, pulling back as the tears spill over her cheeks. Something inside me breaks. It's that fucking heart I didn't know I had.

I contemplate running. But the thought of leaving her is a fresh level of hell. So I decide to do something I've never done.

"Please, baby," I beg, imploring her with my eyes, my voice, not to pull away. "Of all people, I get how fucking hard this must be for you." And I realize right now truth is exactly what she needs. As much as I can give her. "You know how I grew up. Just like you, it made me not trust anyone, not even the man who saved me from the fucking streets." I shift to a sitting position and she mirrors me, almost unconsciously, hanging on every word. "I've had to do some horrible fucking shit to survive. You have no idea. But that's all I've done is just survive. I already told you I've never been in love before. I don't fucking trust anyone enough to get halfway there. Until you. I was lost, Frankie, from the moment I met you. I love you. I'd do anything for you. And I will tell you what you want to know, but I can't right now. I promise you, I will someday. Hopefully soon. Though I totally get if that's not enough for you." I drop my head in my hands, furiously rubbing away the tears forming at the thought of losing her now. It's the most I've ever told anyone about my feelings, and it's a level of raw I can barely stand.

Frankie sniffs deeply, and knowing she's crying nearly sends me over the edge. All of the control, all of the containment I've carefully placed on my emotions has been stripped away. This woman has broken me, and I'm laid bare at her feet.

"It's enough for now." Her quiet voice cuts through the silence, and I look up at her hopefully. She *is* crying. But there's something more in her eyes. "It has to be enough. Because, despite everything I don't know, I want to be with you. I want you in ways I never even knew were possible for me." She presses her lips together, clearly too emotional to continue.

With none of my usual confidence, I tentatively raise my hand to her face. When she allows me to touch her, I can almost feel the shattered pieces of my heart coming back together. But I need more. I also feel like I need her on a level I've never needed anyone. It's both exhilarating and terrifying.

I approach carefully, opening my legs and placing them on either side of her. She does the same, resting her legs over my hips. Still naked, her soft, warm center grazes me. But I'm more interested in getting her in my arms first, in feeling that she's really still here. I reach out and she settles into me, resting her head against my chest.

I cup her face with my hand, looking down into her eyes. But words have left me. So I kiss her softly, letting our mouths meld together. I stroke my hands gently over her back as our tongues dance, tasting deeply of each other. My body craves her in a way it hasn't before, wanting to be connected to her.

She pulls away and places a hand on my heart, as if desiring the same connection. She scoots forward and pulls herself into my lap. Her other hand slips between us, pulling my cock to her. The sudden movement stirs me, and I fully harden as she sinks onto me. Her eyes don't move from mine as she begins to ride me slowly, deliberately. I don't have words for how fucking amazing it feels.

Her arms encircle my neck, as mine encircle her, touching her everywhere I can reach. The slow rhythm we set lets me feel every inch of her inside and out. Her lips part, and her breathing accelerates. And I have to concentrate on not exploding from the mind-numbing pleasure she's giving me, because all I want is for her to feel this good. I pull her hips down as she slides onto me, deepening the reach of my cock as I reach down to gently stroke her clit. She clings to me, her mouth finding mine again as she moans her pleasure. The passion of it knocks me completely on my ass, and I'm speechless as she rides us both to climax.

It's only after, as I feel cum dripping down my shaft while I'm still inside her, that I realize I'd been bare. I look down at our joined, slippery center.

"Oh, fuck," I swear.

She smiles tolerantly. "It's okay," she assures me. "You know I'm safe. And I trust you."

Well, that gets my attention. I reach up and touch her face, unable to convey how much those words mean to me. How much I know they mean to her. "I trust you too."

The rest goes unspoken, but in the wee hours of the morning, Frankie slips into my arms and falls asleep. And it must be the forced connection to my emotions, but it makes me want to cry tears of joy. What the fuck is this woman doing to me?

* * *

Waking up next to her is just as amazing. We spend what little remains of the morning making love. I feel like a pussy even thinking the phrase, but it has definitely crossed over from the fucking we'd been doing. And while it's not my usual mode, it's exactly what we both need right now. There is little said about any of it. Though I don't miss that she never said she loves me.

We go to the diner for a brief, quiet lunch before returning to my apartment to make love again. It's strangely silent, as if all my words were spent the night before, and none of them remain. Not even the dirty ones. Maybe especially not the dirty ones.

When it comes time for her to go to the club, I'm once again uncharacteristically nervous. The lack of discussing anything since last night is starting to unnerve me. But I have things to do, and I sense she needs some time to sort through everything.

I walk her to my door, pulling her by the hand into my arms. I stroke a hand down her cheek, looking into her eyes. Fuck, this woman owns me.

"Thank you," I say simply.

The contemplative look she'd had on her face disappears and she laughs. "For what?" she asks.

"I don't know," I admit with a laugh. "For a lot of things."

She goes on her toes to kiss me softly. "You're welcome, then," she says. "Am I going to see you tomorrow?"

I stare down at her, wondering how, even knowing I'm not lying, she doesn't seem to get how much I love her. That I can't be without her.

"If you want to," I assure her. "I'll be here."

She smiles dimly at me, and I wonder what's going on in her head. This is all so new to me, and it's unsettling.

"Okay, well, bye, then," she says meekly, unfolding herself from my arms.

I resist the urge to kiss her, still sensing that more closeness isn't going to resolve whatever doubts she obviously still has. So I let her go.

"Bye, Frankie."

I've done some hard shit in my life. But letting her leave, with a sense that she may not come back blows it all out of the water.

Chapter 20 — Frankie

After getting to my office and changing clothes, I sit at my desk, staring impassively at the wall as the club bustles outside my door. Despite trying to sort through my feelings, I just feel numb. Unable to think past the fact that while Julian told me he loves me, he's still holding back.

As usual, he didn't lie to me. And while I love that about him, still knowing that he's keeping something obviously huge from me is terrifying in a way I just can't get past. At the same time, the thought of ending things makes me sick to my stomach. Two unreconcilable truths. Lies would be easier — then I could just write him off. I close my eyes.

A soft knock puts an end to my little pity party.

"Come in," I call, rising from my chair and moving toward the door.

It opens and Nils steps in, closing it behind him again. "Francesca," he greets me somberly.

"Nils," I reply warily, stopping in front of him. "What's up?"

He shifts uncomfortably from one foot to the other. "I wanted to check on you. Your behavior last night was … unusual," he replies delicately.

I raise an eyebrow and am about to put him in his place when I consider he might be right. I was so glad to see Julian last night, and so turned on even after having him in my office, that I was uncharacteristically uninhibited with him on the dance floor. Thinking back to the moment, all I cared about was keeping my hands on him, and his on me. But now, in the light of a new day, it actually makes me blush thinking about my employees watching that.

"You're right," I admit, meeting his concerned gaze. "I apologize, it won't happen again."

Nils steps forward, closing the small gap between us. He runs his hand down my arm, grasping my hand firmly in his. His grip is strong and reassuring, but he looks imploringly into my eyes in a way that's more than a little unsettling. His amazing smell reinforces my discomfort.

"I'm worried about you," he says. "You've seemed distracted lately, and not in a good way."

I squeeze his hand, knowing he's just looking out for me. "Again, you're right," I agree with a sigh. "I've had a lot going on. I'm sorry if it's kept me from pulling my weight. But I'm here, totally. What can I do?"

He gives me a small, dangerous smile. And I know I'm going to regret asking.

* * *

By the end of the night, I'm beyond exhausted. While I don't actually regret it, Nils really put me through my paces. But after going over all of the latest financials, reviewing our schedule for the rest of the year, restocking the bar, and seeing the band lineup through another packed night, I'm feeling back in the saddle. Reengaging fully in running the club gives me a sense of organized satisfaction that definitely bleeds over into the other areas of my life. And the deafening sound of hundreds of people enjoying the shit out of themselves is a welcome distraction.

As the night winds down and we start cleaning up, Johnny finds me.

"Hey, boss?"

I hop down from the stage to meet him at the stairs from the bar. "What's up, Johnny?"

He scratches the back of his head self-consciously. "You didn't by any chance go in the security room tonight, did you?"

"Nope, didn't need to, why?" I ask, crossing my arms over my chest with a frown.

Johnny takes a deep breath, his broad chest puffing up. "Fuck. Well, see, I went to reset it for the day, and it was down."

"Down?" I gasp. "Completely?"

He nods, looking sheepish. "I didn't see anyone go in," he hedges, looking everywhere but at me. "But it was nuts tonight. I'm so sorry."

With a heavy sigh, I shake my head. "It's not your fault," I assure him. "You're my head bartender, it's not your job."

Though I get why he feels responsible. Because the door to the security room is behind the bar, he's always kept an eye on it. And with me, Nils, five bartenders, a crew of security guards, and all the other employees milling around, it's not like it's exactly easy to sneak into restricted areas.

Nils walks by at that exact moment, and I gesture for him to join us. Johnny tells him what he just told me, and his response is nearly identical.

Nils's frown deepens the more he thinks about it. "I'll get someone from the company that installed the system to come have a look. Let's lock it up so nothing else goes awry," he says.

"Will do," Johnny agrees. "Seriously, I'm really sorry. I feel like an idiot letting someone just wander in and mess with it."

His words trigger something. "Not just anyone *can* mess with it," I recall. "It takes a code to shut it down, right?"

Johnny shrugs. "I've never done it, only saved the feeds and reset them for the next day."

"She's right," Nils interjects. "But only myself, Ms. Greco, and our security team have that code."

"Uhhh, I think that might not exactly be true," Johnny mumbles.

"Pardon?" I ask sharply.

Johnny pulls a face, then gestures for us to follow him. He leads us behind the bar, through the security door, and to the bank of monitors. He walks over to the mouse, setting it aside and flipping the mousepad underneath over. A yellow sticky note is affixed to the back of it. And on it is the security code.

Nils pinches the bridge of his nose and sighs. "Everybody out," he directs in an uncharacteristically harsh tone. "I'm resetting the code and locking up. After we close, nobody comes into the club until the security company has been in here tomorrow." His eyes snap up to Johnny's. "Am I clear?"

Johnny's eyes go wide. "Yes, sir," he agrees quickly.

"Good," Nils snaps. "Francesca, I trust you'll finish closing and tell everyone else while I take care of this?"

"Of course," I reply.

Johnny and I head out. I take a minute to reassure him first that it wasn't his fault. Then I let everyone else know to go home, and that doors are closed until further notice. That done, I return to my office, sinking into my chair.

My brain spins through the events of the evening, trying to narrow down the time window this would've happened in, besides the obvious of after doors open at ten and sometime before Johnny checked the feeds around three.

It occurs to me suddenly that if Johnny saved the files, I can simply look on our secure cloud server for the time stamp of the last video file. So I do.

The feeds are shut down a bit before one a.m. By that hour there aren't a lot of people coming in and out, as usually everyone who there's space for has been let in, but the club is always packed. Out of curiosity, I check to see when the last person was admitted through the door. I don't have to go back very far, but what I see makes my heart stop.

Julian, walking through the door on the tail end of a group of people I've never seen.

He couldn't. He wouldn't.

But if he did, why?

No.

He wouldn't.

I go back and forth for a good fifteen minutes before Nils finds me.

"It's done," he says wearily as he enters. He stops when he sees the look on my face. "What?"

I contemplate not showing him. I know he already dislikes Julian, considering him a distraction at best. But he has access to the footage too. So, with a sigh, I turn my laptop around to show the frozen image, timestamp and all.

"He was the last one in the doors tonight before the video feed cuts out not but ten minutes later," I say as he stares wide-eyed at the screen. I snap the lid shut, frustrated.

"You think he had something to do with this?" Nils asks. The incredulity in his voice surprises me.

"I thought you didn't like the guy," I grouse.

"And I thought you did," he replies matter-of-factly, settling in the chair across from me looking anything but comfortable.

"I did," I agree. "I mean, I do."

"Do you trust him?"

I let out a deep sigh. "I thought I did."

"But now?"

I look up at Nils. "We haven't known each other that long. There are still things I don't know about him."

"Things that make you think he's interested in messing about in your business affairs?" Nils looks skeptical to say the least. He's right, really. It's a silly supposition and I'm totally jumping to conclusions. Having questions about what Julian is hiding is in all likelihood completely unconnected to what's happened.

"No, probably not," I finally reply. "But then, who?"

Nils shrugs. "It could've been anybody," he points out. "I'm reticent to make any assumptions until we have more to go on."

I huff a small, joyless laugh. "How mature of you," I tease. "I'm just jumpy right now. You're right. We should go home, get some sleep, and deal with this tomorrow."

A tired smile crosses his face. "I'll let you know as soon as I have something."

I lean back in my chair, willing my brain to shut the hell up. "Thanks." Suddenly a thought occurs to me. "Nils?"

"Hmmm?" He tilts his head to the side curiously.

"How come your personal drama never spills over into work? I feel like everyone else around here has been a hot mess at one point or another. But never you."

He rubs his lips together while he considers his answer.

"I'm on a personal drama hiatus," he finally cracks in response.

It does make me laugh. "Seriously? What does that mean?"

He shrugs. "It means you have to have a personal life to have drama."

"Oh," I say in a small voice. "I'm sorry, Nils. You do too much here. What can I do to help?"

He leans forward, looking me intently in the eyes. "While I appreciate the thought, I didn't mean to imply I'm dissatisfied." He pauses, his eyes searching mine. "Everything I need is right here."

I'm unsure of how to respond, so his words simply hang in the air. I decide against saying anything to discourage any unseemly affection he may have for me. Because I think I've made enough assumptions for the night, and I'm probably just being a bit too self-centered on all fronts right now.

Instead, I let him walk me to my car, then I use all of my remaining energy to get home safely. There's nothing left for my endless overanalysis, and when my head hits the pillow, I'm out.

* * *

After I've woken, showered, and eaten lunch, the nagging feeling that Julian might have something to do with this creeps back in. Sick of going back and forth, I decide to just ask him. And driving to his place will give me too much time to vacillate, so I simply call him.

"Hey, baby," he greets me. His deep voice gives me the same chills it always does. I push the feeling down.

"Why were you at the club last night?" I ask immediately, not up for dicking around.

The silence on the other end is unnerving.

"Fuck, you don't miss a trick, do you?"

"That wasn't an answer," I point out. I wonder if he's stalling, thinking he should've asked if my ability works over the phone. But then, maybe I'm not giving him enough credit. Though even feeling like an asshole for asking, I still need to hear his answer.

"I wanted to see you," he replies.

"But you didn't want me to see you?" I ask shrewdly.

"You were on my mind," he says. "But I didn't want to crowd you."

I pause, waiting for the voice. Nothing. He always sounds sincere, so there's nothing to contradict his answer. I've never consciously realized that before now, and I wonder if it's just with me, or if that's always how he is.

"That's the only reason you were there?" I press.

"I was only there because I wanted to see you. I saw you, had a drink, then I left," he says, clearly irritated. That's saying something. He's always unflappably calm and collected. Well, almost always. I recall the things he

142

said to me Friday night, the emotion in his face, his voice, his touch. And I feel like a world-class ass.

"You should've said hi," I grumble, deflated. I'm mostly mad at myself. I've never been able to embrace good things in my life without a heaping side of suspicion.

Julian laughs, that deep, spine-tingling laugh that I know lights up his face. "Trust me, I was tempted," he replies silkily, his hungry tone causing my core to tighten.

"How about you come say hi now?" I ask.

There's a pause before he answers, and I wonder if he sensed and was offended by my previous unspoken accusation.

"You sure?"

"I'm sure," I say with a smile.

"Good," he replies. "Because I'm already on my way."

"You sneaky bastard," I accuse him incredulously. But I can't help the smile that splits across my face. "Did you leave before or after I called?"

"Before," he admits.

"And I called you while you were already on your way here. Damn."

"Yeah," he agrees. "Freaky, right?"

It is, and it isn't. It shows that he thinks about me as much as I think about him. But in his case, he was running toward me. And while I wasn't exactly running away, I was looking for a reason to.

And suddenly it hits me. That's why I suspected him, because I'm looking for a solid reason to run, because he told me he loves me. And even though I wanted to say it back, it's what really scared me. Not that I didn't know what he's holding back. I'm more afraid of what he's not. Because it means I have no reason to hold back anymore, either, not if I really want to be with him.

"When will you be here?" I ask, suddenly very nervous. But in a good way this time.

"Open your door," he instructs.

"Seriously?" I open my door and poke my head out, but he's not there.

"Well, fuck, I'm not *that* good," he laughs. And then he comes around the corner with a grin. "But pretty close."

I can't help it. I pocket my phone as quickly as I can and run to him. He catches me as I launch myself at him, lifting me up to meet his lips. I wrap my legs around his waist and kiss him hungrily. He walks us into my apartment, kicking the door closed behind him. Then he lies me down on the couch, not letting go.

Finally, I break away, panting, as he hovers over me.

"That was a pretty fucking nice way to say hi," he says with a smile.

I grab him through his jeans, and he's already hard for me. "No, *that's* a nice way to say hi," I tease.

He growls at me, burying his face in my neck, sucking hard. As usual, the lust that shoots through me causes me to bow into him.

"Julian," I plead breathlessly, pressing on his shoulders.

He relents, sitting up between my legs. For a moment, all I can do is stare. His hair and eyes are wild and dark, the black T-shirt and jeans he wears fitted around the bulging muscles of his chest and legs. And he's looking at me like he's won a prize. It takes my breath away again. He's good at doing that.

"What, baby?" he prompts me.

I take a shaky breath. "About what you said on Friday —"

He shakes his head. "You don't have to say anything, Frankie."

I shimmy up into a sitting position, and he rests back on his haunches. I put my hands on his taut chest, trying not to be distracted by his strength, his heat. There will be time enough for that.

"I know," I reply. "But I need to." I take a deep breath. "I do trust you. But for me, that's not a single decision. I've gone almost thirty years waiting for that voice in my head every time someone speaks. I know it's not fair, but it's made me used to constantly reevaluating my relationships. It's like a stream of new information that can shake even the deepest trust. So when I choose to trust you, I'm going to have to make that choice over and over again. Does that make any sense?"

Julian scrubs a large hand over his stubble. "Yeah, it does."

"Good," I say, letting out a sigh of relief. "Because I meant it when I said I can't imagine not being with you. I love you." Tears spring to my eyes. I blink them back, waiting for his response.

He just watches me, his eyes calmly roaming my face. When it gets to the point where I'm not sure whether he's going to answer, he leans forward onto his arms, crawling over me, pushing me back onto the couch. He answers with his kiss, pinning me into the cushions, his tongue delving forcefully between my lips.

When he breaks away, his mouth immediately wanders downward, cutting a blazing trail down my neck, to my nipple, grazing the soft sliver of stomach exposed between my shirt and shorts.

"You're not going to say anything?" I tease him.

He catches my eyes as his hands deftly slide my shorts and panties off in one swift movement.

"Oh, I will," he replies confidently. "But only after you tell me that while you come in my mouth."

I gasp as his lips descend on me, his tongue probing feverishly. When it hits my clit, I'm immediately feverish and twitching with pleasure.

"Fuck, Frankie, you taste like heaven," he growls into my core, quickly going back to sucking me senseless. His fingers join in, thrusting me toward the brink.

All I can do is moan and writhe under his skilled touch.

"Tell me, baby," he prompts, flicking my clit with his tongue.

"I love you," I gasp.

He twists his hand, replacing his tongue with his thumb as his other fingers continue to fuck me, making me cry out again. His mouth finds mine, and I lick my slick wetness from his lips. It's his turn to groan into me.

"I fucking love the way you taste," he groans. "And I fucking love the noises you make when I do this." He curls his fingers inside me and presses down on my clit, eliciting a scream of pleasure. "I love you, Frankie."

He pumps me faster, and I grip his shoulders as my orgasm builds.

"Tell me," he demands one last time.

I arch into him. "God-fucking-damn it," I gasp, all but screaming. "I love you."

And with a satisfied smile, his fingers twist and press me over the edge. I scream my release, clinging to him as I ride the wave. He doesn't let up, and it keeps going, and going, until I think I'll pass out from the pleasure. Finally, as he feels my body unclench, he relents, gently stroking me down the receding wave of bliss.

He leaves me to recover for a moment and I glare at him.

"What?" he asks with a laugh.

I give him an impatient look, swiping my foot over the hard lump in his pants.

"Take off your clothes," I demand.

He laughs at me, the bastard. "All in good time."

I raise an eyebrow, sit up, and take off my shirt and bra in one pull. The smile drops off his face as he stares at my chest, followed by the entirety of my completely naked body. A wicked grin of triumph settles on my lips.

While he's distracted, I undo his fly. And before he can stop me, I take him in my mouth. It's no small feat as he's already fully hard. But the gasp he lets out is worth it.

"Fuck, Frankie, be careful," he begs.

I suck hard off his tip, using my hand to continue working him. "No," I reply with just enough sass to make him laugh.

"Have it your way," he replies, resting his hand on the back of my head.

I make him lift his ass so I can completely free him from his boxers.

Cupping him with one hand, I continue to work him with the other hand and my mouth, sometimes together, sometimes one after the other.

He gently caresses my hair as I work, spurring me on to suck him to the edge, then bring him back, all to give him a taste of what he gives me every time he puts his hands on me. To show him that his pleasure gives me pleasure. To show him I love making him come just as much as he does me.

"God, I love watching you suck my cock," Julian groans.

I suck him harder.

"Fuck, Frankie," he moans. "I'm gonna come in your amazing fucking mouth if you keep that up."

I eye him with satisfaction as I twist my grip in time with my suction, and I can feel him clench under the slick pressure. Making him come in my mouth is exactly what I want, and I work him like I mean it.

His head lolls back and his hand slips down my hair, gripping it by the ends. Even when he's about to come, he's so careful. I clench inside, totally turned on as this gorgeous man trembles under my provocation.

I pop my mouth off his cock, continuing to ramp up with my hand as I rub my breasts along the back of his shaft to get his attention. He groans deeply but doesn't look at me.

"Watch me suck you off, baby," I demand. "I want you to watch yourself come in my mouth."

His eyes go wide, and I have to stifle a laugh. He obviously wasn't expecting me to throw the dirty talk back at him. What can I say? He has that effect on me.

His eyes lock on me, so I lower my mouth back over him, satisfied he's doing as I asked.

As my mouth settles back into the mix, he whimpers. I look up to make sure he's still watching. He looks hypnotized. So I go at it with everything I've got. Not moments later I feel the sticky, hot stream in my mouth as his whimpers turn to deep, low groans. He's still watching me, struggling to keep his eyes from rolling back in his head. I open my mouth to show him the last of his load squirting into my mouth, coating my tongue.

"Holy fucking shit," he swears. I gently roll my hand up his length and lick the last, pearly drop off the tip of his trembling cock. At the sight of it he throws his head back and clenches in pleasure under me. "Fuck." I feel him tighten under my hand and one final, huge gush erupts from him as he seemingly has a second orgasm. "Oh, my sweet fucking God. What the fuck was that?" He sinks back into the couch, breathless and truly spent this time.

I climb on him, straddling him carefully. "Say it, bitch," I demand.

Julian laughs, his head lolling tiredly. "I love you, woman," he replies, closing his eyes. "And I have no idea how you did that."

"Me, neither," I admit with a grin. "But it was fun."

He opens his eyes, laughing at me again. "You're crazy," he teases, pulling me into him and burying his face in my neck. "But I think I'll keep you anyway."

I smack him playfully on the arm, blushing at the implication. "If you think you can handle me."

Julian pulls back, looking into my eyes. "I'm serious," he says. "Be my girl, Frankie."

I smile, resisting the urge to point out that that wasn't a question. He already knows how much I dislike being ordered around. Well, when we're not fucking anyway. But this is different, and I know he's not demanding it. He's offering it.

"I'm already your girl," I admit. But I can't help busting his balls just a little. "What did you think, that I go around telling every gorgeous guy I meet at my club that I love him?"

"I'm gorgeous, huh?" He flicks an eyebrow up and leans in, nuzzling into my ear.

"Yeah, but probably not half as gorgeous as you think you are," I tease.

He nips playfully at my neck. "Probably not," he agrees, and it makes me laugh. I can't fault him for being cocky when he's got the cock to back it up.

"Have you always been overly confident?" I ask, sliding off of his lap and retrieving my clothing. I don't bother with the bra or panties, simply tossing them aside in favor of just a T-shirt and shorts. He watches, clearly approving of my choice, and I know he's going to have me naked again as soon as he can. It sends a shiver down my back.

He lifts his tight ass up, sliding himself back into his boxers and pants. "I wouldn't call it 'overly confident,'" he replies with a shit-eating grin.

I roll my eyes and disappear into the bathroom to clean up.

When I come back out, he's leaning against the living room windows, staring outside with a thoughtful expression. He looks up as I approach.

"What happened at the club?" he asks.

I purse my lips together. "What makes you think something happened?" I counter.

He levels a hard stare at me. "Don't treat me like I'm a fucking idiot, Frankie," he says in a quiet tone that's just as hard as his gaze.

I fold my arms over my chest, debating how much to tell him, and the lack of bra pushes my breasts dangerously close to spilling out of my shirt. He resolutely continues to stare at my face.

"Someone messed with the security cameras," I reply.

He stares at me blankly for a minute, running a hand through the tangled, dark mess of hair on top of his head. A muscle in his jaw ticks. "That all?"

I tighten my arms around me, not giving a shit if my tits spill out. Something about this conversation is making me very uneasy. "Yeah," I mumble, averting my eyes. "I didn't really think you did it. I think I was just looking for a way out."

Julian's face falls, his eyebrows tightening together as he frowns. I reach out to reassure him, but he steps back.

"I don't want out, not really," I clarify.

His beautiful, uneven lips settle into a small, sideways smile. "I know," he assures me. "I get you have reason to doubt me. I don't blame you, baby." He shakes his head and crosses his own tattooed, muscled arms over his chest, returning his gaze out the window.

It hits me. He thinks he doesn't deserve me. And my reminding him that I'm not happy about the things he isn't sharing isn't helping. That's a tough one for me. Because I both want to reassure him that I'm still here while wanting to shake his secrets out of him. I wish like fuck that he hadn't ever mentioned there were things he wasn't ready to tell me. But then, knowing about me, he probably thought it was safer to hide as little as possible.

"God, dating me must suck," I muse out loud.

Julian's on me in an instant, pulling my arms away from my chest and dragging me against his hard chest. His hand lifts my chin, then strokes my face. "No," he protests. "You're the most fucking amazing woman I've ever met. Don't doubt that." His lips reach down for mine, wrapping me in the warmth of his affection.

When he pulls away, I can't help laughing. "Thanks," I reply. "But I meant that you can't win. I push you to be honest, then I get impatient when you honestly tell me there are things you don't want to share yet." I shrug. "You've only known me a month. It's not like you owe me your full life story."

He continues to thoughtfully stroke my face, his eyes roaming over me. "Fuck, has it really only been a month?" he murmurs.

The intensity on his face is overwhelming. And I'm with him. It feels like so much longer. Part of me feels like I've always known him. When I'm not fighting falling for him, we just fit. Like he's a piece of me I didn't know I was missing. Because I've never been *that* girl. The one who needed a man to feel whole. But now that I'm his, well, I do. Despite my reservations, that's a difficult feeling to deny. And he looks at me like it's written all over my face, like I'm naked in front of him, not bodily, but my heart and soul.

"Yeah," I breathe. "Just a month."

His thumb finds my lower lip, and my mouth parts for him. His lips pull up in a small smile, and his eyes flick up to meet mine. "Feels longer," he whispers, his eyes darkening.

I nod mutely, unable to do much besides languish in the feeling of his hands on me. I want to remember this feeling for the next time I start doubting him. Determined to commit it to memory, I take in every detail of him as he stares back at me. But when his lips reach for mine once more, when I know he's about to take me in a way that goes beyond the intensely physical relationship we've had so far, I surrender, letting him in completely as I close my eyes.

Chapter 21 — Julian

I open my eyes, wishing away the headache forming in my temples. Fuck, I'm tired. I look around Sal's office, annoyed that he's once again late. I glance over his huge, old oak desk, scratched and scarred from years of use and piled with papers and cigarette butts. His ancient leather chair is peeling and practically falling apart. The standard issue office clock on the wall tick-tick-ticks away the minutes of my pitiful existence. My eyes start to slide closed again like they have a mind of their own.

Shaking myself, I stand up, choosing to pace instead. Anything to keep me awake. My mind wanders back to the reason for my exhaustion. Frankie. Giving herself to me in every fucking way possible. All fucking night. Tired as I am, the thought still stirs me. But I shake my head, knowing she's both my salvation and my damnation wrapped up into one. But I'll be dreaming of those red lips as I burn in hell.

The door flies open and Sal saunters in, a lit cigarette dangling from his crusty old lips. A chintzy pair of aviators sit on top of his greasy, balding head.

"Julian, what the fuck are you doing here so early?" he greets me, tossing the pile of folders in his arms onto the desk. Papers go flying fucking everywhere.

"I left you a message," I remind him.

He shrugs and sits in in his chair, searching the mess on his desk for something. "Yeah, so? I didn't think you meant this fuckin' early," he grouses.

"Well, I did," I say, putting my hands on the edge of his desk and leaning in to catch his eye.

He looks up at me, unimpressed. "So what the fuck do you want?" he asks sharply.

"Why did you send me in for retrieval if you already had someone else on the job?" I demand.

Sal leans back into his chair, folding his arms over his chest with a frown. "I didn't," he says, looking at me suspiciously. "But I take it that means you didn't do what I asked."

I stand back up, folding my arms over my chest. I stare him down, trying to decide whether he's playing me. Fuck, what I wouldn't give for Frankie's ability right now.

"It was too risky," I hedge. "And I don't have time for this shit."

Like lightning, Sal is up and fucking pissed.

"You have time for what I fucking tell you to have time for," he spits, pointing a crooked finger at me.

I don't move, blink, or give him any sign that I give two shits about his temper tantrum.

Breathing heavily, he seems to back down and reconsider.

Good.

"I'm actually glad you're here," he finally says. "There's something else related to this that I need to do this morning. Might make what I asked you to get unnecessary. You're gonna come with me, be my muscle."

Bad. And I know it's bad because I've got that feeling in the pit of my stomach. The one I get when he asks me to do something I know I'm going to fucking hate doing.

"Whatever," I reply with a shrug. "Let's get this over with."

Sal smirks at me. He opens his desk drawer and retrieves his gun. He holsters it behind his back.

"Good. You packing?"

I open my jacket to show him the gun under my left arm. What, does he think this is my first day on the job? Stupid motherfucker.

"All right then," he says. "I think it's finally time we go have a little chat with Samantha Greco."

He saunters past me, thankfully putting his back to me quickly, so he doesn't see the panic on my face. Pushing it down, I follow at a brisk pace. I can't let him know I care. And I sure as fuck can't let him know the last thing I want to do is go shake down Frankie's mother.

* * *

As we walk up the peeling steps of Frankie's childhood home, I can't help wondering where the park is that Frankie used to go sleep in. Dream in. Think of being the child of aliens in. I suppress an ill-timed chuckle. Frankie is hands down the craziest, most captivating woman I've ever met. But everything she's told me about her mother, everything I know, says I'm about to walk into a bad fucking situation.

Sal knocks on the door. I hang back on the top step of the stairs to the porch, wishing I were anywhere but here. Or that I was here with Frankie. Meeting her mother under less fucked-up circumstances. But my life is a lesson in humility.

The door creaks open and an old woman peers out suspiciously. When her eyes land on Sal, her weathered lips pucker, and I get the sense she knows exactly who has come calling. Her eyes flick to me for a moment, then back to Sal.

"Mr. Moretti," she greets him. "I thought we'd be seeing you soon."

"Mrs. Greco," he replies curtly. "Samantha home?"

No greeting, no preamble. Boy, he must really hate this family to treat an old lady with such disrespect.

Frankie's grandmother considers him for a minute. Probably just to keep him on his toes, because she finally opens the door. "Yes, of course, please do come in," she says graciously.

As I step past her, she looks up at me with a glare. "How do you do, ma'am," I greet her with a dip of my head.

She sighs. "I'm well, young man, for now," she grumbles as she closes the door behind me. "But at least one of you has manners."

Sal shows himself into the tidy living room, taking a seat on the couch like he owns the fucking place. I stay standing in the entryway, crossing my arms over my chest.

"Please, have a seat," she says to me, her eyes jumping to Sal in distaste.

"Thank you, ma'am, but I'm fine here," I assure her politely.

She makes a small noise of indifference and disappears down the hallway. I eye Sal, who simply gives me a dangerous smile.

A moment later, a slim, short middle-aged woman appears. Her dark, graying hair is pulled back severely from her face, which has an expression that's as unforgiving as I imagined her to be. Out of habit, I scan her for possible weapons. Though I doubt she needs any. She could cut a man in half with just that nasty look on her face, which she immediately directs at Sal.

"You've got balls, I'll give you that," she snaps at Sal as she stops across from him. She glances at me, then back at him. "Coming here, armed? You always were a disrespectful asshole."

The fucker doesn't even get up, he simply smiles at her.

"Sam," he says. "You're looking good."

"Say what you came to say or get out." She's all business, just like Frankie said.

"Okay. Seems I have a daughter you forgot to mention," he says, menacing tone creeping into his voice.

Samantha continues staring him down impassively, not rising to his bait. Knowing Frankie told her about the DNA test, I know she knows she's not in a position to argue. With that, at least.

Sal doesn't say anything else, seemingly waiting for her to say something. I fight the urge to shift uncomfortably, unwilling to show any weakness.

She considers him for a good long while. "I can only assume you've stayed away because my father threatened you. Even though he's dead, I think we both know that you're still not welcome here," she says carefully. "So I'm only going to say this once. Stay away from my family. Or else."

Sal, ever the suicidal motherfucker, laughs. "Or else what? I think we both know that I've got nothing to lose," he responds. "And since Frankie clearly hasn't joined your little family business," Samantha clenches at his taunt, "I fully intend to fold her into mine."

"You'll do no such thing," she says dangerously quietly. "I've worked too hard to keep her away from you, away from that world."

Sal snorts. "She's running a fucking night club in Hollywood," he chortles. "Did you think she'd be able to stay clean forever? If I don't bring her in, someone else will. You want that for our daughter?"

Samantha clenches her fists but shows no other signs of cracking. "Frankie is too smart to get wrapped up in any of that," she insists. "And she's too smart to fall for whatever line you plan on feeding her."

Before I can stop myself, a wry chuckle of agreement escapes me. Even without her ability, her mother is right. Frankie is way too smart. Samantha's icy glare flicks to me. And though I've faced down men twice her size who were armed to the teeth, the look she shoots me is enough to make me want to run for the hills. She has a terrifying command of the room, and my opinion of Sal's intelligence takes a hit. Why the fuck is he provoking her?

Thankfully, she seems to write me off a moment later, and she turns the heat back on Sal.

"Did you just come here to piss me off?" she asks evenly, voicing my exact thought.

Sal considers that for a moment. He finally stands up, sauntering to a stop right in front of her.

"No, doll," he says softly. "I came here out of respect. Not that you ever had any for me."

Samantha laughs, and it's just as scary as her steely expression. Harsh, and cold, and full of hatred and malice. "You have to earn respect, you piece of shit," she says to him. "Now take your goon and get out of my house."

He smiles. "I've gotten what I came here for," he replies. Then raising his voice, "Nice seeing you, Maria." Frankie's grandmother emerges too quickly to not have been listening around the corner.

"Fuck off, Sal," she replies nonchalantly.

I have to pull my lips into my mouth to keep from smiling. The old lady doesn't miss it and looks me up and down as Sal steams past me.

"You're too good for him, you know," she says boldly.

I clench my jaw, not wanting to agree within earshot of Sal.

"Sorry to have disturbed you, ladies," I say.

They exchange a look. Not wanting to make this worse, I turn and follow Sal out the door. Just in time to witness him crashing into some kid on a bike on the way to his car. The kid bites it on the sidewalk.

"Fuck, kid, watch where you're going," Sal yells at him.

I shoot down the steps, disentangling the boy from his bike and helping him up.

"You okay, kid?" I ask him.

He grips my forearms with wide eyes as he rights himself. I follow his gaze to my jacket, where it's shifted to expose the gun. Releasing him, I stand up quickly. His eyes shift to my face.

"I'm fine, mister," he says, reaching to cradle his left arm with his right hand.

"You sure?" I ask as he winces, clearly in pain.

"Julian, get your ass in the car," Sal calls impatiently from a few feet away.

"Sal, you hurt the kid," I return defensively. I look back to the boy. "Let me at least make sure you're okay."

He nods, sitting down on the curb. I carefully ease down next to him, making sure the holstered gun stays hidden in the folds of my jacket. He extends his arm so I can examine his elbow. It's scraped up and bleeding but doesn't look too bad. I pull a handkerchief from my pocket and press it gently against his elbow.

"It'll be all right," I tell him. "Do you need help getting your bike home?"

The kid blows his dark brown hair out of his eyes and gestures with his head. "Nah, I live here."

My eyes go wide. "You're Frankie's brother?" I say it without thinking. Of course, he is. He even matches Frankie's description of Tony perfectly. All awkward and gangly, every inch the twelve-year-old accident-prone kid he is.

I must say it a shade too loud, because it catches Sal's attention. Fuck, fuck, fuck.

"Yeah! You know my sister?" he asks.

"Sure do," Sal offers before I'm forced to explain. "In fact, I'm her dad. So we're kind of related."

I close my eyes and take a deep breath. He's doing exactly what Samantha just told him not to do. He's messing with her family. And I, for one, don't want to know what "or else" means.

"No way," Tony says with a frown. "Frankie's dad is dead." He glares defiantly up at Sal, who eases his old ass down on the curb next to him.

"Turns out I'm not," he says with a smile. "You can ask her yourself."

Tony eyes him critically. "I'll do that," he says. "Because she knows when people are lying." His words are full of indignant accusation, and if he hadn't just revealed Frankie's biggest secret to a man planning to use her, I'd find his fierce pride in his sister endearing.

As it is, my blood freezes in my veins. He's old enough to know how to keep secrets, but maybe he didn't know that this was one? Whatever the reason, it doesn't matter now. I hold my breath and look over at Sal, who thankfully doesn't seem to know what to make of his comment.

"Yeah?" he says, clearly humoring the kid. "That's cool. I had a grandpa who knew when people were bluffing at cards."

Tony's eyes go wide. "Then she got it from your family," he says excitedly.

Sal gives the kid a look. "Got what?"

"The voice that tells her when people are lying," he presses. "If your grandpa had it, maybe that's why she has it."

Sal looks up at me and catches my eye. I'm not sure there's any hiding the horror in my expression. And I can see the moment it dawns on him that the kid isn't joking. And that I've been hiding something from him.

"Yeah, that must be it," he says, his eyes still locked on mine. I wish I was someone else, so I could kick my own fucking ass. With one look, I've done exactly what I promised myself I wouldn't do. I've betrayed Frankie's secret to Sal.

Tony looks between me and Sal. "Hey, I gotta go," he says nervously, finally sensing the tension. "I only came home 'cause I forgot my math book." He rises and creeps toward the house. "See you around, though, okay?"

Sal snaps out of it and throws the kid a smile. "Sure thing, kid. See ya."

Tony smiles in relief, turns around, and heads toward the house.

Sal is completely silent as we get in the car and head back to his office. When we park, he taps the wheel with his thumbs.

"Anything else you're not telling me?" he asks, dangerously quietly.

"I don't know what you're talking about," I reply. In for a penny, in for a pound, I decide. May as well keep lying.

Sal turns to me. "You think I'm stupid?"

Yes, I think he's very stupid. Especially after the little trip we just went on.

"You think I'm stupid enough to keep things from you?" I counter.

"Why'd you look so guilty back there, then?" Sal asks pointedly.

I shrug, keeping the carefully controlled act in place. "Indigestion?" I offer sarcastically.

Sal pulls his piece out of its holster, laying it carefully on his lap.

"Julian," he says, "you've worked for me a long time. I'd hate for things to end badly."

The threat hangs in the air and I say nothing. What the fuck can I say?

Sal strokes the gun's grip thoughtfully for a moment. Eventually he reholsters it and turns to me.

"I've got what I need now," he says carefully. "Stay away from Frankie. I mean it this time."

I clench my jaw. The only thing I can do. What he means is, he'll be watching me. Or having someone watch me, anyway.

But even though there are other ways I could warn her, there is so much I'd have to tell her first. And I'm not ready to lose her. But if I say nothing, at best Sal will go full-court press to get her under his wing, which would leave her with little choice. And that's not a place I want her to be. Because that's exactly where I'm trapped, and it's ruined whatever life I could've had. At worst, well, we'd get to find out what "or else" means.

Chapter 22 — Frankie

As great as my week started, riding the high of being with Julian, by Wednesday morning it's come crashing down. I haven't heard a word from him since he left Sunday night. Not loving that this is the second time he's done this. Okay, that may be an understatement. I toggle between devastated and furious at any given moment.

To boot, Nils has called me into the office far earlier in the day than I'm used to rising. Needless to say, I'm not feeling terribly optimistic as I head into the club to meet him.

I find Nils in the security room, looking beyond troubled.

"I take it there's been a development?" I say by way of greeting.

Nils looks up from his pensive reverie at the bank of monitors. He flashes the smallest of smiles.

"Yes, there has," he replies simply, gesturing to the seat beside him. I oblige, and he begins to pull up a video file. "This was recovered by the security company."

He presses play, and it's immediately obvious it's the front door cam. The time stamp is *after* the uploaded feeds had cut out. "They erased their own entry," I exclaim. Nils, looking grim, nods and gestures to continue watching. And a moment later, I know why: Jess.

Nils stops the feed after she passes off camera. He shuffles through the files, beginning another clip. This one of the interior of the security room. It clearly shows Jess entering, spending a few minutes manipulating the security feeds, then shutting down the system with the code under the mousepad.

When he stops the feed, I turn to him. "Please tell me we've notified the authorities," I plead.

"Oh, yes," he assures me. "We're pressing charges. I've been assured that due to repeated trespassing offenses she'll at the very least do some community service. I doubt she'll darken our doorstep again. However, it's worth noting that she appeared to have done this so she could go into our computer system without being seen to take files relating to Dave. Depending on what her intentions were, it could dramatically add to her sentence. Unfortunately, it will take some time for them to build their case and prosecute, and they may never know exactly what she had planned."

I lean back with a sigh. "Does it matter? There's no explaining crazy," I mumble, crossing my arms over my chest. But strangely, I find myself relieved by this news. "At least now I know for sure it wasn't Julian."

Nils raises an eyebrow. "You still had doubts?"

I shrug. "Not really, I guess," I admit.

"If you're still unsure about him, maybe it's time to rethink things," he suggests in a tone that's a little too casual.

I shoot him a look. "I'm unsure about everyone, Nils," I reply honestly.

Nils considers that for a moment. "Are you unsure about me?" he asks curiously.

I smile wryly. "No," I admit. Then, with a wink, "Mostly."

Nils laughs, breaking the tension of the moment. "I'll take it."

"You should," I reply. "Anyway, thanks for letting me know. Alas, I need to get ready to have lunch with someone."

"Someone, as in Julian?" Nils asks, the smile dropping off his face.

"No," I reply. "Ugh. It's complicated."

The smile is back. "When is it not, Francesca?" he teases.

I'm a little surprised. Nils isn't much for teasing usually. He almost looks relaxed. I find it kind of strange, given the circumstances, but it works for him. I tell him so, eliciting another laugh from the usually reserved Swede.

Standing, he gestures for me to precede him out of the room. "Onward and upward," he murmurs.

I head to my office and finish some paperwork Nils has for me. That done, I debate for a few minutes whether I really want to have lunch with Sal. The whole situation is just weird, and it's not like I don't have enough other shit to deal with right now. But I'm not that asshole who cancels at the last minute, so I suck it up and head out to meet him.

* * *

I enter the homey little Italian restaurant Sal chose, overwhelmed by the fantastic smell that instantly makes my mouth water. Before I even make it to the hostess stand, I see Sal rise from a table at the back of the restaurant, waving me over.

I admire my surroundings as I pick my way through the sea of checkered tablecloths. It's quaint in that it's totally predictable, with pictures of famous Italian landmarks on the walls, elaborate ceiling murals that hover somewhere between classic art and a cartoonish imitation of them, and customers digging into massive piles of pasta and huge plates of lasagna.

When I reach Sal, he gives me a hug, seeming much more upbeat than the last time I saw him. He smells like cigarettes and sweat, and I try not to wrinkle my nose as I pull back.

"Frankie," he greets me with a huge grin. He gestures to the small booth, inviting me to sit down.

"Sal," I return with a reserved smile. "Nice place."

"Yeah? You like it?" he asks, gesturing around him as he returns to his seat.

"So far, so good," I hedge. "How's the food?"

"Oh, it's fantastic," he assures me.

Having grown up in an Italian-American family, I decide I'll be the judge of that.

"So how you doin', doll?" Sal asks.

I shrug. "Same shit, different day," I mutter as I scan the menu. My eyes flick up to his, noting how overly interested he seems, looking at me intently, leaned forward like he is. "How are you?"

"Oh, I'm great," he effuses. "Just had a development that I think is going to bring some life back to my business." He smiles widely. "How's things at the club?"

Putting my menu aside, I fold my arms on the table. "Club's good," I reply vaguely.

"You sure?" he presses. "'Cause you seem a little on edge."

I huff an unamused laugh. "Just got a lot going on," I say honestly.

"That's owning a business," Sal replies with a shrug. "But hey, if you ever need anything, my services are at your disposal, you know."

I give him a look, unsure of why he'd think I'd use his "services" after making it clear I wasn't a fan of his obviously questionable business practices. But the waiter comes and takes our order, so I have to wait a moment before saying anything.

"I mean it," Sal says as the waiter leaves, beating me to the punch. "We're family. Anything you need, just ask."

I drum my fingers on the tabletop while I contemplate my answer. "Thanks, but I like to keep things above board," I finally reply.

Sal laughs. "Hey, that's all good," he replies. "I go with whatever the client wants."

"I don't think there's anything I need that you can help me with," I say more plainly.

He smirks in response. "Not even security? Or personnel with fraternization issues?" he asks with a cunning glint in his beady eyes. "Because both of those could bring a lot of trouble to your doorstep. And I have plenty of experience with handling stuff like that."

The realization that he's somehow clearly gotten inside information on my business issues does three things. First, it freaks me the fuck out. I mean, who is this guy, really? Second, I'm instantly furious that he thinks it's in any way okay to involve himself in my life that way. Third, it convinces me more than ever that he's shady. And I'm about two seconds from walking out and never seeing him again.

But before I overreact, I calmly confirm whether he's as big of a sleazebag as he seems to be.

"There are two things you should know about me, Mr. Moretti," I say quietly. My formal address at least causes the insipid smile to melt off his face. "First, I can handle my own business, and I don't appreciate when people go behind my back to learn things that are none of theirs. Second, if you think for one second that I'm going to somehow give you access to my operations, you're sadly mistaken."

Sal laughs, leaning back in his seat, casually slinging an arm over the side of the booth. Clearly my outrage hasn't fazed him at all. "You got spunk, doll," he says with a chuckle. "But I think you got the wrong end of things. I'm not interested in your business. I'm interested in you." He continues to stare at me with a knowing smile and a sinister twinkle in his eye.

I give the voice a minute, surprised when it stays silent. He's not lying, and that is surprising.

"Why?"

"Besides the fact that you're my daughter?" he scoffs. I fold my arms over my chest. "All right, all right. You're a smart cookie, obviously. I could use someone like you on my side."

"I have absolutely no interest in being involved with your business. And I'm rapidly losing interest in anything having to do with you, period."

The waiter chooses that moment to return with steaming plates of pasta. And damn if the gnocchi he sets in front of me doesn't smell like heaven.

Sal gives me a knowing look. "At least eat your lunch," he encourages me. "Then I know you're not writing off your old man on an empty stomach."

It's such an Italian dad thing to say, I have to laugh. I decide he's right. At least about the empty stomach part. Shaking my head, I sample the food.

Unfortunately, I can't stop the moan that erupts when the tender, buttery dumplings simply melt in my mouth.

Sal laughs. "See? Your old man knows a thing or two."

Ignoring him, I focus on enjoying my meal. At least I'll have that to remember him by. Though I'm sure as hell coming back to this place without him. I try not to think about how much Julian would love this, because that's a fresh wave of shit I don't want to think about right now.

It doesn't take long before I've cleaned my plate. It's probably the best meal I've had, possibly ever.

"Okay, I'm full now," I respond. "So if I write you off, you'll know it wasn't hunger."

Sal gives a rueful laugh and shakes his head. "C'mon kid, it could be great for the both of us," he urges. "We both have things we could offer the other. Let me make up for all the time I couldn't be there and help make things better, easier for ya."

I go to protest again, but he holds up a hand. "You don't gotta say yes," he allows. "But at least don't say no. Just think about it for a while. I'll drop it, okay?"

He's a persistent old bastard, I'll give him that. But I know my answer isn't going to change. I also know, though, that fighting him on it isn't going to do any good. If I decide to, I can just never speak to him again.

"Fine, whatever," I reply, getting out my wallet.

Sal waves me off again. "Put that away, kid," he chastises me. I open my mouth to argue, but he waves at me dismissively. "Neither of our money is any good here. One of my clients owns the place." I can't help but raise an eyebrow, at which he smiles widely. "What? You didn't think there were upsides to getting into business with old Sal? Not everything is muddy, doll. I've got plenty of legitimate clients."

"If you say so," I reply evenly.

He stands up, still chuckling at me. At least my rejection amuses him.

"We'll talk soon?" he asks as he walks me out.

I shoot him some serious side-eye. "We'll see," I hedge. "Thanks for lunch."

"Anytime, Frankie. You take care, now."

I step out onto the sidewalk and try not to shudder as I feel his creepy gaze follow me until I'm out of sight. Yuck. I decide then and there that every instinct I had about the guy was dead-on. And I have no intention of wasting any more time being subjected to his sleazy attempts to fold me into his sketchy "business."

As I get in my car, I half want to go home and shower off the icky feeling. But I'm also still on edge over Julian. So I just text him. *Haven't heard from you. Everything ok?*

And if that isn't giving him the benefit of the doubt, I don't know what is. I sit there for a few minutes, fiddling with the radio, but there's no response. With a sigh, I start the car, lower the ragtop, and head home. I try to let the crisp November air blow away the heaviness in my heart. But it's only wind.

* * *

161

I end up sullenly drinking a fair amount that night. To the point where I'm so indignant at not getting a response from Julian that I foolishly make the decision to go to his place and tell him off in person. But even in my tipsy state I'm not stupid enough to attempt to drive, so I call for a ride, ending up at Julian's door around midnight.

Not giving a shit about the late hour, I bang on his door as hard as I can. What I don't realize is that it's a bad idea to come over unannounced, making a ruckus at the door of a big, rather scary man. At least, not until he opens the door with a gun pointed at my face.

As soon as he sees it's me, he drops the weapon to his side. "Fuck, Frankie, what the fuck do you think you're doing?" His dark hair is in a tangle on top of his head, his stubble thickening toward a beard, and he's shirtless, displaying his muscled, tattooed chest and arms, and that gorgeous "V" pointing to the top of his low-slung sweatpants.

He shakes his head, turning away and depositing his piece on the counter, leaving the door open. I take it as an invitation and step inside, closing the door behind me.

"What the fuck am *I* doing?" I slur. "What the fuck are *you* doing? I don't hear from you for days, *again*. I text, you don't answer. That's not how you treat your *girlfriend*." I drunkenly spit the word at him with the malice born from three days of being ignored. Again.

Julian sinks into his couch, gesturing for me to sit with him. I fold my arms over my chest and stick my bottom lip out.

"Don't be like that, Frankie," Julian grumbles, running his hands roughly over his face. I finally take a good look at him. He looks worn out. And sad.

I walk over to him, standing to the side of his knees. He uses the opportunity to hook his leg around mine and pull me in. Toppling onto his lap, I throw my hands out and grab him to slow my fall. I end up in his arms, cradled in his lap with my hands on his shoulders.

He runs a thumb roughly down my cheek. "I'm sorry," he says simply, offering nothing further.

I push against him, trying to free myself. "Let me go, Julian," I insist.

His hands close around my wrists, pulling me even closer. "No," he replies with a smirk. "Now that you've woken me up, I get to make it up to you."

"Make it up to me? You think it's that easy?" I ask, wriggling in his hold. "How about an explanation first?"

Julian leans into me, and the smell of his skin is beyond enticing. "I'd rather just fuck you." I don't even have a chance to protest that that's his answer for everything before he pulls my arms behind his neck, dropping his hands to my chest as his mouth latches on to my neck. He works fast, squeezing and working my breasts as his tongue slides down my body.

I press my hands against his chest, but my protests grow feeble as my body responds to him. "We can't solve all of our problems with sex," I manage to breathe out. It's barely convincing, because there's a dripping wet part of me that obviously would rather just let him fuck me too.

Julian looks up at me. His dark eyes are stormy, tormented. "I know." His hands wrap around my back, and he lies me down on the couch, sliding down with me. His head rests on my chest and he squeezes my body to his. "I'm sorry, baby."

I'm not sure if he's sorry for not calling or for trying to distract me. But he sounds so sincerely miserable that all the fight leaves me. I wrap my arms around him and kiss the top of his head.

"I know," I whisper.

We lie, silently soaking each other in. I close my eyes, letting the feeling of his warm body against mine soothe me. I feel myself drifting off, and I try to fight it. But it's useless, and as I slip into unconsciousness, I vow not to let him off the hook this time.

Chapter 23 — Julian

I wake up around six fucking a.m., still wrapped around Frankie. Or at least, I'm guessing it's that early because the sky is just starting to lighten. I carefully slide an arm out from under her and use it to prop up my head so I can watch her. She's a fucking stunner. Even drunk and sloppy as she was last night.

I fucking hate that I let Sal bully me into staying away from her this week. As I watch her breathe lightly through her open lips, something inside me snaps. The timing couldn't be worse, but I'm done. I can't be Sal's bitch anymore. It's time to tell him exactly that, and where he can shove this job. And if I survive, I'll tell her everything. Then I just have to hope like fucking hell that she'll forgive me.

I've never been comfortable living in the shadows. The nastier aspects of my life are what they are. Violence, intimidation, doing whatever is necessary to survive, to come out on top, that's just how life is. But having to keep people at arm's length because of it hasn't ever cost me anything. Until now. And I'm fucking over it. I'm not letting this girl go. She's the kick in the ass I needed to set my life straight.

Even if that's easier said than done. But I'm sure as fuck gonna try.

First, though, I need to be inside the gorgeous creature in my arms. To hear her say my name as I fuck her. To get her off on my hand, my face, my dick. Just the thought makes me hard as a fucking rock. I free my other hand and trace her jaw, skimming down her neck, between her breasts, down the line of her jeans. My teeth find the nipple resting under her shirt as my hand rubs between her legs. She stirs under me. I let her nipple go, running my nose over it.

"Julian?" she murmurs.

"Hey, baby," I reply, sinking my mouth back over the fabric covering her breast.

She groans and bucks into me. Such a good girl.

"What time is it?" she asks, her beautiful eyes opening and searching the dim room for a clock.

I sit up, settling between her legs.

"Time for this," I reply, undoing her jeans and pulling them down. She gasps and starts to reach for me, so I leave them around her thighs, dipping my hand between her legs.

164

She's silky soft in my hand, but I waste no time enjoying the feel of her. I go straight for her clit, rubbing hard circles until her hand falls, and her back arches into it.

"That's it, baby," I sigh, slipping a finger inside her, feeling her juices rise to my touch. "Goddamn, I love how wet you get for me."

The heat rises in her cheeks at my words, and with a satisfied smile I plunge two fingers into her tight, wet little cunt. She cries out, and the sound goes straight to my dick. But I keep control, finger-fucking her as I watch her orgasm build. She grabs desperately at her tits, squeezing and pinching her nipples.

"Fuck, baby, if you keep touching yourself like that I'm going to have to join in," I growl at her.

She nods, panting, unable to speak but clearly silently begging me to do exactly that. I reach over and grab one of her tits, pressing into its tip with my thumb. I don't stop my assault on her pussy either, letting my other thumb push on and off her clit as I stimulate her inside and out. Finally, when I can tell she's ready, I clench down with all fingers, on her nipple, clit, and G-spot. She bucks wildly into my hand as I press hard circles. The screams that come out of her make me glad I'm wearing a pair of sweats I couldn't give a shit about. Because I'm so fucking hard for her, I'm about to rip through the fabric.

"I need you to fuck me. Now," she demands after she catches her breath.

Everything inside me tightens. "Don't have to ask me twice," I groan, ripping my sweats off. She kicks her pants off at the same time, and as soon as we're both naked, I grab her legs, roughly pulling her to the edge of the couch.

I run my hand up my shaft, mostly just so she can see how fucking turned on she makes me. She watches me with hungry eyes, and I can't help the smirk I give her. "You like that?" She nods, biting into her lip hard. "You want this big fucking cock in your pussy?" And I swear I see her nipples get harder.

"Yes," she begs.

I seat the tip at her entrance. I can feel her slick warmth waiting to suck me in, but I hold back. I rub her from clit to ass, spreading her juices all over us both.

"Please," she whimpers.

"You want it?"

Her head bucks backward. "God, yes."

"How do you want it, baby?"

"Deep and hard. Now. Please, now," she begs.

It almost undoes me, but hearing her beg is fucking next level. I slide in excruciatingly slowly, stopping short of fully immersing myself in her before I pull back out.

"I think I need to teach you a little patience," I mutter, continuing to go shallow and slow. She twitches beneath me.

"Just give it to me, Julian," she moans.

"Hmmm," I tease, trying to decide how best to drive her crazy. And I remember. It's face next. It takes everything I've got to pull out of her and see her look of despair. But I know she's going to like what comes next, and it'll make her last orgasm that much better if I wait to give her what she's asking for.

For now, I drop between her legs, plunging my tongue into her, hungrily sucking and lapping at her juices. The unexpected move has a string of curse words flying out of her mouth. I laugh, even though my mouth is full of her pussy.

Getting back to business, I focus on tongue fucking her this time, wrapping my hand around to thumb her clit as I do. As soon as she comes, I spring up and plunge into her, fucking her deep and hard just like she asked, as the last of her orgasm clenches her around me.

I tilt her ass up so I can reach every last sweet inch of her as I pound her into oblivion. Her tits bounce back and forth in a way that would make me come on the fucking spot if I didn't have such good control.

"That what you want, baby? Deep and fucking hard? You want my hard cock fucking your sweet little pussy?"

She arches off the couch, and a fresh gush meets my pounding cock. I clench my teeth, pull out, and flip her over. She turns her head, so she's not buried in the cushions as I plunge back into her relentlessly, continuing to lift her ass in the air so I'm drilling her so hard and deep the force is shaking the furniture with each thrust. Her low moan becomes one continuous sound that grows louder each time her gorgeous ass slaps against me.

"Fuck, Frankie, you feel so fucking good," I tell her. I start to feel the orgasm building behind my cock. I press deeply into her, using a tilt of my hips to slam the head of my cock over the spot inside her as I reach around and rub her on the outside.

"Fuck, fuck, fuck, fuck, fuck," she screams as she comes on my dick, her legs shaking, her pussy clenching harder than I'd dreamed possible. She milks me, and fire licks through my body as I empty into her.

I want to collapse. I want to wrap myself around her. Claim her. But I pull back. Some of the wetness between us drips onto the floor. I stare at her trembling backside, mesmerized as our combined juices drip down her red, swollen pussy.

"Shit, baby, now that's a view," I pant. She lets her ass fall onto the couch, turning her head to give me a teasing glare. But she's still clearly unable to form sentences, so I laugh, turning and going into the bathroom to clean up.

Since I'm already naked, I decide not to half-ass it, and jump in the shower. When I'm just about done, Frankie saunters in. Watching her through the glass as she prowls toward me, naked, has unbelievably given me a semi.

"You are too fucking gorgeous," I tell her as I wash myself.

She opens the door and climbs in. Without a word, she's on her toes, her mouth on mine, her tongue demanding a response. Never one to shrink from a challenge, I lick her tongue, then spin her under the hot stream of water.

I pull back, watching the hot water cascade over her perfect chest, her nipples clearly still hard.

"Still want more, do you?" I tease her, clamping down on both of her nipples between my fingers and thumbs.

She hisses in pleasure. "Apparently, I can't get enough of you," she agrees. "Even when I'm hungover and pissed off."

I raise my eyebrows. Well, good that I at least have a weapon to distract her with. And I don't fucking waste it. I drop to my knees in front of her, lifting one of her legs with my left hand, and using my right hand to both support her and finger-fuck her. My mouth latches on to her lips, her clit, and anything else my tongue can lap at as I bring her back up to climax.

She leans her back against the tile, and the water pours down her delicious curves. Her taste, her need for me, her hot, wet pussy in my mouth drives me fucking crazy. I've never worked this hard to please a woman before and loved every minute of it. As she comes apart for me once again, I say a prayer that I get to do this to her always. That she'll let me do it to her always, even once she knows everything.

That thought sobers me considerably, and as I let her down, I don't respond as her hand finds my cock.

I stroke a hand down her face. "I think he needs a break," I say lightly.

Frankie's blue eyes, those deep, dark pools that fucking slay me, stare up at me, ripping away my defenses.

"You can't make me come four times and not expect a good blow job in return," she replies matter-of-factly.

Now that makes me laugh. I draw her to me, tucking her under my chin.

"Maybe later," I reply. "Some of us have to get to work."

Some of us for the last time.

Her bottom lip pops out. "Boo," she comments.

167

I smile, running my hands down her sides to grip her ass. "You're too fucking cute," I murmur, burying my lips in her neck.

It takes a few more minutes to stop touching long enough for us to get out and dry off. When we're dried and dressed, I walk her to the door.

"We'll talk later," I assure her.

She looks surprised. "Yeah?"

I hold back a sigh. "Yeah," I promise.

"Well, I'm at the club early tonight. Deejay competition. But I might be able to go in late tomorrow." She looks up at me, all fucking sweet and hopeful. And I hope I'm not about to make a promise I can't keep.

"Sounds good," I reply. "Tomorrow, then."

She gives me one last, sweet kiss before she leaves. I have to lean on the door after I close it behind her to catch my breath. And steel myself for what's next.

* * *

"What do you mean, you quit?" His voice is too calm. His eyes narrow as they hone in on me trying to look as blank as I can sitting across from him in his peeling leather chair. He even puts his half-finished cigarette out in his ashtray. All sure signs that he's dangerously pissed off.

I take a subtle deep breath in through my nose. "I mean, I'm done. I'm out."

Sal leans back, tapping his fingers on the arm of the chair. "You got another offer."

"Fuck, no," I protest quickly. "I mean I'm done, done. Out of the game."

Sal snorts. "There's no getting out of the game. So you've either turned on me, and I should kill ya right now, or you've lost your nerve, in which case I can't trust what you know to stay with you," he says, sizing me up. "Either way you cut it, there's out, and there's staying alive."

I shake my head. "Really? You think I'd turn on you after all this time? I've only stayed this long out of loyalty. I want a life," I respond, some of my anger finally seeping through as I gesture around. "This ain't no life, Sal."

Sal taps his chin in thought. "You're a good kid, Julian, or you were. But if you leave it'll spook everyone. We're already losing this war," Sal points out.

You've already lost, old man, I can't help thinking to myself. Though he's not wrong. I'd be like a rat leaving a sinking ship. And I'm almost sure others have already or would more than willingly turn on him.

"That's not my problem anymore," I say as evenly as I can.

That gets a laugh from him. "Says you," he chortles. "But you forget who the boss is here."

"C'mon, you've got Paul and Dino," I point out. "And even they're more muscle than you can afford right now."

"Good point," he says easily. Too easily. "Maybe I'll go cut one of them loose right now."

Now I know he's desperate. It's an empty threat. He can't cut them loose. Their families are one of the last pillars of support of what little is left of Sal's once vast empire. And it fully hits me that this is the best thing. The necessary thing. Because even without Frankie waking me up to what life could be like outside of this world, Sal is a sinking ship. I leave and maybe I die now, or I keep working for this cocksucker and maybe I die a few months from now instead. My odds fucking suck either way.

"I don't think you'll do that," I insist. "And I don't think, after everything you've done for me, you'd keep me from living my own life."

"And a year ago you would have been right," Sal admits. "But times are different now. If I go down, you go down with me."

Well, that fucking seals the deal. I rise, knowing I'm rolling the dice either way.

"Good luck, then," I say flippantly as I walk away. When I get to the door, I look at him one last time. "For what it's worth, I hope you survive this." I might even bet money that he does. He's a fucking cockroach. My only hope is that he has enough fatherly affection for me to just let me go. But I'm not stupid, and I don't turn my fucking back as I close the door.

When I leave, I sure as fuck don't go home in case Sal plans to immediately make good on his threats. Instead, I drive out to Santa Monica, hitting up the pier. The one place Sal's never thought to look for me. The place where I can feel free, remembering the short time of my life between escaping the hell that was foster home after foster home and getting caught up in the even worse hell that Sal rained down on me when I was too young, cocky, and stupid to know any better.

I sit on a bench all afternoon, watching tourists lose money at the carnival games, kids run amok everywhere, and couples making out on the Ferris wheel. I'd already been thinking of that early date with Frankie here only a few short weeks ago and watching them go at it makes me close my eyes and think about being with her. Touching her. Tasting her. Fuck, that woman's gotten under my skin fast. A month with her and I've found the courage to do what I've wanted to for years. I say a prayer that I survive this, so I can see what a lifetime with her would do.

By the time I head home, I realize it needs to not be home anymore. And fast. I should've thought of it before, but what can I say, I've had a lot on my mind. Either way, I need to evade Sal long enough for him to let me go.

I case my apartment building, going in only when I don't see anything out of place. But as I enter my apartment, I know I wasn't careful enough, and that I sure as fuck should've handled this *before* I quit, because Sal sits on my couch, with a gun pointed at me. My own is holstered under my left arm. I'd have no hopes of drawing it in time. Fuck. I'm losing my edge, being so careless. I let the door swing against the frame behind me, leery of even looking like I'm turning to close it.

"Couldn't find Paul or Dino?" I ask nonchalantly.

Sal smiles wryly. "Nah, I know they're your boys," he admits. "I doubt they'd have the balls to do what needs to be done."

He's not wrong.

"Is that you asking me to change my mind?" I ask.

Sal tips his head back and forth as if considering it. "If I asked, would you?"

"No."

"Didn't think so," he replies. "You made your peace with God, kid?"

Sal has always mocked my beliefs on sin, faith, and God. And it's always gotten under my skin, despite myself. He knows that. The fucker is kicking me when I'm down. I shouldn't be surprised. I always knew he was a piece of shit.

"No, but thankfully God's made his peace with me," I reply.

Sal's brows pull together. "Whatever, kid," he replies.

"I have a request," I spit out, stalling. If I can distract him, I might be able to get the drop on him.

His aim doesn't waver as he laughs. "You got some brass ones," he says. "Go ahead."

"Leave Frankie alone," I reply bluntly. "Whatever you have in mind for her, however you're planning to use her in this little game of yours, don't. She's your fucking daughter, Sal."

If I thought that would appeal to his emotional, fatherly side, I'd obviously forgotten that he's about to kill the closest thing to a son he's ever had.

"Answer one question, and I might consider it," he counters. And I know he won't either way. But I need to buy more time and hope to the fucking Almighty that he screws up.

"Go for it."

"Can Frankie really tell when someone is lying?"

I stare at him blankly, unwilling to confirm it, but unable to deny it believably. Sal stares back. Until comprehension dawns on his face.

"You're *protecting* her," he says incredulously. "Holy fucking shit, Julian, you *love* her."

I remain impassive. Again, I don't trust myself to deny it, knowing I wouldn't be able to keep the emotion out of my voice. Not when it comes to Frankie.

Sal shakes his head. "And here I sent you after her because you're the most coldhearted motherfucker I've ever met. Did you get her to fall in love with you too?" he asks.

He's getting the better of me, and I'm beyond furious. I'm sure it shows on my face.

"This is fucking perfect. I can work this to get her to use her little ability for me." He looks me up and down. "Maybe you haven't outlived your usefulness after all. I take it you haven't told her you work for me. That you only met because of me."

A loud thud in the hallways startles us both. On instinct, I take the opportunity to slip out the partially open door. I don't waste time, bolting around the corner to pass the elevators and take the stairs. As I whip by, I see the doors closing. I catch a glimpse of dark hair, a tear-streaked face, and gorgeous red lips.

Chapter 24 — Frankie

As I approach Julian's building, I look up to see him heading inside from the opposite direction. I run to catch up, but when I get inside, he's already disappeared. I push the elevator call button, in a hurry to get the wallet I didn't realize was missing until I got to the club. I just hope it's actually in Julian's apartment.

He's obviously faster than me, because the hall is completely clear when I get upstairs. Rounding the corner, though, I can see his door is cracked from afar. Curious, I approach, but I freeze when I hear voices coming from inside.

"...God's made his peace with me." Julian's voice is clear, and I realize he must be standing just on the other side of the door.

"Whatever, kid." The other voice is muffled, as if the speaker is across the room, though I can still make out the words. And there's something familiar about the voice.

"I have a request," Julian says. He sounds panicked. I freeze in place. Julian is unflappable. If he's unnerved, nothing good is going on behind that door.

The other man laughs. "You got some brass ones," he says. "Go ahead."

"Leave Frankie alone," Julian replies. My heart slams in my chest at the mention of my name. "Whatever you have in mind for her, however you're planning to use her in this little game of yours, don't. She's your fucking daughter, Sal."

The name and the voice click. My throat tightens and tears spring to my eyes. What the ever-loving fuck is going on? My head pounds as I struggle to comprehend how these two parts of my world could possibly be colliding. The truth hits me like a goddamn sledgehammer. This is what Julian has been hiding.

I reach out to grab the door handle when Sal's next words freeze me in place once again.

"Answer one question about her, and I might consider it."

Beyond confused, I search for something Julian might know about me that Sal would care about. I realize what just as Julian speaks again.

"Go for it."

"Can Frankie really tell when someone is lying?"

172

It feels so much like someone just punched me in the stomach that I nearly vomit. Julian told him my secret.

Or did he? I place a hand silently on the door frame, trying to hold down my dinner. Julian doesn't say a word.

"You're *protecting* her. Holy fucking shit, Julian, you *love* her." There's a pause, but I'm still reeling too much to process any of this. Not that I have time to, as Sal keeps going. "And here I sent you after her because you're the most coldhearted motherfucker I've ever met. Did you get her to fall in love with you too?"

And there it is. Confirmation of the truth that causes all the blood to drain from my face. Now I know this *is* what Julian was hiding, and why he's in there having a conversation with Sal. With my biological father.

Suddenly sure I'm going to be sick, I put my hand over my mouth and breath quietly and deeply through my nose.

But the hell continues. "This is fucking perfect. I can work this to get her to use her little ability for me. Maybe you haven't outlived your usefulness after all. I take it you haven't told her you work for me. That you only met because of me."

It starts to sink in. Sal sent Julian in ahead to check me out. Julian has been playing me this whole time. Getting me to fall in love with him so he could what, soften me up to do Sal's bidding? I stagger backward mindlessly, not even realizing I'm moving until I smack into the wall behind me and the voices inside stop abruptly.

In a panic, I run. I skid around the corner, ready to fly down the stairs when the elevator doors ping open ahead of me. I crash inside, mashing the button to close the doors. As they begin to slide together, the tears fall. And just as they close, I catch a pair of dark eyes look my way as they flash past.

* * *

I don't know how I make it through the night. I'm a zombie, mechanically pushing through my tasks for the evening. When it's all over, when the club is finally closed, I slump into my office chair, pulling a bottle of whiskey out of my bottom drawer.

But before I can open it, Nils walks through the open door without a word. I look up at him blankly, unable to form a sentence. He stays silent, rounding the desk and dropping to his knees, turning my chair so I'm facing him.

His hand reaches up to cup my face. "Do you want to talk about it?" he asks. There's a vulnerability in his eyes I've never seen before. It would scare me if I weren't so numb. If I didn't still feel like vomiting.

I shake my head wordlessly. His eyes roam over my face one more time before he stands, opening the bottle of whiskey and handing it to me. I take a giant slug, then hand it back. The burn reassures me that I'll be relieved of my ability to think about any of this very soon. Nils takes a more measured drink.

Somehow, a good number of drinks later, we end up on the leather sofa in the VIP lounge. He sits with me, matching me drink for drink, if not drinking as deeply as I do, until the words finally begin to pour out. When I've finished my story — well, as much of it as I can share without telling him anything I don't want him to know — he sets the whiskey down on the table in front of us, then turns to me.

"He's a fucking idiot," he seethes drunkenly. "If you were mine, there's nothing I would keep from you, nothing I wouldn't do for you."

I stare back at him, not comprehending those words from Nils's mouth. Somehow, he takes my confused silence as an invitation, and next thing I know his lips are on mine.

With my defenses down, I don't stop him. His mouth is warm, and skilled. So skilled. His tongue joins to mine, gently stroking me in sensual invitation. Part of me wants to let go, to fuck Nils on this couch, to use his body to erase Julian's hold on me. But a bigger part of me knows that would be a mistake on so many levels.

I disengage gently. "Neither of us is thinking clearly," I slur, offering him the out.

"No, Francesca," Nils breathes, his long, gentle fingers stroking my face. "I think I finally am. I've been in love with you all this time, but I didn't want to ruin things here. When the brooder came along, I realized I'd been playing it too safe. I don't want to do that anymore." His ice blue eyes search mine.

But there's nothing in me for him to find. Everything in me belongs to Julian. The realization triggers all the emotion I've been suppressing, and I start sobbing uncontrollably.

Nils sits patiently with me, stroking my back until it's over. I stand up to grab a fistful of tissue from my office. When I emerge, Nils is leaned against the bar looking considerably more sober.

"I've called a cab for you," he says softly as I approach him.

I sniffle, then hiccup loudly. His eyes go wide for a moment before we both burst into laughter.

"Thanks," I finally manage between giggles. I rest my hand on his arm. "Some night, huh?"

"Indeed," he murmurs, looking at me sorrowfully.

"Nils —" I start, but he holds up a hand.

"Let's just move on, shall we?" he suggests.

I press my lips together and nod. The service bell rings.

"That'll be your cab," he says, sliding his hand into mine and walking me out. Sure enough, it is, and he sees me into the back. "Forgive me if this is out of line," he pauses to smile ironically, "but you may want to stay with a friend for a day or two."

I hadn't even thought of it, but he's right. I could use the support, and it's better if Julian doesn't know where to find me. Or Sal, for that matter. I nod my thanks, and with another small, sad smile, Nils goes back into the club. I push everything that just happened between us down in my mind, in the same dark hole I've shoved everything else, completely unable to deal right now.

I give the driver Emma's address, texting ahead to make sure she's there.

OK if I come crash at yours for a couple days?

And even though it's an ungodly hour close to dawn, it takes only a minute for her to respond.

Yah, of course. U ok?

I blink back the tears that form at her question.

Eh.

Not sure what else to say, I pause, wondering how to prepare her for the hot mess that I am. But she beats me to it.

Get ur sweet ass over here, I bet ur tired. We'll talk later.

With a grateful sigh, I reply simply with *thx* and lean back into the headrest for the rest of the ride.

It goes by in a blink, though I may have dozed off for a few minutes on the freeway. When I get to her door, Emma pulls me inside and gives me a huge hug.

"Sorry if I woke you," I manage. As the booze wears off, I'm finding it harder to control my emotions. And as soon as the words are out of my mouth, I realize talking isn't the best idea. I just want to be unconscious, so I don't have to deal with the flood of emotion I no longer have the energy to hold back.

She shakes her head. "I was up. Not sleeping too well these days," she admits.

With a sigh, I look her over. She looks tired and sad. I realize she's probably missing Ben, even though we've talked and agreed over and over that it's for the best. Just like leaving Julian behind is for the best. Doesn't mean it doesn't suck.

I nod, pulling her in for another hug.

"C'mon," she says, pulling me into her bedroom. She points at the bed. "You. Sleep. Now. I'll be here when you wake up, okay?"

I look down at myself, realizing I'm sticky and smelly with dried sweat and all kinds of other crap that comes from a night of work. "I'm a mess. I'll shower first," I insist.

She looks me over. "Yeah, probably for the best," she agrees. She catches my eye and we both chuckle.

A quick, hot shower leaves me feeling considerably less of a mess, and I let the small amount of relaxation it gives me take over, so sleep finds me before anything else can.

* * *

I wake to afternoon sunlight and the smell of coffee. Trudging out into the main room, I find Emma in the living room watching courtroom drama TV and eating donuts.

"This looks like my kind of party," I say drily.

She looks up and smiles half-heartedly. "Thought you'd be up soon, so I made you a fresh pot of the darkest roast I have," she offers.

"You're a saint, Emma," I breathe, following my nose into the kitchen. I find the largest mug in the cabinet and fill it to the brim. No cream or sugar for this girl. Give it to me black. Like my heart right about now.

Ignoring the heat, I gulp it down and shuffle back to the living room, snagging a chocolate frosted cake donut.

We eat in companionable silence while the show's participants battle it out, screaming at each other over the judge.

"I love this shit," I say to Emma. "Makes my drama seem less drama-y."

Emma gives me a skeptical side glance. "Really? Because seems like there might be some seriously drama-y stuff going on about now."

With a sigh, I put my nearly empty mug down on the coffee table.

"Touché."

"Ready to talk?"

"No." I shift uncomfortably in my seat.

"Maybe you should anyway," Emma urges. I look up at her. It's hard to argue with the voice of experience. So I tell her everything.

When I'm done, she looks into the empty donut box. "We're going to need another few dozen of these before we can even start dealing with that shit."

I shake my head and laugh. I stop myself before it turns into crying. "Yeah, that's about where I'm at."

"I'm sorry, babes," she says softly.

I look down into my hands. "I have no idea what to do next."

Emma rises from the armchair she's been occupying to plop down next to me on the couch.

"Oh, I do."

I give her a curious look.

She smiles tolerantly and tugs at the end of my hair. "Time for a change," she says with a glint in her eye.

"You know what? You're abso-fucking-lutely right," I agree.

Emma gets back up. "Then let's get this shit show on the road before you have to be back at the club."

* * *

Emma is a genius. Not just about the hair color, as that's really just her knowing how temperamental I am and that changing my hair is often part of my coping with changes in my life. But it also gives me something to do until I have to work. I've never been one to endlessly rehash what went wrong in my relationships, and Emma is respectful of that. I always feel like it makes me wallow longer. Actually doing something, distracting myself so I can just move on, works best for me.

When I show up at the club that night, it's with a new red ombré dye job that flows down from the close-to-natural chocolate color on top to a flaming, bright color at the ends that, in the shifting light, really does resemble flames. It completes my dangerously pissed-off look that matches my mood exactly.

However, I work hard to be as sweet as pie to my team because of it. It's not their fault half of my genetic makeup is from the biggest dirtbag I've ever met. Or that I fell for Dirtbag Junior.

The thought makes me physically ill. I can only assume everything he did from the moment we met was for his boss, to get me to fall for him for whatever advantage they think that gives them.

But then, he fell for me too. I doubt that was part of his plan. Surely being with me is getting in the way of being the coldhearted motherfucker Sal expects him to be, of him doing his job.

I decide it doesn't really matter. Fuck them both.

I physically force myself into the ebb and flow of managing the club to distract myself. Nils somehow manages to completely avoid me, communicating through Ace and Johnny when needed. I try not to pick at that hornet's nest, hoping it'll just fade back into the background. It's not like I hadn't suspected. But even without Julian around, I never would've let anything happen. Hopefully, now that he's professed his love he can realize and accept that it's not going to happen, and it's better for everyone if he just moves on. For now, I'm happy to give him distance, and tonight it doesn't seem to be interfering with anything.

When the band for the night is in full swing and the bar has died down a bit, I find myself with nothing to do but scan the crowd. It's not enough to distract me, and the anger starts to seep through my veins. Aggravated as hell, I go to my office and grab the pack of smokes I keep in my bottom drawer, slipping out of the side entrance. I sink down into my usual spot, lighting up as I look up at the sky, imagining the stars I can't see.

"I knew you'd come out here eventually." The voice cuts through my reverie. I tip my head against the building, holding back tears. Why did I not realize he'd be out here, waiting for me?

With one last, deep drag on the cigarette, I stomp it out under my boot and climb to my feet. I don't even look his way. I simply turn around to go back inside.

"Don't go," Julian pleads, his voice just behind me now. But he doesn't make any move to stop me. He doesn't have to. I'm completely frozen in place. My heart burns with anger, but the part of me that's still his responds to him, still wants to believe there's hope. It's the thing I love and hate most about love: Hope dies last.

"I've got nothing to say to you," I reply, turning to face him. It's as big of a mistake as I knew it'd be. He's right there, towering over me with his tight black T-shirt and jeans, his intensely dark eyes filled with sorrow and longing, smelling like cigarettes, alcohol, and *him*. It makes me clench, but not in the good way. My heart squeezes hard in my chest as the broken pieces work to tear me apart from the inside out.

"Yeah, well, not to sound like a fucking cliché, but I've got a lot to say to you," he pushes, his voice husky and tired.

I laugh, tilting my head up to the heavens. "That's just great," I say to no one in particular. I look back at him evenly. "Fine, talk." I remind myself that I don't give a shit about his explanation. I can tell he sees it in my eyes, but he presses on anyway.

"Yes, we only met because Sal sent me to you, to get information," he offers. "And I still don't know exactly what he wants with you," he pauses, letting me listen for the voice, or in this case, lack thereof, "but I've wanted out for a long time." He stares at me longingly. "Falling in love with you gave me the courage to do what I should've done a long time ago. Because I may have been a stupid kid who fell for his shit all those years ago, but I haven't been that kid for a long time." He looks down at his clenched fists. "So I quit. But I can't stick around, Frankie, or he'll find me. And in case it wasn't obvious, he's not exactly a kiss-and-make-up kinda guy. He's more of a bury-his-problems kinda guy." He lets that sink in before adding, "Literally."

Clearly, Sal is into even worse shit than I thought. But it still doesn't add up. "Why would he want you dead? As long as you're willing to stick around and keep softening me up for him, shouldn't he be happy?" My words are pure venom.

Julian shakes his head, stepping dangerously close despite my obvious anger. "I was never supposed to soften you up," he murmurs, looking down into my eyes. "You softened me up, baby, don't you see? I'm no good to him anymore. I don't want to be any good to him anymore. I just want my own life back. And I want you in it, even though I know I don't deserve you."

Believing him isn't a choice. I have no doubt he means it. He's spoken to me more plainly than he ever has to demonstrate his veracity. But truth and trust are two different things. And how can I possibly trust him when he kept something this big from me?

"No," I agree. "You don't. Goodbye, Julian."

And before the tears can fall, I close my eyes, purposely not subjecting myself to the look on his face as I turn around and go back inside.

Once I'm alone in the hallway, I don't crumble. If anything, seeing him, hearing what he had to say, has given me the closure I needed. I square my shoulders and stand tall as I walk back into the club, putting the whole thing behind me, literally and metaphorically.

* * *

"Yeah, but is it really behind you?" Emma points out the next day as we repeat our coffee and donuts ritual.

"Yes," I reiterate.

"Really?" she presses. "You're just gonna let Sal off Julian for sticking up for you?"

I look over at her skeptically. "If he does, it'll be because Julian refuses to work for him anymore, not because of me."

She shoots me back a cynical look. "Po-tay-to, po-tah-to," she replies. "To-may-to, guy-who-loves-you-standing-up-to-a-killer-so-he-can-be-with-you."

I shoot her a dirty look. "What, you think I should go order around a guy who apparently kills people he doesn't like anymore?"

Emma waves her hand dismissively. "He's not gonna hurt you — you're his daughter. Plus, regardless, it sounds like he needs you, for whatever reason. I mean, he's gone to a hell of a lot of trouble to learn about you, to get in with you."

I think about that. "You're right. I have the leverage to save Julian's ass," I realize.

"Exactly," she says firmly. "So what are you waiting for?" I shoot her a sharp look. "Okay, bad assumption that you actually want to help him. You obviously don't. Forget I said anything."

With a sigh, I shake my head. "You're not wrong. He did ask Sal to leave me alone. And I do want to tell Sal that I know what he's up to, and that he's not going to manipulate me into working for him. While I'm at it, I might as well ask him to leave Julian alone. You know, out of respect for whatever feelings we had for each other."

Emma rolls her eyes. "Oh, please, Frankie."

"Oh, please, what?" I snap.

"I want you to say these words out loud," she directs. I glare a warning at her but let her go on. "'I no longer have feelings for Julian.'" I open my mouth to protest. "Say it!"

I scrunch my face at her. "I no longer have feelings for Julian." *Lie.* "You're a bitch, Emma."

She cackles evilly. "I know. It's why you love me." She gets up and grabs my coffee mug, bringing it with her to the kitchen to refill. When she comes back and hands me the cup, she picks my phone up off the table in front of me and hands it to me as well. "You love him. You may not be willing to take him back, but you're gonna hate yourself if you don't do something."

Ugh. Well, lord knows I can't say she's wrong. After all, I know I'd be lying.

* * *

I meet Sal the next afternoon at the Italian restaurant. I picked it because it was in public, but if I'm being honest with myself, the thought of eating that gnocchi again is pretty appealing too. And definitely mitigates the steaming pile of shit I'm about to step into.

Like before, he's waiting for me at a table in the back. I dressed for the occasion, in fitted jeans and a black blazer over my red shirt to conceal the gun at my back. Just in case. After practicing with Mac all morning, I'm ready for anything. Thankfully, Mac didn't ask about my sudden, intense need to practice, and I sure as hell didn't offer anything up. In any case, as I approach Sal, I feel confident.

He stands to greet me, opening his arms for a hug. I stop and give him my best "you've got to be fucking kidding me" look. It's my opening salvo that all's not well.

"Or not," he says as I take a seat at the table. He slides back into his chair. "Everything all right? You seem a little out of sorts, doll."

His response answers the only question I had; whether he was aware I heard everything that day. Clearly, he's not. I don't waste time enlightening him.

"Well, when I found out my boyfriend's just some hired muscle sent by my dad in an elaborate ploy to get me to do God only knows what, I get a little tetchy," I snipe.

Whatever he was expecting to hear, it clearly wasn't that. He only raises his eyebrows for a moment, quickly working to wipe the surprise from his face.

"I knew that kid was a rat," he laughs, shaking his head.

"He's not," I counter. "Not that he's in my good graces, either. But for what it's worth, I overheard you at his apartment on Thursday."

"Ah," Sal responds curtly. "That."

"Yes," I reply hotly. "That."

Sal spreads his hands over the checkered tablecloth. "So you came here today to do what, exactly?" He looks at me, and it's the first time I notice that his eyes are the same shade of blue as mine. It makes me sad.

"If any harm comes to Julian, you'll never see me again, much less get me to work for you," I promise carefully. Not mentioning I have zero intention of ever doing either.

"That a fact?" Sal asks nonchalantly, leaning back. He pulls his hands back into his lap and looks up at me again. "What if I told you if you don't come work for me, he'll be the first to pay, but definitely not the last?"

I've been threatened before. I'm not easily intimidated, and I expected something of the sort from him. But the absolute casualness of his manner, how easily the words roll off his tongue disturbs me on a level that makes my blood run cold.

"You really think threatening me is going to help? Do I seem like the kind of person who bows to threats?" I reply.

"Don't make them if you can't take them," he replies with a smile, crossing his legs. "And sure as hell don't make threats you aren't capable of following through on."

I stare back at him impassively. "I don't think you'll risk it. You need me." I probably shouldn't be so sure of myself, but for some reason I am. Habit maybe? Whatever the reason, I somehow sense I'm running out of luck at getting away with being so cocky. Not that I've ever been very good at learning my lesson.

"What gives you that impression?" he asks, arching an eyebrow.

"Really? That's how you're gonna play this?" I ask with a laugh. "You've gone to lengths to dig up dirt on me. But I bet even you didn't realize how much you'd hit the jackpot until you found out about my ability.

181

And the fact that you're willing to threaten to harm people I care about to get me to do what you want …" I let my words hang in the air.

Sal leans forward, dropping his voice. "You're a smart cookie, but there's something I know that you don't." I look at him quizzically and he gives me a leering grin. "There's nobody I care about more than me. You, on the other hand, well, there's lots of people you care about. People you don't want to see hurt. Your boyfriend. Your mother. Your grandmother." He pauses. "Your brother. He's a sweet kid, that Tony. You wouldn't want anything to happen to him, would you?"

"You bastard." The words slip out of my mouth before I can stop them. My heart pounds in my ears, and I'm practically seeing red. How *dare* he threaten my family.

Sal chuckles. "Technically, you're the bastard here," he points out. "But yes, I know I'm an asshole. Don't take it personally. I'm just doing what I've gotta do to survive, doll."

My eyes flick around the restaurant. We've been quiet enough to escape notice, but the place is packed. The urge to punch the fucker in his smug mug fades as the sea of faces around me come into focus. No need to make a scene.

I rise, trying to quell the shaking in my limbs to no avail. "Stay away from me. Stay away from my family."

"Not gonna happen, doll. You'll see. One way or the other, you'll see." He almost looks regretful. I shake my head and walk away. No. I don't know what the expression on his face was, but it wasn't that. He's a monster. And monsters don't feel regret.

* * *

I sit in my car, shaking with anger for a solid hour before I decide that there's only one person I can talk to. One person who was there at the beginning, who will listen without judgment, and who might be able to tell me what to do.

I drive carefully to my mother's house, still unsure if I should be driving in my state. I can't shake the anger, but it's abating enough so I can feel what's under it: fear. When I park in the blessedly empty driveway, I realize I need to call Nils. It's already past the time I'd normally be at the club on a Saturday, and I'm not sure when, or if, I'll make it. He's more curt than usual, but thankfully he's still his generally composed self, assuring me that he'll take care of everything.

I take a deep breath, put my gun in the glove compartment, lock it, and get out of the car, thankful at least that my mother isn't here. It takes Nonna a minute to answer the door after I knock.

"Frankie," she greets me, clearly surprised. She steps back, gesturing for me to come in. "Everything okay, dear? Shouldn't you be at the club right now?"

I put my keys on the table by the door, taking the few steps into the living room. I stare at the couch, too nervous to sit down. Nonna comes up alongside me, laying her hand on my arm. I turn to face her, trying like hell to stay calm.

"No, Nonna, everything is not okay," I reply, struggling to keep control. "Mom was right about Sal."

Nonna's weathered face hardens. "What did he do, Francesca?"

I bury my face in my shaking hands. Nonna only calls me by my first name when things are serious. And it's exactly why I came to her. Because I knew she'd take me seriously. But hearing her call me that drives home exactly how bad this situation really is.

"I don't know how to tell you this, Nonna, but Sal is beyond bad news," I hedge, realizing this may be harder to explain than I thought.

Nonna shakes her head. "There isn't anything you can tell me about Salvatore Moretti that I don't already know, dear. So out with it," she directs sternly.

"He's been trying to get me to work for him. He was threatening someone I care about. And tonight, I went to meet him, to get him to back off. And he threatened all of you," I say. "Mom. You. Even Tony. I don't know what to do, Nonna."

Nonna looks back at me in horror.

"What exactly did he say?" The controlled anger in my mother's quiet voice rips across the living room. I look up in surprise.

"But your car —"

"Is in the shop. What did the bastard say, Francesca?" my mother demands again, her eyes full of quiet fury.

I know it's pointless to keep the truth from her. Not that she's ever given me the same consideration. But I tell her anyway.

"That he has nothing to lose, but I do. And I'll lose all of you if I don't do what he wants from me," I admit.

My mother is terrifying under normal circumstances, but her small frame seems to swell with the rage that emanates from her. "And what, pray tell, does he want from *you*?"

I'm too shaken to be overly disturbed by the implication. "I don't know," I admit. Then, with a cringe, I tell her the worst of it. "But he knows about my ability."

"You *told* him?" she rages at me. All the years she lectured me to keep my gift hidden, all the times she tanned my hide when I let even the idea of it peep through around anyone who wasn't family comes rushing back to me.

It snaps me out of my fear. "Of course not," I return hotly. "I don't know how he knew."

"I know," a small voice says from behind my mother.

Mom whirls around to reveal Tony cowering in the hallway. "I saw him outside with the big man. He said he was your dad. That his dad knew things too. I thought that's where you got it."

My mother's jaw practically hits the floor. "He saw you? He *talked to you?* When?" she demands. Tony shrinks against the wall under her fury. In my concern for him, I still register that Julian was here with Sal, doing God knows what. So Sal clearly knows where they live and what Tony looks like. This is so much worse than I'd even imagined.

"On Monday, I came back for a book I forgot, and he was leaving," Tony squeaks. "I'm sorry, Ma, I didn't want you to get mad that I left school, so I didn't tell you."

Nonna looks between me and my mother. "Let's all try to calm down. That man has always had a big mouth and little to back it up," she says as soothingly as she can. But one look from my mother shuts her down.

My mother looks at me, and I can see the calculating malice behind her eyes. "Stay here," she directs to no one in particular. With that she heads to the door, snatching my car keys from the table.

"Hey!" I protest, bolting through the door after her. But she's too fast. In a flash, she's started my car and is pulling out of the driveway. I chase her halfway down the street before she's out of sight. Winded and out of my mind, I drop to the ground. Once again, I can think of only one person to turn to at this moment.

Chapter 25 — Julian

I sit in the dark, the soft clicking noises of the engine cooling breaking the quiet of evening suburbia. My eyes flick back and forth between the road and Frankie's mom's house as I consider the events of the day and how fucking messed up Frankie was after leaving that restaurant.

It's a place I've been a thousand times, so I know exactly who she was talking to. And what the motherfucker must've said to her to make her look as upset as she was. There's nothing Sal wouldn't do to have power over his enemies. And if you're not his friend, you're his enemy. He's got a lot of them these days.

I know I shouldn't be here. Still in L.A. I should've hit the fucking road after Frankie made it clear she wanted nothing to do with me. But the primal energy that has existed between us since day one, the underlying thread that binds us together, that led to us falling for each other, won't let me walk away from her. Even if I know some serious shit is about to hit the fan. Or, perhaps, especially because of it.

So I'm not surprised when shortly after Frankie goes into the house, her mother comes tearing out, hops in the convertible, and peels off with Frankie herself hot on her heels. And when the convertible outruns her and Frankie drops to her knees in the middle of the street, I'm out of my car before I know what I'm doing.

As I get closer, I can hear her panicked breathing as she scrambles to type something on her phone. But she's shaking so fucking badly it drops out of her hands onto the asphalt.

I reach down and snatch it up, offering it to her. As she takes it from my hand, her eyes flick up to meet mine. Deep, sad pools of stormy blue stare at me, confused.

"How ...?"

I shrug, offering her my other hand to help her up. "I knew this wasn't over," I say softly.

She brushes off my hand, hauling herself to her feet.

"No, I meant, how did you show up just as I was trying to text you?" she clarifies.

I raise an eyebrow. "Same answer," I reply.

She looks at me, clearly mystified before shaking her head. "Whatever. You have your car, right?"

I hook a thumb back over my shoulder, pointing out the sedan parked under the dark cover of a tree just down the road. The door is probably even still open.

"Good," she says grimly. "Because we're going after her."

She marches off toward the car and I haul ass to keep up with her.

"Where's your mom going in such a hurry?" I ask as I get ahead of her in time to open the passenger door.

"I have my suspicions, but I don't know how she plans to find him," she says sadly as she gets in.

Once I've gotten in on the driver's side, I grip the steering wheel as I absorb what's happening. "Your mother is going after Sal."

It's not a question.

"Pretty sure."

"He threatened you."

Still not a question.

"Yes. And everyone I love," she says softly, her eyes flicking to meet mine. And I know she's including me in that. Reminding me once again that I'm the biggest fucking asshole on the planet for hurting her.

"Heaven help him when she finds him," I mutter, starting the car. "I know his usual haunts, I'll start —"

"This will tell me where she is," she interrupts, holding up her phone.

"How's that?"

She opens it, selecting an app and punching in a code. "I set it up so I could track the car if it was stolen."

A smile tugs at my lips. This chick.

"You sure you want to do this?"

She looks at me apprehensively. "No. But it's my fault. I've got to stop her from getting hurt. He's dangerous."

I take a deep breath, not sure that putting ourselves between those two is a good idea. But it's past time this all ended, and it might turn into the exact opportunity I need. "Tell me where to go."

She gives me directions, not speaking otherwise. The tension is unbearable.

Finally, we pull up to a building I know all too fucking well. Frankie's car is parked just up the street.

"What is this place?" Frankie asks at the look of recognition on my face.

"Sal's apartment," I reply shortly, parking in a spot across the street.

I pull my 9mm out of the holster under my left arm and check the clip.

"You got another one of those?" she asks. "Mine was in the car, and I can't get it without the key."

I raise an eyebrow at her but say nothing. I reach down under my pantleg and grab the .38 Special that's concealed there. When I hand it to her, she frowns.

"Sure, give me the girl gun," she mumbles, checking the cylinder.

"If you don't want it, give it the fuck back," I tease.

She rolls her eyes and gets out of the car, shoving the gun in the back waistband of her jeans.

"That's a good way to shoot yourself in the ass," I murmur, following her out. But she's already jogging across the street. "Fuck, wait up."

She stops on the sidewalk, letting me catch up. "Look, I only needed you to bring me here and tell me what I should expect going in there. Beyond that, you should just wait out here. I only went to Sal in the first place to save your ass. If he shoots you now it was a complete waste."

I look her up and down. She's tough, but she's no match for what's probably going on up there.

"I know Sal. It was a complete fucking waste anyway."

She scrunches her face angrily, and I know she knows I'm right.

"Just tell me where to go," she demands.

I roll my eyes and hold the front door open for her.

"Fourth floor. Second door on the right. He's just as dangerous as you think he is, so I'm going in first," I insist as she waltzes past me.

She stands in the rundown lobby looking around. "We'll see. No elevator?"

I smirk as I stride by her toward the stairs. "No such luck, princess," I reply, taking the stairs two at a time as she struggles to keep up.

When we get to the fourth floor, I give her a minute to catch her breath. Putting my finger to my lips, I start down the hall, but she grabs my hand. I turn back and she's looking up at me. Her expression is raw and vulnerable. "Thank you," she whispers. "For being here with me."

It fucking guts me, and I can't help myself. I push her into the wall, lifting her up by her soft, beautiful ass as I bend down to kiss her. I don't have time for gentle, or long. It's rough and short, and she tastes like fucking heaven, as usual. I let her go before she has time to protest, taking her by the hand and leading her down the hall. But before we can get two steps, a muffled bang reverberates from behind the door just ahead.

"Mom!" Frankie shrieks, diving for the door. It springs open at her touch, and even though I clamber to catch her before she runs in there, she somehow slips through my fingers. Pulling out my gun, I barrel after her in time to tumble into Sal's empty living room.

She goes to scream again, and I wrap a hand around her mouth from behind. I bring the tip of the gun to my lips to tell her to keep fucking quiet.

When she nods, I let her go and point with my free hand at the half-closed bedroom door.

It's been only seconds since the bang, but it feels like hours as we slowly approach and my heart hammers in my ears. Holding the gun up, I use my foot to swing the bedroom door open quietly as Frankie clings to my back.

The sight that greets me isn't pretty. Frankie's mom is looking down at her phone as she stands at the foot of the bed. The bed Sal is lying on, dead from what appears to be a gunshot wound straight through his motherfucking heart. I can feel Frankie peeping around me. When she sees that her mother is okay, she rushes out from behind me.

"Mom," she cries again, heading toward her mother.

Samantha looks up in surprise, starting to reach for the gun lying on the bed in front of her when she realizes who it is. Frankie crashes into her, wrapping her arms around her, and I lower my gun.

"You're okay," she sobs.

Samantha pushes Frankie off of her. "I'm fine," she says shortly. But when her gaze slips over Frankie's shoulder and locks with mine, she dives for the gun. Instinctively, I raise mine.

In seconds flat, she's shoved Frankie aside and has her sights set on me. Frankie looks at her in horror.

"Drop your gun," Samantha demands.

"You first," I respond.

"Both of you, stop it, now," Frankie commands.

"Be quiet, you stupid girl," her mother seethes. "This brute works for the bastard that just tried to kill me."

"*Worked* for," I stress. "And looks to me like you came here looking for a fight. And won."

"Julian!" Frankie gasps.

Samantha sighs. "I'm not going to even ask how you know this thug, Francesca. But for once in your life, do as I say and stay out of this."

"Mom, come on, put your gun down. Julian is not going to shoot you," Frankie presses.

"That's right, Samantha," I agree. "Unless you try to shoot me first. Like you did with our old pal, Sal, there."

"It was self-defense," she hisses through her teeth.

"Tell that to the pillow with the bullet hole through it," I point out.

In my peripheral vision I see Frankie's mouth drop open in horror as she finally looks around at the evidence. Clearly there was a fight here. Things are knocked over, and the bed is a mess. But the bloodied lamp lying on the floor matches a lump on Sal's balding, greasy head. And the pillow was clearly used to muffle the sound of the shot that killed the poor, likely unconscious bastard.

"Aren't you happy he's dead? If you tried to quit, surely he was about to kill you anyway?" Samantha replies drily.

I shake my head ever so slightly, so as not to take my eyes off of her. "I'd be happy, except you plan to kill me anyway," I respond.

"No," Frankie pipes up, finally finding her voice again. "Nobody else has to die tonight. Mom, please."

"Shut up!" Samantha screams at her daughter, finally losing her cool. "You know *nothing*, Francesca. Nothing about what I've had to do to keep you and your brother safe. He has to die. He knows too much. You can't trust him. Our family isn't safe while he's still alive." Samantha's knuckles are turning white, and I want to caution Frankie to back off of her, to not push her too far in her current state. She's only beginning to see what her mother is capable of.

But Frankie always surprises me. She steps between us, backing up with her hand extended to me, silently begging me to stand down. I lower my gun. There's no fucking way I could ever keep it up with Frankie in my line of sight.

"You want to talk about family? About feeling safe?" Frankie asks. Though I know she's crying, she amazingly sounds perfectly calm. Her mother's aim falters ever so slightly, trying to find a way around her daughter. "I've never felt more loved, more accepted for who I am than he's made me feel. He's acted more like family to me than you ever have."

My heart twists in my chest. Because I feel the exact same way. I reach out for the hand Frankie is still offering and squeeze it tightly. Her return squeeze gives me the first ray of hope I've felt since we walked into this mess.

Samantha looks utterly fucking horrified. "You're making a huge mistake," she spits at her daughter. "And I'm going to fix it for you." She steps to the side to retrain her gun on me, but Frankie anticipates it.

She drops my hand, grabs the gun at her back, and steps in time with her mother all in one movement. And when she's done, I'm not the one pointing a gun at Samantha Greco anymore — Frankie is.

"Don't do this, Mom," Frankie begs.

Samantha lowers her gun, but it doesn't make me any fucking less alert. "Frankie," she says softly, almost lovingly.

Frankie starts to lower the .38. But it's all a trap. Sensing her weakness, Samantha quickly raises her arm, retraining her aim at me in an instant. Before I can even register what's happening, I hear the shot. I close my eyes, so I don't have to see the look on Frankie's gorgeous face when I die.

But the hot sting of a bullet entering me never comes. A low moan comes from across the room and my eyes fly open. Bright red blood blossoms over Samantha's crisp white shirt right over her heart. As the life leaves her, her face freezes in an expression of betrayal and anger. Her body slumps to the floor and the gun in Frankie's hands slips. I grab it from her before she can drop it, turning her to cradle her against my chest.

"Don't look, baby," I mutter into her hair. "Just don't look."

Frankie melts into me, her hands balling into fists over my shirt. She looks up at me, terrified.

"What have I done?" she asks as a sob rips out of her.

And even now, with almost all of the secrets I'd been keeping from her laid out on the table, I still don't have the heart to tell her the worst one of all. The one that wasn't my secret in the first place. That her mother stopped one crime boss tonight. But Frankie stopped the other.

Chapter 26 — Frankie

I hear sirens. They're coming for me. Good. I'm a monster, I should be put away. I murdered my mother. Strong hands hold me up, but everything else blinks in and out as I struggle to wrap my head around what just happened. She was going to kill Julian. I had to. I had to. I had to.

"Shhhh. Yes, you had to," Julian whispers.

I blink up at him. Was I saying it out loud?

Crashing. More loud noises. Police officers. Julian in handcuffs. Someone ushering me out of the room, telling me not to look at all the blood. Not to look at the bodies. *The bodies. Oh, God.* I fall to my knees and vomit. Cool hands hold back my hair, stroke my back.

I wipe my mouth and look up in time to see Julian being dragged away by two burly cops.

"No," I cry, reaching for him. I need him. Who else is strong enough to hold me together? I'm falling apart. Bring him back. But I can't make any more words come over the wretched sobs.

The female officer beside me motions for the men to stop. Julian drags himself across the room to me. Drops to his knees for me.

His warm lips press against my forehead. Yes. He's my glue. Please don't take him away.

"I promise everything will be okay," he whispers. "The worst part is over."

I look up at him, shaking my head, still unable to speak. *No. The worst has only just begun.* The fresh hell I'll live in forever. I killed my mother. What have I done?

Murmurs in the room. "Samantha Greco ... her daughter ..." Fear. Of me? I don't think so. I don't understand.

Blink, blink. I'm in the back of a police car. No handcuffs, just cold leather on my cheek.

Blink, blink. I'm in a room. All by myself. Yes, stay away from the murderer.

Blink, blink. Weathered hands hold mine. "Frankie," Nonna whispers lovingly. I shake violently. *No. I killed her. I killed your daughter. Don't love me.*

Blink, blink. I'm holding my knees against my chest. No more tears. Just pain. I hear Nonna ask me something. Just leave me alone. Lock me up. Go away. I put my hands over my ears.

Blink, blink. Warm, rough hands. Familiar. *Him.* "Frankie," he whispers. My fractured mind won't let me answer. "Take these." Cold, smooth. He puts the pills on my lips. "Please, for me." I open my mouth. *Only for you.*

* * *

A voice pulls me from unconsciousness. My mouth is dry, so I dart my tongue around, trying to moisten it. My eyelids are heavy, but I push against the weight. It's so bright.

A hand slides over mine, giving me a reassuring squeeze. "Slowly," someone whispers.

I blink until my eyes adjust, my tongue flicking again, this time to wet my lips. "Where am I?" My voice sounds like I ate sandpaper.

"You're still at the police station, dear," the voice says louder. I realize it's Nonna. And it all comes flooding back.

I snap upright. "Oh, God," I croak. "Mom."

Nonna snaps her fingers in front of me. "Look at me," she commands. I've never heard her so stern. It grabs my attention away from the panic that's starting to overwhelm me. "There's a lot you need to know, but not just yet. Suffice it to say that you've done *nothing* wrong, my dear. Do you understand me?" She looks down at me sharply.

Tears well in my eyes. How can I possibly believe that?

"I'm serious, young lady," she says in a slightly softer tone. "Don't shut down on us again. You're strong. You will get through this."

The truth of her words sinks in, and not just because of the absence of the voice. But because I know that. I am strong. I close my eyes and take a deep breath. When I open my eyes, I turn to her and nod to show her I understand.

"Where's Julian?" I rasp.

Nonna hands me a glass of water that I gulp gratefully. "He's skulking around here somewhere," she replies.

I want to laugh, but it hurts my throat. "How long have I been out?"

"Just the night," she says dismissively. "It's Sunday morning." She glances at her watch. "Quarter of seven."

"Then why do I feel like I haven't had a drink of water for a week?" I ask.

"They gave you something to calm you down. I'd wager it dried you out, too," she replies, offering the glass again. "Drink."

After I've done as she asked, I realize Julian must be free. "They let him go," I gasp.

"They did," she agrees. "Once they got his story, they had nothing to hold him on. He had no gunpowder residue on his hands. You, however ..."

I bury my face in my hands, but she tugs at my arms. "They'll want to speak with you, dear, but there's a good deal you don't know. They want me to wait to tell you until you've given your statement."

"Oh, so suddenly it's fill-in-Frankie time? Why now?" I snap.

Nonna gives me a disapproving look. "Well, I'm glad you seem to be doing better, at least." She sighs. "There were promises I made to your grandfather, and your mother after him, that I'm no longer bound by. But I'm an old fool for not having told you sooner anyway. I'm terribly sorry, Frankie. I hope someday you'll be able to forgive me."

I give her a long, hard look. "I'll let you know after you tell me whatever it is you've apparently conspired to hide from me my whole life."

Nonna presses her lips together, clearly trying not to smile. "Oh, dear. It sounds like my odds of forgiveness are rather low."

Her usual, graceful manner undoes my anger. I can't trust my emotions right now, and the last thing I want to do is make this worse. With a sigh, I swing my legs off the padded bench I'd been laid on. "Let's get this over with and we'll find out," I reply evenly. The motion makes me acutely uncomfortable. "But first, where's the bathroom?"

With a smile, Nonna points to a door in the corner of the room.

I do my business, and when I emerge a policewoman has joined Nonna. She looks at ease, but I don't miss her hand resting on her gun. Their silent stares are unnerving. I swallow hard and brace myself for what comes next.

* * *

I'm not allowed to see anyone else until they're done with me. It takes a full two hours of questions. Well, more like about ten questions, repeated in different ways. Like they're trying to catch me in a lie, or get me to contradict Julian, or even myself. It's exhausting, but, in a way, it's also liberating. As I relive the experience over and over again, I realize that my mother truly left me no choice. The guilt I felt at first has been replaced with extreme sadness, in large part over the relationship I never had with my mother. I find myself completely unable to understand why she did what she did because of it.

So when I'm done with questioning and am released, I'm eager to hear what it is Nonna has to say. When I meet her in the front lobby, I notice Julian hovering in a corner, clearly unsure of what to do.

193

As we leave, I approach him, taking his hand in mine and leading him out behind me.

Apparently, someone recovered my keys, as Nonna hands them to me as soon as we're out of the building. My convertible sits gleaming in the parking lot, my first visual reminder of the night before. With a deep breath, I head toward the car. But Julian's hand tugs against mine.

"You sure?" he asks. I look at him, bemused. "I mean, are you sure you want me to come with you?"

"Yes," I reply succinctly.

He gives me a sideways smile, but still throws a reluctant glance over at Nonna.

I turn around fully, placing myself in front of him.

"You're part of this whole thing," I explain, only touching him through our joined hands. "You have pieces of this story that only you know. And I need to know. I need to understand what's been going on. How long it's been going on. And what it all means. Do you think you can help me with that?"

Julian looks down at me intensely. "Of course," he murmurs. The scent of him washes over me, and I have to work to focus. "I'll tell you anything you want to know."

"Good." And with a determined pull, I drag him to the car. Nonna climbs in too, and we all head back to … well, I guess it's Nonna's house now.

When I pull into the driveway, I realize I haven't seen my brother. "Nonna, where's Tony?" I ask, suddenly anxious.

She lays her hand on my arm as Julian climbs over the side of the car to get out. "He's fine," she assures me. "He's staying with friends for a few days."

I breathe a sigh of relief, and we all head into the house.

Nonna tells me to go shower and change, not having been able to do so since yesterday. I see the wisdom, but I do it as quickly as possible. Unfortunately, the only clothes I have here are from years ago. I slip into the most fashionable thing I can find, a body-hugging blue sweater dress, hoping it's warm enough without leggings.

I emerge into the kitchen to find Julian sitting at the dining table while Nonna puts together some food and drinks. Julian eyes my dress appreciatively. Blushing, I sit down across from him, fidgeting with the hem of the dress as Nonna works. We all continue in the silence I suspect has ruled since I went to shower. After she's laid everything out on the table, she sits with us. We all eat mindlessly for a few minutes.

"Goodness, where should I start?" Nonna muses.

I shrug. "At the beginning."

Nonna shoots me an impatient look and shakes her head. "Have it your way, then." She takes a deep breath. "I suppose it started with your great grandfather. He and his wife immigrated here just before your grandfather was born. They opened a restaurant, but times were troubled then. They banded together with people they knew, other people who owned businesses in the community, to protect each other."

My eyebrows jump. "Protect each other? What does that mean?"

When Julian lays his hand over mine trying to soothe me, I realize it must have come out more shrilly than I intended. But seriously, does that mean what I think it means?

"It means they did what had to be done to make people leave them alone and to find the resources they needed to succeed. These days they call it an organized crime syndicate. And while they were less focused on crime back then, they were, nonetheless, still highly ruthless and ambitious," Nonna explains tightly. "When it was time, your grandfather took his father's place in the organization. Luca, God rest his soul, was an especially heartless man. He wasn't afraid to exploit others for his own gain. Under him, the organization grew in leaps and bounds. He became very powerful. And I'm afraid as your mother grew, she found it all very enticing. She and your grandfather had very similar dispositions." Nonna grimaces, clearly reliving her disappointment.

I wonder, not for the first time, how my gentle, kind grandmother was ever married to a man like that. Different times, I suppose. I stay silent as she goes on, still reeling from the revelation of my dirty family history.

"From a young age, and against my wishes, Luca involved Samantha in almost everything he did. He made sure she had around-the-clock protection because of it. Salvatore Moretti was one of her bodyguards."

Julian's face reflects the shock I'm sure is on my own. Sal didn't exactly seem like the strong protector type. And even the need for a bodyguard says Nonno was into some seriously bad shit. Like, it's-going-to-take-me-a-while-to-fully-wrap-my-head-around-it kind of shit. I shake my head, wondering if I'll ever believe that my mother had this whole other illicit life I knew absolutely nothing about.

"I know," Nonna agrees. "Sal was a little weasel of a man, even then. But he was ambitious. Unfortunately, he wasn't very smart. Before we even knew they were together, she was pregnant. Your grandfather, er, dismissed Sal." She shifts uncomfortably in her chair, and I sense there was a lot more violence in that act than she's comfortable discussing. And definitely more than I'm comfortable hearing about. This whole thing is just bizarre. "We decided it was best if Sal never even knew about you, which your mother was especially adamant about. What we didn't count on was your ability."

She folds her hand over mine. "The very first time you asked about your father, your mother panicked. You were so little. Not even two. She wasn't expecting to have to answer questions that soon, so she said he was dead. When she explained what that meant, you wouldn't accept it. We thought you were simply stubborn. But looking back, it was the first sign. There were no others for a good long while, though."

"So I just went along with it after that?" I ask, puzzled.

Nonna shakes her head. "You never asked again, to my knowledge."

I lean back in my chair with a frown.

"Nonno and Mom didn't run a cleaning business." As the pieces start to come together in my mind, my stomach roils. "They were gangsters." Even saying it is beyond crazy. Though, thinking about it, it fits my mother to a T. Her commanding, stern manner that suffered no dissension. The strange men who would hover in our sphere for a short time only to disappear. Her strange "work" habits. Cleaning business, my ass.

"No, dear," Nonna admits. "Not as such."

Julian snickers. I throw him a sharp look and he snaps up in his chair.

"Sorry, I just ..." he laughs, then claps a hand over his mouth, getting ahold of himself before he continues, "I grew up hearing your mother's name spoken in fear. To think about her daughter being under the impression she cleaned houses or something ..." He struggles again to suppress an ironic laugh.

"Samantha worked very hard to keep that all away from her children," my grandmother replies waspishly. "She'd make an example of anyone who came anywhere near her family. I'm sure you know that."

Julian nods his agreement. "That I knew. But the rest, not really. It explains why Sal was always so determined to take over her territory. He hated her, and your grandfather. He had a fucking party when he died." His eyes snap up to my grandmother. "Sorry, ma'am."

Nonna rolls her eyes. "Don't be, I had my own party."

Julian's eyes go wide. I look at Nonna and we both start laughing. "Nonno was horrible," I explain to Julian. "Only mom was sad when he died." I don't feel the least bit bad saying it, though it's always been an unspoken understanding between my grandmother and me. The man was a complete terror, and it only got worse the older he got.

Though a lot of that makes more sense now. And I suddenly realize I don't feel much different about my mother's death than I did his. It makes me wonder how Nonna feels about it.

"How are you doing?" I ask her. "She was your daughter."

"And yet my relationship with her was no less complicated than yours," she sighs. "Perhaps even more so. I loved her dearly, of course. What mother doesn't love their child? But I prayed every night for her to step away from that life. Or for her to find someone who cared enough for her to help soften her edges." She looks meaningfully between Julian and me. A brief ache rolls through me, but I push it down. Whatever we are, or aren't, it can wait. "But she craved power. And that's a neverending cycle that only leads to self-destruction. I'm just sorry her end involved you like it did." Nonna's eyes fill with tears, but she quickly wipes them away.

I reach over and wrap my hand around hers. "I'm sorry for all of us," I agree. "But I'm glad I know now. It explains so much about our relationship, about my childhood. I just wish it hadn't ended like this."

"No, child," she assures me. "This is just another beginning." She rises from the table, clearly done with her story as she starts to tidy the empty plates. I'm sure I'll have more questions for her once I really start to absorb all of this, but for now I have other questions.

I glance over at Julian, who is leaned back in his chair with his arms crossed over his massive chest, quietly contemplating all that's been said.

"Walk with me?" I ask, standing up and offering a hand.

He takes it, rising to tower over me. "Sure." His voice is subdued, and he follows me quietly out the door.

We walk, hand in hand, in the cool November evening. I lead him to my park, and we sit down side by side on the bench I'd sleep on as a child.

"This is the place, isn't it?" he asks, running his hands over the weathered boards.

"Yep," I reply.

We're silent for a few minutes. I'm unsure of how to begin. Because this could be the end. Or not.

"Do you remember how hot and cold I was when we first started talking?" he finally asks.

I laugh sharply. "How could I forget?" I look over at him. "It wasn't that long ago, really." He's staring up at the sky, his arms splayed out on the back of the bench.

"I was only supposed to stake you out. Ask a few questions. Sniff around. See what your deal was. I wasn't supposed to get close," he explains. "But it was impossible to resist you. Even now, whenever I'm near you, you're like a star. You have gravity I can't seem to escape."

"But you wanted to?" I ask.

He shakes his head. "No," he replies flatly. "If we'd met under any other circumstances, I'd have tried to get you in bed that first night. But I was working. And Sal made it perfectly clear I wasn't to touch you."

"Except you did. A lot," I recall with a smile.

He turns his burning gaze on me. And despite the heaviness of the conversation, I can still feel it. The gravitational pull. That unshakable, deep-seated attraction I've never felt with anyone but him.

"Yeah. And it was fucking torture," he admits. "Knowing I shouldn't. Then being told not to. Then giving in anyway. Back and forth. It drove me nuts. I imagine it was even worse for you."

I give him an appraising look. "You're underestimating your appeal," I tease. "But yes, it was confusing, to say the least. And then awful, once I knew you were still holding something back." I heave a sigh. "I never imagined it was this huge."

Julian leans forward, staring at his fingers as he works them between his knees. "I'd say it was dangerous for me to tell you. To drag you into that world. But it was just selfishness. I didn't want to lose you," he admits. "And then I did anyway."

"You didn't," I correct him.

"Oh, yeah? What about that whole schtick where you told me to fuck off and agreed that I didn't deserve you?"

I shrug. "I'm an enigma."

Julian laughs. "That you are."

"What do you think Sal wanted with me?"

Julian doesn't seem surprised by the abrupt change. I'm sure he was expecting the question at some point.

"His organization was dying. You were the last play he had against your mother. Beyond that I'm not sure exactly *how* he planned on using you in that game. I'm not sure he even knew. He was just desperate, and like your grandma said, he just wasn't smart enough to pull it off. Not effectively going up against both you and your mother."

"So what happens to you now?"

"What do you mean?" he asks with a furrowed brow.

"Are you still in danger?" I ask, hoping some good may have come from all of this.

"No," he breathes out. "What little was left of Sal's organization will dissolve, or reorganize, or whatever. But my obligations died with him. Nobody will care what I do now. I'm a free man."

I try to understand the life he's lived. An abused foster child turned runaway turned lackey in a criminal organization. The things he's done. And I realize I can't. It's the world my mother shielded me from. Not that I ended up any less fucked up for it.

"What about you? What happens to you now?" he asks softly.

"The sad truth is, I don't know if this really changes my life much," I admit. "Learning that I had a father made me question everything. But at some point, I remembered I am who I am. My past may have shaped me, but I choose what my life is now. And as huge as this has all been, knowing what was really going on that whole time doesn't change what I want to do. I want to keep running my club. Maybe even expand someday. See where it all takes me."

"If I haven't lost you, does that mean I get to come along for the ride?" he teases with a smile.

I look at him analytically. "I don't know. Let me check one thing. Tell me you don't love me."

He looks at me like I'm nuts. "I don't love you."

Lie.

I grin widely. The voice is still there. And Julian still loves me. Despite everything we've been through, or perhaps because of it, the knowledge makes my heart soar. "I might keep you."

He turns toward me, hooking one of his legs behind my back and pulling me into his arms. He stares down into my eyes and strokes a thumb down my cheek.

"Good. Because I'm going to be your fucking shadow, baby." He leans in and kisses my earlobe. "I'm going to be with you as long as you'll have me." His mouth moves down, and he kisses my jaw. "I'm going to love you with everything I've got." His fingers tilt my chin up and he kisses my neck. "I'm going to pleasure you in ways you never even dreamed possible, then I'm going to wait on you hand and foot until you recover enough for me to do it all over again." He kisses my collarbone. "Every. Fucking. Day." He nuzzles into my neck, pulling me tight to his chest.

I close my eyes and breathe deeply of his scent. His words, his lips, his arms around me, it all penetrates the shield I've had around myself today. Oh, who am I kidding? I've always had that shield around me. I needed it to deal with my ability, and then to get through this ordeal.

But I have him now. And with everything we've been through, I can't imagine what could shake us. I love him. Body and soul. Despite his holding back the awful truth. Or maybe because he loved me so much, he couldn't bear to have it separate us. But it wasn't of his making, ultimately, and I can't say I'd have done anything differently in his shoes. So there's absolutely nothing left to hold me back.

I realize suddenly what my ability has been trying to show me all along. People lie for all kinds of reasons, but all those lies fall into one of two categories: selfish lies and unselfish lies. Julian's have all been the latter, the ones I don't need to worry about. He'll always be there for me, to protect me, to love me, to drive me fucking crazy for better or for worse.

"I think I can live with that," I reply casually. "I have just one condition."

Julian laughs. "Oh, yeah? What's that?"

"Lots of dirty talk," I reply with a grin.

Julian looks up at me with a predatory glint in his eye. "Are you trying to get me to fuck you on this bench?" he asks huskily.

A shiver rolls up my spine and I bite my bottom lip. His eyes zero in on it.

"No. I'm trying to get you to tell me *how* you'd fuck me on this bench," I tease.

Julian goes still and I don't even have to look to know he's hard as a rock. And I'm just as ready for him. And I know deep down, I'll always be this ready for him.

I'll always be his. And he'll always be mine.

THE END...FOR NOW

TO FIND OUT WHAT BECOMES OF FRANKIE AND JULIAN, GET *AFTER THE LIES*, A SHORT STORY AVAILABLE EXCLUSIVELY BY SIGNING UP FOR MY NEWSLETTER AT:
https://mailchi.mp/melanieasmithauthor/signup

A Note from the Author

If you enjoyed this book, I would greatly appreciate if you would take a few moments to leave a review, even if it's just a sentence or two saying that you like the book and why. Reviews are valuable feedback that let both the author and other readers know that the book is an enjoyable read. When you leave a positive review it also lets the vendor know that the book is worth promoting, as the more reviews a book receives, the more they will recommend it to other readers. Regardless, thank you for reading this book, and for your support!

Acknowledgements

First, always, a huge thank you to my husband for his support on every possible level. After being married nearly a decade, I know he didn't originally sign on for this, and I'll be nominating him for sainthood soon with his unending patience and bringing of the sugar and caffeine that fuel my marathon writing sessions. Not to mention distracting our mini-me, which is no small task.

Next, to the amazing and talented Jenny Gardner, editor, friend, and all-around woman extraordinaire. I love going through this journey with you, and you've been not only one of the best sources of support but also taught me so much through this process. Here's to almost twenty-one years of amazing friendship, may we have at least that many more!

A huge thanks to my fabulous beta readers, who are also both amazing authors — Lindsey Powell and Katie J. Douglas. Check out their books, y'all, you won't be disappointed!

Also, I don't know if I've ever included this in my acknowledgements before, but I must mention that I wouldn't be anywhere without the saving grace of God. Being a fairly private person, I'm not exactly vocal about my faith, but through writing this I've oddly felt His presence calming me through my less confident moments. Proof that you can write smut and still love Jesus. Just sayin'.

And, as always, a huge thank you to everyone who buys, reads, and/or reviews my books. It's my biggest goal and pleasure to share my stories with those who will enjoy them, and your support means the world to me!

Want more? Check out Melanie A. Smith's romantic suspense series, starting with…

The Safeguarded Heart

Read on for a sneak peek!

Prologue

The threat of imminent death fills my senses, my brain clouded with pain and terror. I can't help but wonder if, knowing where it would lead, I would do anything differently. Knowing myself, likely not. My stubbornness knows no bounds, and my natural ability to persevere is what got me here in the first place.

In any case I know it's pointless to speculate, and this journey has been ten years in the making. And just as it seems like it will end in suffering and horror, so did it start, when I was only nineteen years old and broken to my core. My mind tears through memories, struggling to make sense of it all, taking me back to the time when, the pain of loss fresh once again, I turned to my grandparents. Remembering how they took me in and gave me comfort, wisdom, and direction as I climbed out of my pit of despair to finish my business degree.

My grandfather, especially, gave me so much more. His cheerful, round, and wrinkled face flashes across my memory, and warmth spreads through me, my emotions mixing in a confusing swirl. A wealthy real estate tycoon since well before I was born, Grandpa was also a patient teacher. At his side I learned about the power of cash flow, how to negotiate from a position of strength with the simple ability to say "no" and mean it, and how to build a team that would start me down the same path he had walked more than four decades ago.

I made my fair share of mistakes in those early years, and he was there to see me through them all. Those small defeats had pushed me to grow, to adapt, and at the time had seemed like natural discomforts that I needed to endure to find my way. But looking back at the costs, I lament my thick skin, my acceptance of what "came with the territory."

Because, as the moment of my demise approaches, I realize with startling clarity that the real estate business, with its many facets and complexities, is ultimately about people. It's so easy to forget, amid the drive to succeed, that people's lives are in your hands.

My strength has always been in facts and figures, the bones on which the industry operates and grows. Learning how to handle people was always the most difficult part for me. So I used the same tactic I'd applied to everything else. I compartmentalized, quantified, and planned for it. Emotion and empathy were enemies to reason and logic.

And I realize only now that approach was an illusion. A coping mechanism for my ruined ability to care deeply. To trust. To love. Perhaps the lack of those abilities is what led me here.

But that wasn't something my grandfather could teach me, and I had to learn this lesson myself.

And while my grandfather lived to proudly see me start my own business at twenty-five, I'm suddenly thankful he wasn't here to see me learn this lesson too late.

My gut wrenches at the thought of his disappointment. And at the thought of disappointing my nearly four dozen employees, who helped me build a full-service real estate investing support company. It was a niche I'd long hoped to carve, and it had just begun to bear real fruit.

As if it were a sign, in early February on nearly the anniversary of my grandfather's passing, we acquired two new major clients: The first, a large company looking for centralized property management. The second, another young but rising company that had moved into the Seattle area from San Francisco only a couple of months prior.

But nothing could have prepared me for what came next. For meeting Alessandro Giordano, the company's owner. Unspeakably handsome, with a thick Italian accent and a disarmingly charming demeanor. At least, at first.

As past events continue to spin through my frantic brain, I can't help but try to cling to the memories of those early months. The countless meetings, site visits, and rejected proposals that often brought us head-to-head in heated exchanges about almost everything. He is one of the most challenging people I've ever met. As stubborn and intelligent as he is handsome.

I remember, also, shutting down his flirtations from the start, noticing the appreciative glances from nearly every female in the office, and how frequently he returned them. It was clear from the beginning that he was a man who lusted voraciously after what he wanted and was used to getting it. I overestimated my ability to keep that part of me shut down. Or perhaps I merely underestimated his persistence.

Tears fill my eyes, and I wonder if I'll have another chance to tell him how I feel one last time. And that I forgive him.

Chapter 1

As I ride the elevator up to my company's suite on the 30th floor, I breathe deeply, steeling myself for another challenging day. Another day of arguing with Buone Case, with Alessandro Giordano. I can't decide if I'm exhausted or thrilled by the prospect. Probably a bit of both. But, as it's Friday, there is a light at the end of the tunnel.

The elevator doors open, and I get the same small thrill I do every morning to see my company's name, Evans Realty Services, over the entryway of our reception area.

Though it's well before her usual start time, our receptionist, Lucy Drummond, has already arrived. Just, from the looks of it, as she removes her coat and starts her computer.

"Good morning, Lucy," I offer as I enter.

She looks up, momentarily surprised, her dark eyes jumping to meet mine. "Oh, Ms. Evans," she responds, "good morning. I didn't hear the elevator."

I smile warmly. "Sorry if I startled you," I apologize. "Why are you in so early?"

"I have to leave after lunch for a doctor's appointment," she explains, then adds in a dry tone, "Don't worry, there will be someone else in this afternoon to cover the phones."

Lucy has always been a bit mouthy for the year or so she's worked here, but I frankly find it kind of refreshing. And far preferable to the fake deference so many people show me.

"I have no doubt you have everything under control, as usual, Lucy," I reassure her. "I'll be in my office." Secretly, I do doubt it, as I doubt everything, but as the company grows I've had to learn to let go of micromanaging every dimension.

As usual, I don't see anyone else as I head to my office. Besides my general feeling that as the boss I should be here first, I like to be in before everyone else to have some quiet time to get ready for the day. I set my bag on my desk and hang my coat on the back of my office door, glancing at the dull, misty Seattle skyline out the window before taking a seat.

After sending a few emails, I review the latest briefing I've assembled for our weekly tag-up meeting with Buone Case. It's a summary of the relevant regulations governing build size based on property zoning. I'm hoping to use it to convince Mr. Giordano to scale back his plans or increase his budget. But the real trick will be convincing him he can't have both.

At first, I chalked up his insistence on waiting for perfection to a cultural difference — perhaps Italian real estate development is easier, more adaptable to the developer. But with several years of developing in the San Francisco Bay Area under his belt, and his clear shrewdness and business acumen, it's become clear that it's merely stubbornness. In a way I admire his tenacity, but it's bordering on being a nuisance, and in any case is impeding our ability to move forward.

A few minutes before the meeting I hear a small knock on my door. I look up, expecting to find my assistant, Maggie, checking in to remind me of the meeting, but instead am startled to see Mr. Giordano.

His dark brown hair carefully mussed, he looks more like a male model than a real estate developer leaning casually against my door frame. His fitted, tan slacks and black buttoned shirt open at the neck would be fitting for a casual Friday if they weren't clearly designer and impeccably tailored to his tall, slim frame.

"*Buongiorno,*" he greets me, and as usual I must suppress a shiver of enjoyment at his deep, lilting accent. "Do you have a minute?"

"*Buongiorno,*" I respond, glancing at the clock. "Of course. We have a few minutes before the meeting. Let's head to the conference room and we can talk."

I rise, bringing my laptop and folio. His appraising glance at my white button-front shirtdress belted over navy leggings reminds me why I never let him get me alone in my office.

"As you wish," he responds, hesitating in the doorway for a moment as I approach. I slow and stop a respectable distance away. "You look lovely today."

"Thank you," I respond evenly, maintaining stern eye contact. "Shall we?"

He cocks a half-smile, one he's used to disarm me before, and stays put. But I'm practiced at ignoring his flirtations by now, so I simply stand my ground, waiting impassively for him to move.

For a moment we remain motionless, staring at each other, the tension in the room palpable. His smirk deepens, and he sighs lightly, stepping aside to end the standoff and let me pass. Most days I think he just enjoys the sport of it.

I breathe an inward sigh of relief, ignoring the tingling down my spine as he walks next to me, our hands swinging closely, threatening to brush against each other in the tight hallway. I hug my things to my chest, wrapping both of my hands around the warm laptop.

Before we can get very far, Jackson Williams, my assistant for the Buone Case project, spots us on his way to the conference room and joins us.

Relieved not to be alone with Mr. Giordano, I pull Jackson into a discussion that continues into our meeting.

But by the end of the hour we've made little progress, and both Jackson and I are struggling to find new ways to explain the contradictions at hand.

"Marco and I will review the legal descriptions this afternoon," Mr. Giordano finally promises as we wrap up the meeting. "But I'd still like to find a way to stick with our original scale."

I can see Jackson ready to beat his head against the desk.

"Again, the regulations simply don't support that," I insist. "You would need a significantly larger parcel."

"We're pushing our investors to their limit as it is," replies Maria Greco, Buone Case's finance lead. "We have no room there."

Mr. Giordano narrows his eyes at the report in front of him, as if challenging it to a staring contest will change what's on the page.

"Mr. Giordano, please," I say pleadingly, "review the data objectively. We'll get back together on Monday afternoon and try to find a path forward."

He leans back in his chair, his jaw twitching. He clearly has issues conceding defeat. I'd find it endearing if it wasn't so infuriating.

"It's time for lunch anyway," he finally says dismissively. "I'm sure we could all use a break."

There is a noticeable sigh of relief from everyone in the room, and I can't help but chuckle to myself. As everyone files out, Mr. Giordano stays fixed in his chair, running a finger slowly under his chin in thought.

"Ms. Evans, please stay," he asks quietly as I'm about to leave.

The last person files out in front of me and I glance back at him apprehensively. "All right," I concede slowly, leaving the door open and setting my things back on the table.

He rises, circling the table to close the door, then drops into the chair next to me. I attempt to control the pounding of my heart as he crosses his legs thoughtfully, leaning back in his chair.

"Serafina," he starts, and I'm jolted by his use of my first name. I've been very careful to keep things as formal as possible, so I'm wary of what he'll say next. "You are obviously an incredibly capable and knowledgeable businesswoman. Otherwise, I wouldn't be using your services. But surely you didn't get where you are by settling?"

I consider my response for a moment. I know he's trying, under the guise of flattery, to trap me into letting him persist with chasing his ideal.

"Mr. Giordano," I reply pointedly, and a smirk settles across his luscious pout, "I got where I am by working within the established system. What you're holding out for isn't going to work. I strongly urge you to review the data I've provided before we continue to discuss this further."

"Are you telling me what I want is impossible?" he asks shrewdly, with a look of such intensity on his face, I wonder for a moment if we're only talking about business.

"No," I admit, "but I am telling you what you want is going to cost you more than you have to spend."

He laughs suddenly, jarring me. "Despite what Maria says, there is always a way to find more money," he replies dismissively.

I shake my head. "You misunderstand me, *signore*," I persist. "The biggest cost here is *time*. You've already spent more than two months pursuing your ideal, to no avail. It's April. If you want to build in the Seattle area, you're going to need to start. Soon."

His eyes darken a shade as he weighs my words, and he shakes his head lightly. He leans forward, placing his elbows on his knees.

"I appreciate your conservative approach," he allows, speaking into his lap at first. "It's a useful counterpoint to my methods, I see that. But what you must understand about me is, once I study a market, I have instincts about where and how to enter. I've found ignoring those instincts to be very dangerous." He looks up into my eyes for a long moment. "I'll review the data," he finally says. "But I'm not one to give up easily."

I regard him quietly. From everything I've heard of his success in San Francisco, one of the toughest markets on the planet, I can't argue that he must have good instincts. And his words make me realize my usual tenacity may have been replaced with reservations as a counterbalance to his dogged pursuit of what would amount to one of the best deals I've ever seen. But I'm hard-pressed to encourage him, as I know how often that kind of deal comes along and what the cost is of waiting for it.

"I'm sure you'll do what you feel is best," I reply reservedly, switching the cross of my legs as I fidget under his heated stare.

"I know I'm a difficult bastard," he admits, smirking again. "I can't help that I'm used to getting what I want." He leans back in his chair, tilts his head, and cocks an eyebrow suggestively.

I bite back a snappy retort by reminding myself that it's his deal. His decision. And there's no way in hell I'm giving him the satisfaction of rising to his coy taunt.

As I remain silent, he purses his lips, and for a moment I think he looks disappointed.

"I'm sure we could do this all day," he says, abruptly changing the subject, "but you must be hungry. Can I take you to lunch?"

It's not his first invitation, and I'm sure it won't be his last. But my answer is always the same, and I'm sure he expects it.

"*Grazie*, but no," I reply lightly, rising from my chair. *Thanks, but no thanks. On all counts.* "I have work to do."

I can feel his eyes on me as I leave the room. Not for the first time I consider that his interest might purely be the simple intrigue of there being a female who spurns his advances. While he's not my usual type when I do bother dating, I'd have to be blind not to find him attractive. I'm just not sure why he's so interested in me. I'm pretty, in an average sense I suppose, with long, wavy brown hair, hazel eyes, and strong features, but I'm also thicker through my arms, chest, and thighs. Despite regular exercise and a decent diet, I'll never be the thin, gorgeous model type I imagine him with.

As I enter my office, I glance back to see him heading toward the elevator. His confidence radiates off him, his charm obvious even from the small greetings and interactions he has as he goes. If I know anything, it's that giving in to him would only bring trouble.

* * *

That evening I drift toward sleep on the couch while watching an old movie. Between the tensions of the day, and my half-asleep mind, my thoughts drift back to Alessandro. I roll the name over my tongue and giggle.

Two months of working together, and he still continues testing my resolve on every front. The business side I can handle. The flirtation, though, unseats me more than I'd like to admit. He drops his hints shamelessly, though never publicly, and I wonder again if he's merely seeking the thrill of victory.

But in my drifting state I don't stop the thoughts like I usually would. Instead I dangerously start to wonder what might happen if I allowed it. The surprise on his face might just be worth it.

But then, things would get complicated. And I don't like complicated. Though it has been far too long since I've done, well, someone. I giggle again sleepily and push him and any thoughts of unleashing those desires back into their cage in my mind.

About the Author

Melanie A. Smith is the best-selling author of *The Safeguarded Heart Series* and other contemporary romance fiction. Originally from upstate New York, she spent most of her childhood in the San Francisco Bay Area before moving to Los Angeles for college. After that, she spent almost fifteen years in the Seattle Area, and now lives in the Dallas-Fort Worth area of Texas with her family.

A voracious reader and lifelong writer, Melanie's writing began at a young age with short stories and poetry. Having completed a bachelor of science in electrical engineering at the University of California, Los Angeles, and a master's in business administration at the University of Washington, her writing abilities were mainly utilized for technical documents as a lead engineer for the Boeing Company, where she worked for ten years.

After shifting careers to domestic engineering and property management in 2015, she eventually found a balance where she was able to return to writing fiction.

Melanie is also a Mensan and enjoys spending time with her family, cooking, and driving with the windows down and the stereo cranked up loud.

Links

For updates on my books, exclusives, giveaways, freebies, and more, sign up for my newsletter here: https://mailchi.mp/melanieasmithauthor/signup

For exclusive swag, updates, giveaways, ARCs, and more, sign up my street team here: https://mailchi.mp/melanieasmithauthor/romancereadersquad

Follow me on
Instagram: instagram.com/melanieasmithauthor
Facebook: http://fb.me/MelanieASmithAuthor
Twitter: https://twitter.com/MelASmithAuthor
Goodreads:
https://www.goodreads.com/author/show/18088778.Melanie_A_Smith
BookBub: https://www.bookbub.com/profile/melanie-a-smith
Tumblr: http://melanieasmithauthor.tumblr.com/

Books by Melanie A. Smith

The Safeguarded Heart Series
The Safeguarded Heart
All of Me
Never Forget
Her Dirty Secret
Recipes from the Heart: A Companion to the Safeguarded Heart Series
The Safeguarded Heart Complete Series: All Five Books Plus Exclusive
Bonus Material

Standalone Romance Novels
Everybody Lies (audiobook also available on Audible and iTunes)

Life Lessons: A series that can be read as standalones
Never Date a Doctor
Bad Boys Don't Make Good Boyfriends

CPSIA information can be obtained
at www.ICGtesting.com
Printed in the USA
LVHW101547240223
740349LV00006B/135